KU-731-705

STARFISHING

Nicola Monaghan graduated from the University of York in 1992, and went on to teach for several years before taking a job in the City of London. A career in finance took her to New York, Paris and Chicago, before she gave it all up in 2001 to return to her home town and pursue an MA in creative writing at Nottingham Trent University. *The Killing Jar*, Nicola's first novel, won a Betty Trask Award, the Author's Guild Club First Novel Award and the Waverton Good Read. She is currently a fellow of the National Academy of Writing, based at Birmingham City University, where she runs a diploma course in Creative Writing.

ALSO BY NICOLA MONAGHAN

The Killing Jar

NICOLA MONAGHAN

Starfishing

VINTAGE BOOKS
London

Published by Vintage 2009

2 4 6 8 10 9 7 5 3 1

Copyright © Nicola Monaghan 2008

Nicola Monaghan has asserted her right under the Copyright, Designs
and Patents Act 1988 to be identified as the author of this work

This book is sold subject to the condition that it shall not,
by way of trade or otherwise, be lent, resold, hired out,
or otherwise circulated without the publisher's prior
consent in any form of binding or cover other than that
in which it is published and without a similar condition,
including this condition, being imposed on the
subsequent purchaser

First published in Great Britain in 2008 by Chatto & Windus

Vintage
Random House, 20 Vauxhall Bridge Road,
London SW1V 2SA

www.vintage-books.co.uk

Addresses for companies within The Random House Group Limited
can be found at: www.randomhouse.co.uk/offices.htm

The Random House Group Limited Reg. No. 954009

A CIP catalogue record for this book
is available from the British Library

ISBN 9780099507925

The Random House Group Limited supports The Forest
Stewardship Council (FSC), the leading international forest
certification organisation. All our titles that are printed on
Greenpeace approved FSC certified paper carry the FSC logo.
Our paper procurement policy can be found at:
www.rbooks.co.uk/environment

Printed and bound in Great Britain by
CPI Cox & Wyman, Reading RG1 8EX

FOR JULIA CASTERTON

A Higher State of Consciousness

You walk through the door and into a wall of sound.

It's so loud it sends you off balance, makes it difficult to put one foot in front of another.

The room is immense and lofty, the size of an aircraft hangar, and it boils with people pushing and shouting and clambering over each other. The air crackles. Static moves the tiny hairs on your arms and the back of your neck; you feel it sweep your body.

The clothes people are wearing make your eyes dart about, they send you dizzy with their blues and reds and stripes and stars. The hot pool of bodies oozes sweat, which fills the air and floods your senses. Everyone's squashed against each other with their arms in the air and as you walk through, they suck you in. Your heart's pounding, you're pumped full of chemicals. You don't run and you don't fight and they build and build and it makes you light-headed. High.

People shoot past you, on a mission. They fly at you and seem to go past sooner than they get there and it's all you can do to keep yourself upright with the force of it all. The world glows radioactive; electric blue, shocking pink, the colours have a charge to them.

Then you're in the middle of it, arms stretched out to some random god. You're shouting and waving and making the room change. You pull something from the air, not solid or liquid or an object you can hold, but real nonetheless. Hard to define and gone as soon as you've touched it. It's like you're earthing a charge that flows right through you and, when you get it right, turns gold all over your fingers.

There's a lull. People move to the side of the room, they whisper to each other. The air is thick around you, the way it is on the kind of summer's day that has to break, the kind when you wait and watch for the sky to moan and scream as lightning cuts it open.

You hold your breath.

Then it's off again and it's madder than before and you didn't think that was possible but it is. It's like the floor's pulled out from underneath and you all fall through, out of control, and you've got no fucking clue where you're going to land or how hard. People scream and scratch like pigs. All round the room the lights are going mad, flashing and changing and flashing and changing and mashing up your brain with the input. It's too much to take in so it bypasses the front of your head and goes right to where it's needed. The room smells of bodies and fear and instinct. It smells of animals hunting, and being hunted.

A bell rings and it all stops. The screens and the walls are splattered red with all the numbers that have gone down, down, down, down. Like it's been sprayed with blood from a slaughter, from the hunt.

You feel blooded too, can almost smell the iron of it, feel it smeared across your face.

2

The floor is littered with debris. You walk, watching your feet as they crunch through abandoned trade cards. They remind you of autumn. They remind you of betting slips at the races.

LIFFE (lahyf)

The London International Financial Futures and Options Exchange. An open outcry exchange based at Cannon Bridge in the City of London. Open outcry traders face each other in a 'pit' and agree deals, using hand signals to clarify. They often wear brightly coloured jackets, signifying the companies they work for or the jobs they do.

Life (lahyf)

1 the general or universal condition of human existence; 2 a person or thing that enlivens: *the life and soul of the party*; 3 effervescence or sparkle, as of wines; 4 what happens when one is making other plans.

Life (lahyf)

We were all off our faces.

It was a club somewhere in Amsterdam, that was about all I knew, that and the fact I was steaming. A load of vodka Red Bull on the plane. We'd flown over for a night out, on a whim, me and a couple of clients and some other mates. There were still a few months left of 1997, but we were partying like it was 1999. I was being good by my standards because I had a big day in the office on Monday and wanted to be sharp for it, so I was only drinking. Everyone else was soaring high. They'd double dropped on the Dam's finest

Ecstasy, purchased from a dodgy-looking guy in a road down by the canals, a big fat wobbler of a whore watching us through the whole deal and sticking her tongue out the corner of her mouth at the boys.

Iain was dancing on a podium with two tanned and shiny girls. He'd taken his top off and looked good; ripped with muscle and his skin glowing gold from the sun he'd been getting on regular trips home to South Africa. He was out of bounds for me, though, because he was one of my clients. You don't go there. But a girl can look.

Merrick was right next to me, trying to be a sexy dancer. It made me laugh because he was so serious and intense, and although he was wearing the right clothes, he looked like a troll from a fairy tale who'd dressed in disguise and not very well. Hair sprouted from the cuffs of his designer shirt and his thickset legs refused to move in time to the music, despite the amount of MDMA he had in his body. His pupils were dilated so wide you could see only the thinnest blue outline, the very edge of his irises. I'd had to brush off his attentions a couple of times. This annoyed me because I'd made my position known. Told the boys in no uncertain terms I wasn't going to sleep with any of them and that it would piss me off if they tried it on. Not that it stopped them. Traders are too into games, which is exactly why I'm not into playing with them, but telling them that was a big mistake; red-rag-to-great-big-rhino kind of error.

The club was one of those huge places that used to be a warehouse. Despite its size, it was packed and sweaty; so humid it felt tropical. As I danced, the heat and moisture smothered and slowed me. It was a hard house night and everyone was going as mad as the beats per minute. The music thumped and kicked at my eardrums. Everywhere you looked there were people stomping. Boys baring their chests, hair gelled into thick spikes, tanned girls in bikini tops and hotpants, glitter winking from their skin as the light hit. Beautiful people dressed in blues and reds and pinks that shone on the edge of the spectrum, making them glow with something ethereal and spooky.

Jason came over and was dancing with us. He wasn't a client of mine but I wanted him to be. Jase traded Bund futures on LIFFE, had his own account there and was making plenty of money. Not just from dealing contracts on the trading floor but from dealing other stuff too, to his mates. Other stuff on the floor of the exchange too, if rumours were to be believed. He was a typical Essex lad, tall and skinny, with pale skin, nothing special, on paper. There was a promise in the way he smiled, though, that was just so sexy. We'd nearly got together a couple of times, but I kept holding back because I wanted a business relationship with him. I hadn't got him to sign any contract yet but we'd become friends. He put an arm round me and we stomped to the music together. His eyes were wet with what he was on, and he looked like he'd never stop grinning. I was jealous and wanted what he was having.

'Got any more pills?' I said.

Jase didn't just smile; he shone at me. ''Course,' he said, and went digging in his pocket. He handed me a small white tablet. I always check to see the picture. This one was a Playboy bunny and that made me smile because it really summed Jase up, him and the rest. I was looking at the pill, and Jase was passing me water, and I thought – *do I really want to take this after all that booze?* Then I thought *fuck it* – and shoved it right to the back of my mouth, grabbing the water and washing it down. It tasted like hairspray and the nastiness lingered on my tongue. I passed the water back to Jase and grimaced. He took another sip. I immediately felt different. I knew this wasn't the pill, that they didn't work that quickly. It was anticipation, excitement about the way my night would change now.

I was tired of the music and went over to the chill-out zone to wait for the drugs to kick in. Merrick followed and sat cross-legged right next to me, close enough that one of his legs touched mine. I moved so we weren't touching.

'You having fun?' he said.

'S'all right.'

'Had any disco biscuits?' he said. I didn't answer. He went off on one then, going on about all the drug experiences he'd had like he was the king of it all. He reminded me of a thirteen-year-old telling someone all the dirty words he knew, thrilled with the idea he was being naughty.

As we sat there, Merrick gabbing away and me half focused, I felt the chemicals being churned and released in my stomach, the fizz from them burning at my insides. I was already feeling the high, though, and it was enough to dampen any worries I had about what might be happening to the soft tissues of my digestive system. I was relaxing and got chattier, was less wary of Merrick and his wandering hands. As the feeling built, I thought I might be sick. I got up and went to the loos, but a long queue trailed the door and I couldn't be arsed with waiting. I stood bent double for a minute, then the pain went off. I was about to go back to Merrick in the chill-out area when the music grabbed me. Round me the colours that had been bright before shone out like they had lights behind them. The strobes pulsed in time to the music and made my head go funny and then I heard the opening chords from 'Born Slippy NUXX'. The song threw me back to the previous year, to good times with Darren.

A few people shoved past me but it didn't matter. They were just going where they were going. I turned to see a girl next to me with shiny blonde hair and told her she looked beautiful. We exchanged smiles and then I let the music take me. The words didn't make much sense but that didn't matter. *Drive boy dog boy dirty numb angel boy in the doorway boy she was a lipstick boy she was a beautiful boy* . . . I let it all wash over me, the chords, the voices, the drugs inside and the colours around me, and it was all I could do to stand there on the edge of the dance floor and hold my arms in the air.

Then I was on the floor and dancing in the crowd, though I didn't feel the people as I pushed my way through. The noise pulsed out from the speakers and vibrated through me. The sound was like colours, the bright, big, crazy colours everyone was wearing. It was like that sour, fruity, sugary taste you get from some sweets that takes over your tongue so you can't think of anything else except how good your mouth feels.

Iain came over and danced behind me, grabbing my waist. I was going to tell him to get off like I knew I should, but I didn't. It felt so good; everything felt so very, very good. I was waving my arms in the air and the lyrics were racing on, *shouting, lager lager lager lager, shouting, lager lager lager lager, shouting . . . lager lager lager, shouting, mega mega white thing, mega mega white thing, mega mega white thing, mega mega, shouting lager lager lager lager,* the singer kind of rapping, kind of singing, the drums going fucking mad. I got this feeling in my head, like an orgasm in my brain. Then, like after an orgasm, the way your body aches and you feel tired but in a lovely, satisfied, How-Great-Thou-Art, birdsong-and-bright-sky-on-a-spring-morning kind of way. Well, that's how that pill was bringing me up, only times about a fucking hundred.

The next thing I knew, I was sitting in the chill-out area with Iain. I had a black hole of time missing but was too high to care. Damn, these pills were good. Iain was massaging my scalp with the tips of his fingers. I lay back and enjoyed his hands, all over my head, my neck, then down further to my back and my belly. As his fingers swept down it was almost too much and I had to flick him away. He leant round to kiss me but I moved out of his way, so he planted his lips on the side of my face. He hugged me in close and I could feel the way he was grinding his teeth. I turned to look at him.

'It's great here, innit?' I said, and he nodded. I swallowed. My jaw was so tight it was hard to speak. 'It's completely amazing here in my head,' I said. I smiled, and he smiled too, leaning back and supporting himself on his elbows. It looked like he was staring up at the lights but his eyes were closed, and his face was lopsided. He looked like someone who'd climbed into a warm bath after a long, hard day.

His eyelids snapped open. 'What's in that head, Francesca? That's what I wanna know, Francesca.'

I smirked. 'Francesca, Francesca. No one calls me Francesca.'

'It's a beautiful name.'

I nodded. It was, I just hadn't noticed.

'What you wanna be when you grow up, Francesca?' He was singing my name.

I hesitated. 'I don't ever wanna grow up.' We both laughed. Then I said, 'I want to be a trader.'

'You already a trader, hon.'

'Nah, I mean, like, a proper trader. On the floor with those special jackets, waving your arms round and going crazy for a living.'

'Innit?' he said. And he pulled me back into him and squeezed me hard. 'Y'know, I know people. I can get you an interview if you really interested.'

'You betcha,' I said. And I didn't think about it much more than that. Sure, Iain could get me an interview. People tell you ten kinds of crap when they're on a pill so I didn't take much notice. And I was on a pill too. I'd never even thought about trying to get a job on LIFFE before. The only thing I was really bothered about right then was being touched some more and Iain was doing a wonderful job in that regard. I lay back against his good strong chest and enjoyed it.

A week or so later I got a phone call from a bloke called Tom.

Spoof

Spoof is a guessing game, often played in pubs or bars to establish who should buy the next round of drinks. One of the unusual things about Spoof is that there are no winners, only an eventual loser.

The game is played in rounds by any number of players. Each takes or pretends to take up to three coins from his or her pocket and holds these in an outstretched fist and players take turns to guess the total number of coins. Then everyone opens their hands to reveal the coins and these are counted. If any player has guessed correctly they are eliminated from the game. This process repeats until one player remains: the loser.

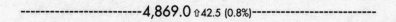

------------------------4,869.0 ⇧42.5 (0.8%)------------------------

Sexy. That's what I'd say if I had to sum up Tom in a single word. That was the first thing I noticed about him – I have my hidden shallows. He was typical of the sort of man I was attracted to: strong-looking, not a pretty boy, with a certain aura of trouble about him. I remember following him all the way up those long, long escalators, then through a corridor to a back room, and it was all I could do not to put my hand out and touch his thigh. I had to make myself look away, up to the back of his head, but even then the curls tickling his neck got my attention. All I could think was how I'd love to push my hands through his coarse wiry hair and feel his body against mine.

He shut us in his office, gestured at a chair and was off talking, firing questions and ideas so fast into my face it felt like assault. Even with the door closed I could hear the noise from the trading floor, but it was muffled, like I was listening underwater. If I was hoping for any relief from my attraction as we got down to talking business I was very much mistaken. Everything about him struck me at once; the muscle straining under the skin of his biceps and against the silk of his shirt as he leaned towards me, his sexy Midwestern drawl (Chicago? Michigan? I'd known enough Americans to just about place it), that typical orthodontic smile, the ten years or so he had on me and the experience that promised, his intense psycho stare that should have freaked me out but turned me on instead. I had to work hard to focus on his questions. Then he said he would take me on a tour and he was up and out of the office so fast I was left dizzy in his wake.

I knew we were getting close to the floor when the squashed-down noise began to sound less easily contained, like it might burst into the corridor any moment. Then Tom opened a door and it was like an explosion. The room had a floor area the size of at least a couple of football pitches with a ceiling so high that staring up gave me vertigo. Everywhere I looked there were people waving their arms. There was so much noise it made a buzzing in my head, as if a bee was trapped inside my ear. I was holding my breath.

We stood on the edge of the trading floor and watched. There was no point Tom trying to explain anything, tell me who was who or what was going on; it was just too loud. People barged and pushed past. My eyes darted round, catching glimpses of the action, a hand here, the glint of cufflinks there, then the edge of the room, then Tom's neck again. It must have all gone in but so fast I couldn't get a handle on what I was seeing. Then Tom was off ahead of me and I thought I'd better try to keep up. I breathed deep, sending air shooting into me and making my head spin with the force of it and I thought – yay – free high!

Tom made this sign with his hand and I knew he wanted me to stay where I was and wait. I wondered where he was going – off to do a deal or something? As he disappeared into the thick crowd I was bursting inside to follow, but I knew it was important I did as I was told. I felt silly standing in the middle of all this activity, my arms pinned to my sides. I felt like I should be going somewhere, waving my hands or shouting, moving with a purpose like everyone else. I felt a curious detachment, like I was watching through glass.

No one noticed me. They just got on with it, pushing and shouting and jostling in a way that made me think of busy markets in foreign places. An assault of colour reinforced this image: the trading jackets. There were the functional yellows and reds that were the basics of the exchange, and the team strips of various companies too, so that the overall effect was the clash and mix of a spin cycle. It stung my eyes to look for too long, so I looked down, at suit trousers and shoes, the dull floor, for some relief.

I felt a tap on my shoulder and turned; it was Tom. I wondered if he'd come back via some convoluted route or if I'd moved somehow, shimmied along by the crowd. Calm was settling across the room, the noise bubbling down to a gentle hum. As the floor emptied, I saw guys standing around, chatting, comparing trade cards or flicking them across the room, having a laugh. That was when I heard a couple of shouts, bold as you like: 'Beaver!' I knew right away they were aimed at me. The same sort of thing had happened when I went to my dad's factory, back in my teens, so I knew what it was about.

'Don't take no notice,' Tom said. 'It's their fucked-up way of saying you're hot.' He smiled, catching my eyes so firmly with his it was hard to look away.

I turned my head, shrugging off Tom's flirting. I was there for an interview, not to get it on with some trader, no matter how sexy he'd turned out to be. Now the room was clearer I could get a better view of the action. Hanging from the ceiling there were displays of red and green lights showing the prices for the different options and futures that were trading. The FTSE index, a number I knew people were buying and selling right in front of me, but also feeds from Frankfurt of the DAX, and the French CAC 40. Prices too from the American markets, frozen solid at their close from the previous evening. There were rows of computer screens and men sitting at them, telephone handsets pressed into their faces. There were figures listed on the screens too, and charts that ticked in real time, the lines getting longer and axes adjusting every time someone did a deal. It took your breath away to think about it, people watching and inputting data to their computers, sending the numbers via the office of some software company so it could all come back so close to where it was happening. There was so much information twitching around me, I couldn't make sense of it. I stared at Tom's face, watching the numbers flash in his eyes. He turned and caught me. Laughed. 'Don't worry about it. Each trader has to concentrate on just one or two contracts.'

I smiled at him. Then I switched focus from the outside of the room to the middle. Trading areas were hexagonal; raised around the side up to metal barriers, like the ones on football terraces, steps leading back down into what was called a 'pit' but was level with the floor around it. Trading was picking up again and men piled in and out of the pits, yelling and falling over each other. The scene reminded me of TV footage I'd seen of bees crawling over honeycomb. In a nearby options pit I could see market makers, stood in the middle facing out, quoting prices to the other traders.

The room was streaked with yellow, the colour of the runners' jackets, the worker bees who dashed everywhere with trade cards, checking, reconciling, passing on messages. Their bright yellow stood out from the other colours but you would have picked them out without this. They were really young, and many of them were stunning-looking girls. I'd been worried that this was what Tom was after when he got in touch, some runaround, and I was already doing quite well for myself thank you very much without taking a step backwards like that. But I'd asked him straight out and he'd said I'd have to train, of course, and it was entry level, but that he was looking for a trader. Despite what I'd said to Iain when we were both high, this wasn't something I'd ever imagined myself doing. I was ambitious, viciously and unashamedly, but I hadn't had a focus for it before now. That had changed since Tom rang. Now I knew exactly how I wanted to make my millions. Seeing it in all its vibrant glory right in front of my eyes just made me more sure.

On the edge of the action there were guys stood around watching, waiting. A few of them were chatting or reading newspapers.

'Why aren't they doing anything?' I asked. My words disappeared into the air.

'Can't hear you.' Tom put his mouth so close to my ear I could feel his curls against my cheek. 'It's better here to get close and whisper if you wanna be heard.' My nerves had been sparking like crazy the whole morning, but Tom's latest little trick sent an electric shock down my arms and legs, making me shiver. I put my lips right next to his ear and repeated the question.

'They're brokers waiting on orders. My brokers, some of 'em, for what it's worth. When that guy over there, we call that the booth.' He pointed at the men on the phones. 'That guy'll signal and they'll be off quicker than you can count to one.'

'One,' I said.

And then it went off, exactly like Tom had told me it would; he couldn't have set it up better. He threw his head back and beamed. 'Beautiful, ain't it?'

I nodded and I meant it.

Tom led me away from the trading floor and back to the office. 'What d'ya think then, babe?'

I put on my smoothest voice. 'Like I said, I'm fully committed to a career in traded derivatives and think UBF are the best possible—'

'Enough already.' Tom was waving his hand across his face. 'I've heard all your interview bullshit. But this ain't no normal job, this is the LIFFE trading floor, baby. Do you wanna work here? Do you really want it?' He brought his face right up to mine, staring like some sociopath right into my eyes. It freaked me out and I wanted to look away but had a feeling that was totally the wrong thing to do. I looked back and threw him the biggest smile I could. My eyes flicked down from his for an instant, down to his chest, where I saw his ID badges, moving as he breathed. I saw his trader pass for long enough to notice his mnemonic – TAP – and think how he was kind of tapped in the head as well, but sexy with it.

'God, I want it. I've never wanted anything more.' And I meant every word.

'That's what I needed to hear. Are you hungry? Are ya?'

'Tom, I'm starving. Ravenous.'

'Ravenous,' he repeated, trying to imitate my accent and going all Dick Van Dyke. 'I like it.' He was grinning like a fool.

I braced myself for what was coming. I could go down the pub with the lads and talk about sex in terms so crude it shocked them, and it didn't embarrass me one little bit. But I still felt uncomfortable in salary negotiations. I knew this was something I needed to get over if I was ever going to make it the way I wanted to. I made myself push the word out. 'Money?'

Tom laughed, a sound that had enough amusement in it for me to know my stress had come across in my voice. 'Gwaan, then, what you after?'

'Thirty.' This would be a pay cut, but still I was pushing the boundaries for a trainee position.

Tom's lips stayed curled and he raised one eyebrow. 'I was thinking closer to twenty-five.'

So was I but I didn't say yes, yet. I stared at him, trying to get from his expression if I had leverage. All I could see in his eyes was mischief.

'You're one badass negotiator,' he said, but his tone and widening smile told me he was making fun. 'Tell you what; spoof you for it.'

I let out a shock of laughter. 'You serious?' His face didn't change. 'I've got no coins.'

He held eye contact as he dug in his pocket and handed me three. 'Call it an advance. Heads up, best two out of three, age before beauty. You ready?'

I nodded. Spoof was the sort of game you play to decide

who buys the next round in the pub, not what salary you're getting – but what choice did I have?

We held out our balled-up fists. Tom called first, the way he'd set the rules, and he called 'five'. It told me too much. I knew he couldn't possibly have less than two coins, and that he might well have the maximum of three. It also told me he was taking it easy on me, at least this round, and I couldn't help thinking – *false sense of security*. I had two coins, so it put me on the spot a little. You can't dupe so I called 'four'. We opened up our palms and there they were – four. I'd won the first round.

He raised his eyebrows and dug his hand in his pocket again. I tried to concentrate on the game. This was worth money. I slid my hand in my pocket and let go of the coins. Tom counted again and I held out my fist. He called 'one'. I felt hot and sweaty all of a sudden. The five grand stake and the difference that would make to my life made my mouth shut tight.

'Tough, ain't it?' he said. 'This is exactly what it's like out there.' He nodded with his head, back in the direction of the trading floor.

I gritted my teeth, forced the corners of my mouth up and called. I couldn't choose one, which meant I had to go for zero. It was my only chance and it was fifty–fifty. We opened our hands. I saw a coin nestled in Tom's palm and there was a lurch in my chest. Then I panned back and took in the whole picture. There was one in my hand too; I hadn't dropped them all into my pocket after all. My hand was wet with sweat and that must have stuck the coin there. We were both still 'in'. I went back into my pocket ready to continue.

'Fuck it,' he said, words that kicked me in the stomach. 'You held your nerve so well, I think we'll leave it at that.

Thirty it is, babe, you've fleeced me. You better be worth it.' He looked me up and down then, and I felt the force of his innuendo and tried not to smile. 'I'll leave you to sort out the logistics and that shit with my secretary.' He shook my hand hard. I felt sick but I made sure I held on tight, and gave him one more tight smile for the road. 'Francesca Cavanagh, welcome to LIFFE.' And just like that, I was reborn.

---------------------------**4,879.2** ⇧52.7 (1.1%)-----------------------

I came out onto Cannon Bridge and headed up to the main road. Across from me I saw a brass statue of a trader on a mobile phone and I thought – *that's me, that is.* At least that's who I'm going to be. A thrill rocketed from my stomach to my neck at the thought of it. It crossed my mind that Darren would have said they were all wankers but I couldn't have cared less for his opinion. His inverted snobbery was one of the many reasons he was no longer my boyfriend. I headed back towards St Paul's. Towards work. I was in no hurry to get there.

My desk was a mess when I got back. Littered with the yellow squares of telephone messages and scribbled notes. I sat down and unlocked my computer screen, knowing my inbox was going to fill up with mail as soon as I opened it. I probed my handbag for the fat brown envelope Diane Cooper had given me. She was one of the UBF yellow-jackets and had not looked pleased to see me. I had a feeling we would not be sharing make-up tips and gossip about the boys. She was the sort of girl who'd wear white trousers and make it to the end of the day still looking like she'd crawled straight out of the washing machine. She wouldn't ever spill her breakfast down her blouse or come to work with smudged mascara, or get so wasted she fell over and sat drooling in the corner. I could just picture the kind of underwear she bought, and knew she would always smell of expensive perfume, not last night's red wine. I knew her type. The place I came from was their breeding ground: Dagenham and Ilford and all those little towns near where my dad lived. And they flocked to the City, not to forge careers and earn money for themselves like I was doing, but to find a bloke who was loaded and marry him. They'd take any job, any old crappy admin or secretarial position that would get them close to eligible men. I'd seen it all before.

I found the envelope and pulled it from my bag. Inside was a thick wad of forms. They looked pretty standard: medical questionnaire, referees, the job offer subject to both turning out right. A credit check and the SFA registration, but I'd been through all that with my last job and it was just a formality. The standard drugs and alcohol tests were part of the deal, but it was just a urine sample, and it was common knowledge this was easy enough to get around. As long as you didn't smoke weed or do coke, the stuff that stayed in your system, and you were careful for a week or so beforehand, you could get away with it. I kept leafing through the papers, looking for problems. I hadn't been stressed before about not getting the job but now I had an offer on the table I had something to lose.

'Dentist okay?'

The voice was right in my ear and made me jump. It was Peter, my boss, close enough to my face that I could smell his breath, a sour mix of alcohol and coffee. The letters and forms from UBF were right in front of his nose. I thought about covering them up and sticking to my story, but I knew there wasn't much point. He'd seen enough to guess what was going on.

'I didn't go to the dentist.' I shuffled papers round my desk. This wasn't how it was supposed to work out. I'd been looking forward to telling Peter but I had my plans for how and when and they didn't go like this. I grabbed the mouse on my desk and clung to it, trying to stop my hand from shaking.

He raised his eyebrows and placed a hand on my shoulder. I had to work hard not to jerk away.

'I've been offered a job.'

Peter pulled over a chair and sat down, holding his head at the listening angle, that way he did. It was one of the million things I hated about the tosser, like he thought tipping his ear over made the words go in easier. In my experience they just fell right through the space where his brain should have been and out the other side.

'It's a trading job, on the LIFFE floor, with UBF.'

Peter didn't move much from his listening position. He held his stubbly little chin in one hand and stroked at it. 'Open outcry, huh?' he said. He paused and looked like he was considering it deeply, then smiled, but not in an open or generous way. The smile was all about him, his games. 'And they think you can do this?' he said.

I turned and made my eyes meet his, giving him all the attitude in the world right back in his face. 'They know I can, else they wouldn't have offered the job to me, would they?'

'Well, good luck with that.' He threw an arrogant shrug in my direction. 'You'll have to work your notice here, though.'

I heard myself laugh, that weird choked sound that comes out when you hear something that is far from funny. Since I'd worked at Peter's dump of a brokerage, a good number of my colleagues had jumped ship. The market was

21

flooded with work if you had the right skills and experience. The blokes who'd left had been sent on gardening leave after they resigned, just in case they photocopied the client list and sent it to every bank in the square mile. I had half a mind to do that, to teach Peter the lesson he deserved. I knew what this was all about. Same as the way I got passed over for promotions and stuck 'watching the fort' for whole afternoons while all the lads went out on the piss together. I wasn't having any of it. I'd done my research.

'You can't make me stay, you know. All you can do is get a court order to stop me working till my notice is up. And if you do that, you have to pay me.'

Peter's features froze below his pencil-grey hair. His head moved to a less friendly position. I'd seen this happen in about a hundred meetings, just before he laid into whichever clerk or IT manager or other less important colleague had challenged him. I was ready for it and didn't back off a millimetre. 'You'll be expecting a reference from me, then?' he said.

''Course.'

'Then you better work your notice.'

'I don't think so.'

I turned to my computer and clicked around until I found the file I needed. There was a chance that Peter would go for me and I glanced at one of the many cameras that watched our every move. He followed my gaze, which was what I'd hoped would happen, for him to be reminded they were there. I opened up a file I'd saved as 'back office', a cheeky title he never would have thought anything of because it was the name for one of the bank's departments.

'What the fuck?' Peter said, but then he stopped talking and looked at the Word document I'd opened. It was a 'fuck me please' collage I'd collected over the three and a bit years I'd had to put up with his leering attention when he came back half-cut from the pub. A veritable cut-and-paste of lewd suggestions I'd had via email, and from verbal comments I'd recorded in a diary.

'That's not all I've got, matey. I kept all the original email messages, and an answerphone tape, and it's all backed up and being looked after by a solicitor,' I said. It had not been hard. Peter behaved the same way whenever he'd had one too many and I was around; even outside of work he'd got into a habit of calling my home and my mobile. I'd tried to discuss the issue with him when he was sober but he'd always looked embarrassed and said he didn't know what I was going on about. So I'd kept everything.

I smiled at him. 'What were you saying about my notice?'

'I'm sure we can come to some kind of . . . ' He cleared his throat. 'Agreement.'

'I'm sure we can.' And I beamed at him, and pressed control-alt-delete twice so that my PC closed down.

I crossed Cannon Street feeling like I could walk up into the air if I wanted to. I looked round for somewhere to go and All Bar One caught my eye. I dug in my bag for my mobile and called Lorna. She worked for a City law firm and could usually swing one in the afternoon if she told her boss she needed to go and meet clients.

'Hey, it's me. Fancy a nooner?' I said.

Minutes later I was in the pub with two glasses and a bottle of white wine, awaiting her arrival. I'd sent texts to the few people from work I liked, to let them know my news and say I'd keep in touch. And to Iain and Merrick and the client boys, even though Peter had said I wasn't allowed to contact them. They were my mates, though, and there was nothing he could do about it. My phone was still beeping with replies when Lorna spun into the pub like the Tasmanian devil from the cartoons. She was itchy after an ashtray, dashing over and dumping her bag, then hunting like her life depended on it. She'd straightened her hair and it swung round her perfectly made-up movie star eyes. She lit a cigarette, then sat down, taking a big drag and relaxing. She beamed at me. 'So?'

'Celebration,' I told her. This was a ritual of ours. One of us had to say 'celebration' or 'commiseration' and come up with something to justify the afternoon session, the flimsier the better. 'That sexy bond trader I'm into smiled at me' or 'Email's gone down' or 'I left my umbrella on the DLR'. Today I had a solid gold reason and no heart for invention. 'I got the job.' Lorna let out a little squeal, and picked up her glass.

'To your new job, girl.' We clinked glasses and threw wine down our throats like we needed to empty the bottle and get the deposit back. It was Chardonnay, and nothing special. The kick as it slipped down my throat made me gag, but I kept swallowing.

Lorna went into interrogation mode. She asked what colour the jacket was so she could advise me about make-up and accessories. She dealt with the challenge of blue and gold stripes then asked me other stuff, like what I'd be paid and what exactly I'd be doing. I muttered something about client orders and hand waving, using my arms to demonstrate as if she'd never heard of open outcry before, making her spray wine over the table. I told her how I'd been made to play spoof for my salary and her eyes widened. 'Interesting. So this Tom chap, what's he like?'

'Much nicer than Peter.'

'Nooo!' Lorna gave my hand a playful smack. 'You can't fancy your boss.'

'I can't not fancy him, I'm telling you. You'd understand if you met him.'

'Ring finger?'

'I didn't look.'

Lorna's face turned stern and her voice went serious. 'Ring finger?'

I shrugged and felt teeth escaping into a smile, despite myself. 'Yeah, there was something shiny there.'

'Don't go there.'

'He's my boss and I don't intend to. But a girl can look.' I could see from her face she wasn't convinced. 'How's Steven?' I said, to remind her she couldn't preach.

'Different,' Lorna said, wagging her wine glass in my general direction. 'That was kismet or something. You can't compare that with your new boss.'

'That was too much Chardonnay the way it always is with you.' She was opening her mouth to say something back but I didn't let her. 'Anyway, maybe me and Tom is kismet.' This was supposed to be a joke.

'Maybe, but is it worth the risk he might be just another one of those men who will never leave his wife?'

I laughed. 'I was just teasing, you daft moo. You know me, I don't go there on my own doorstep. It's my one rule.'

'Okay, but don't come crying to me when it all goes wrong.' Lorna held her hand up, palm out. It made me wonder if she was listening to me at all.

'How is Mr Kismet, anyway?'

'He's fine. Be here in a bit. But I want to know more about this job, Frankie.' Lorna switched the topic back just a bit too fast. She'd mentioned a few weeks ago that things hadn't been great between her and Steven. That's as much as she'd said, though. We were good-time girls, me and Lorna, we didn't do the heavy stuff.

'I start next Monday,' I told her.

'Good God, that's bloody quick. How did you wangle that one with Peter?'

I glanced up at her and I touched the back of my neck. 'Gentle persuasion?'

'Did you sleep with him?'

'No!' The idea made my face screw up. 'Dirty cow.'

'Then what?' Lorna paused. 'Nooo!' she said. 'You black-mailed him or something.'

'I wouldn't exactly say blackmailed.'

'You really are terrible,' Lorna said, but there was admiration in her voice.

'Just getting what I want from the knob for a change. I've put up with his fucking boys' club long enough.'

'I'm surprised you didn't push for gardening leave, then.'

'I could've. But I want to start the job. I just can't wait.'

Lorna looked at me and beamed. 'Good for you, honey.' She squeezed my arm and I could feel that I was glowing with it all. 'I wish I could get properly motivated about any job,' she said.

The bottle of Chardonnay was soon drained and Lorna was off to get more. She was glugging down the liquid like it was lemonade even as she walked back to the table. The new bottle was a Chenin Blanc and tasted better, though I couldn't be sure I hadn't just knocked out enough taste buds not to care. Steven arrived soon after we hit the second bottle, and beelined for us. Lorna fussed over him for a bit, and got an extra glass from the bar so he could share the wine. He lit a small cigar and swallowed the smoke, swilled it around like mouthwash.

'Good day?' he said to me.

'Oh yeah,' I said, and explained about the job. I got

rapid-fire questions from him then, asking the same things Lorna had and some because he was an IT contractor, working with traders, so he knew more about the markets. Even just the second time I'd said it all, I was getting bored explaining. I'd reached the limit of my attention span which said a lot about me, given this was my own good news. Lorna nudged Steven when I blushed at the mention of my new boss and it made him laugh.

'What's his name?' he said.

'Tom Phillips.'

'Yank with black curly hair, talks like he's spent too much time surfing on a beach in California with all that dude and babe bullshit even though he's from Chicago or something?'

'That's the guy. How the fuck do you know him?'

'The City, my dear, is a small place, teeny-tiny. Deutsche I think, a way back. Good bloke, even though he's a sickening bastard with all that tall-dark-handsome shit going on. Bit of a lad though.' Steven blew a ring of smoke and smacked his lips. 'Just watch yourself.' I felt a jolt of attraction for Tom when Steven said this, strong enough to move me in my seat. Tom was just what I was looking for in Mr Right Now. If only he hadn't been my boss.

'You not worried about the Germans?' Steven asked me then.

I swigged my drink while I thought about it, then I laughed. 'Fuck the Germans.'

'Yeah? There's whispers at our place that something might happen. They're sick of being shafted by the wide boys down there. Don't say I didn't warn you.'

Lorna was looking puzzled. 'The Germans,' I told her, 'invented this new exchange. All computers.' This wasn't entirely true, the DTB had been around for a while and had recently got regulators to allow their screens in London, but none of this seemed worth the explanation; Lorna didn't care. I turned to Steven. 'It's all bollocks. We got the liquidity.'

'For the moment.'

I put on a documentary film voice. 'Only Chicago's Board of Trade did more business than LIFFE last year.'

'They got you programmed, then.'

Lorna looked up at us, her face made plain by boredom. 'Can we talk about crap again now?'

'Two world wars and one World Cup,' I sang. Lorna leaned forward and lifted her glass to that sentiment with a broad smile.

Steven's face stayed serious. 'I got two words for you, Francesca. Penalty shootout.'

'I got three for you, Stevie. Traitor bastard swinehunt.' I poured more wine. I noticed the bottle was getting on for empty again and got up to buy another.

Two bottles on and the session was getting messy. Lorna was slurring and leaning over the table, her eyelids hanging half down over her big green eyes. Her hair was sticky and untidy because she'd let it drop in her drink a few times. Most of her lipstick was stuck to fag butts in the ashtray. I was so drunk the room was blurred. I thought about getting some food to try to dilute the effects of the alcohol but it was an effort to focus enough to read the menu. Then Steven suggested we hit Fuegos, this place a few minutes away on Pudding Lane. Lorna lapped up the idea with a clap and an excited noise, but I reckon she would have agreed to anything right then, she was so bladdered. I suggested a Ruby down Brick Lane might be a better idea, but got outvoted. We got our stuff together and headed for the door.

We stepped outside and Lorna hooked her arm under my elbow. Steven lit up another cigar and walked behind us and we all kept up the pace trying to stay warm. We were soon at Pudding Lane and got in the queue. *Fuegos* is Spanish for flames, I told Lorna, and she said something about wishing she'd done languages at uni too. The bar stood in an historic spot that had some connection with the Great Fire of London and it was as if the place had never properly cooled, stayed hot enough to ignite little fires, between men and women who shouldn't go there, and destroy marriages. It was infamous that way.

We were let in and went downstairs, into a packed room that stunk of booze. Most of the girls were wearing knee-high boots and had a scorched blonde look about them. Steven went to the bar and we went to dance. You could almost hear eyes turn as we walked onto the floor, which made us both laugh, but no one came over to chat to us. We didn't look the City bird type, not like the girls around us. Steven came over with the drinks. He put his arm round Lorna and squeezed her in, and they drifted off.

'Get a room!' I shouted after them, laughing at my own joke. Looking at them now, I couldn't believe they had any problems.

I danced on my own, didn't care, too pissed to even notice what other people were up to. The DJ was cheesing it up to the max and I lost myself jumping around to Madness and the *Grease* soundtrack. I found myself acting out 'Summer Nights' with some random bloke and knew it had gone too far. I was feeling tired and a bit sick. Steven and Lorna were all over each other. I tapped Lorna on the shoulder and told her I was going. She smiled and made a token effort to persuade me to stay, then they both kissed and hugged me goodbye. The hugs smelt of alcohol.

I walked out of the club. It must have still been cold, but I didn't notice, though I could feel my face glowing red.

This was another thing that often happened when I'd had too much to drink; Lorna and I called it the 'beer coat' even though it was usually because we'd been on the vino. As I walked out of the door, I was sucked into a crowd of taxi drivers, all pushing and hassling to give me the best price. It made me think of the trading floor, those thick layers of people shouting prices at each other. I thought it'd be a laugh to try out a trade.

'Five for one, pay five for one,' I yelled, signalling like crazy, making up hand movements based vaguely on what I'd seen. I got wrapped up by a huddle of drivers. There were about thirty of them hanging around looking for a fare and just one of me and I thought – *ace, buyer's market*. One of them beckoned me towards his car. 'Fifteen pounds to the Docks,' he said, and I said, 'No fucking way.' I told him five again, and held out the fingers from one hand hard at him. He shook his head and walked off and I thought – *tosser!*

I stood round for a few minutes shouting out my price and looking out at the sea of eager faces. I remembered what Tom had said was the most important thing about trading. About 'life', he'd said, though I couldn't tell if he was talking about the exchange, or something more general. He'd told me that a commodity, anything – a car, a book, someone's services, whatever – is worth only and exactly what someone's prepared to pay for it. So I stuck to my price and what Tom said worked. I did my first trade, and bought a cheap ride home.

--------------------------4,986.2 ⬆10.0 (0.2%)--------------------------

It was raining outside but nothing in the world could have put a dampener on my mood. I walked from my bedroom to the lounge and turned the music up loud. I heard thumps on the wall, my next-door neighbour throwing his toys out of his pram again. That was the thing about living in London, for most people, getting used to a paper-thin layer of separation. My neighbour needed to learn to ignore things. I'd mastered this skill a long time ago; you do when you grow up on a council estate. In my dad's house, you could hear it if the bloke next door unzipped his flies. When I was young, it struck me as strange that you could close your eyes but not your ears, that you had no choice but to hear what people said or the sounds they made, if it was within a certain distance of you.

I set the bath running, both taps turned on full, and went to the bedroom to sort out some clothes suitable for clubbing. It was Saturday night and everyone was up for a big one. Well, almost everyone. I'd tried hard to persuade Lorna to come but, as always, she'd said it wasn't her scene. She'd suggested I take it a bit easy to make sure I was fresh for starting the new job on Monday, but I'd said – fuck that, I can sleep long enough when I'm dead.

I walked back to my bath, which was getting full. I stood in the doorway and caught my breath. Just for a second I was thrown back to the phobia I used to have about baths, well, about the old bathtub at home. This scratched enamel thing that the council must have put in when they built the house. I used to scream and shout and buck and kick when my dad tried to put me in there; I even bit him once. He would usually give up and wash me in the kitchen sink instead. Twenty-odd years since I was small enough for that and I was still left with the residue of my fear. I held my breath and climbed into the water. The heat of it felt amazing against my skin and I lay right back. I closed my eyes and any thoughts I had about my dad's house were washed right away.

31

The weather scratched against the window behind me. It was stormy and the rain was coming down as hard as pellets from a paintball gun. My flat was right on the edge of the dock and I could hear the sound of water hitting water. My eyes tight shut, I listened to the thunder laugh. It sounded like the villain from a black-and-white movie. The thunder and lightning and thumping rain threw me right back. To another storm. The rain skating as it hit the ground hard. Me, standing in a bus shelter talking to Darren.

'I wanna go to bed with you now more than anything else in the whole fucking world, 'course I do, babe. I keep thinking how easy it'd be. How nice, but I'm holding out cos I think it's for the best.'

That was exactly how he'd put it; that it'd be easy. That we shouldn't in case it spoilt our friendship. It made me laugh, thinking back, this idea that there was ever anything deep enough between us to warrant such caution. Me and Darren Matthews: drink, drug and fuck buddies extraordinaire. It was all a line, fake as plastic trousers, like everything about Darren. It haunts me that I was ever that naïve, but Darren's protestations had the desired effect, dragging me in because he seemed noble and wanted to do the right thing. It dusted off the last specks of doubt about trusting him with my body. Then we'd kissed and I'd gyrated against his leg and that was enough for him to forget about our friendship. Something animal broke through his skin. 'You've done this a hundred times before,' he'd said, and I hadn't put him right.

Darren without his clothes had been an unexpected treat. I hadn't thought I'd like the way he looked naked, but it made my breath quicken. His body was smooth, and curved from shoulder to waist, then back out to his hips. He'd reminded me of those marble statues. Greek and

Roman gods. Michelangelo's *David*. His body was as close to perfect as those cold, white statues, except warm and breathing and standing right in front of me. I didn't tell him this. I might have been naïve but even then I recognised the kind of ego that didn't need feeding. I lay there looking up at him, shaking a bit. Some of that was nerves, but mostly I was cold and wet from the rain. He sat on the edge of the mattress, moving his hand rapidly. I can't help smiling every time I remember this, because I hadn't got a clue what he was doing.

'Are you wet?' he asked me.

'Yes.' But I thought he was still going on about the rain.

It'd thundered outside as Darren pushed inside me for the first time, making us both giggle it was so on cue. He'd pulled me close then, and the laughing turned into sighs from both of us. It didn't hurt. I'd said something lame like, 'Oh, yes, yes,' because I was so young, I didn't know the right noises. Then there was more lightning, making the curtains flash like a Halloween lantern. He'd pulled my hair back, yanked it so my neck and back were arched. I felt a jolt of pleasure at this, getting past the mechanics of it for a moment. Then he'd let out a grunt and rolled his eyes. And I thought – so that's all it is.

Thunder jerked me back to my bath, which was fast turning cold. I could feel static in the air, it moved the surface of my skin and made my cilia stand to attention. I touched myself, trying to remember how it felt back then. Trying to feel it again. I struggled for the memory of his lips. His touch. There was a time when just the thought of his fingertips on my skin would make me shiver. Not any more. The years had passed so fast, and here we were, hurtling towards the end of the millennium our separate ways. And thank God for that. We'd broken up plenty of times but this one felt permanent. I hoped so, anyway. I'd escaped before, for two whole years when I first went off to university, but he'd sucked me back in again, that way he was good at. My on-off, up-down relationship with Darren was enough to make my whole being conspire against what I called the 'love thing'. Not that I was ever in love with him. I thought I was, at the time, but looking back I could see that was nonsense. They talk about the power of love, but it doesn't even come close to the nasty spines of lust and ego.

I thought hard about Darren, tried to fix him down with words like bastard and wanker. It would be so much easier if I could hate him. I knew he wasn't a bad man, though. He was just like me, like all of us, complex, over-evolved animals struggling to cope. Flashbacks of our sex life came to me; his cock in my mouth; my nipple between his teeth; him pinning me to the bed by my wrists. I could see it all in my head, play it through like it was a film. But I couldn't feel it. It was just like a movie; I could only watch. I rubbed hard against my clitoris, tried to make it catch fire and burn for him the way it used to but it wasn't happening.

Then I thought about Tom.

My mobile rang, vibrating hard against the bathroom floor and startling me out of my reverie. I got out the bath and wrapped myself in a towel. It was Tom's number flashing on the phone, as if my lusting after him had conjured him up. Then everything sank inside me as it struck me that all might not be well. Why would Tom be ringing me? Had my new employers discovered one of my dark secrets, the things I thought I'd managed to bury? The debt I'd left behind when I moved to London, my dad sending back the letters to the bank 'not at this address'. The time I was cautioned, when I was thirteen. I was a juvenile then and it was supposed to be wiped from all records but what if someone had found out? I was shaking as I picked up the phone. The vibrations went right through me like an electric shock.

Tom's voice sounded slurred, as if he'd been drinking. He said he was calling to check on me, to make sure I was still 'pumped' about the job, and all set for an early start Monday. I told him no worries, that I was, and hoped to fuck my voice didn't shake too much.

'I was in the bath.' I didn't have a clue why I told him this, it just came out.

'Really? All wet and naked?' I could hear a smile in his voice, like he knew what I'd been up to.

'Yes.'

'I'd better not think about that too much,' he said, and he hung up.

We had arranged to meet at a place near the club for drinks-'plus' before we hit the queue. I walked to Crossharbour; there was no Underground service out where I lived on the island, just the DLR. A train pulled into the station and its doors sighed open. I got on, then floated above the East End on the Disney Land Railway. It was nice to travel in the sky like that, at least as far as Bank, where the train nosedived into the bowels of the City and I had to change onto the tube.

I resurfaced at Elephant and Castle; what a hole of a place. The ugly pink elephant outside the shopping centre looked as though it had been painted with leftover emulsion. I'd never been in and looked at the shops and I didn't intend to change that. We came down here clubbing a lot because it was a good venue but, if it hadn't been for my religious calling, it was a part of London I would have avoided. I could see up the road that people were already queuing for the club. I was surprised because the pubs weren't kicking out yet, and I knew right then it'd be a head banger of a night.

I walked into the bar and scanned round. My mates were over in the corner. Merrick spotted me and waved.

'You seen the queue already?' I said.

'I know,' he said. His eyes were already dilated wide as they'd go, black and shiny with pleasure. I looked at Iain and Jase and they were the same. I felt miffed to be on catch up.

'Took your time, didn't ya?' Jase said, passing me a playboy like the one I'd had in Amsterdam. 'Shall we off?'

I grabbed it off him and downed it with the dregs of his beer.

'Animal. Honestly, you're the worst out the lot of us,' he said. He thumped my shoulder lightly as he spoke. 'Hear you're coming to work at our place. Congratulations, honey.'

I nodded and smiled and swallowed. The pill felt trapped in my throat.

'Well, you'll make a very nice little addition to it, I can tell you,' he said. I got the feeling he was implying I'd brighten the place up, rather than improve it in some deeper way. I didn't dwell on it. I'd come out to have a good time.

We left then, and headed up Newington to the end of the queue. It stretched a long way from the door.

There was a bite in the air that made me feel uncomfortable as I stood waiting. 'I'm sure they let people in as slow as they can,' I moaned, 'just so the queue builds to make it look like there's a huge crowd. I bet there's about three people inside but they've barred the doors, just to make out there's something worth waiting for.'

'I bet,' Iain said, laughing and hugging me. I wished my head was in the same place as his. Merrick gurned at me and I noticed hair sprouting from his nostrils. For a terrible moment I thought he might try to kiss me, but then he looked away, towards the street.

We queued for close to forty minutes. My stomach started aching and I felt a chill crawl over my skin. I was coming up. I bent double with gut ache, but five minutes passed and so did the pain. By the time we got in I was off my box. I dumped my coat on the floor against a wall and headed for the dance floor, climbing over the loved-up couples who were sitting and lying all over the place.

Everyone looked amazing. Spiked and sprayed and outrageously dressed, their eyes wet and faces glowing with pleasure. As I squeezed past people towards the middle of the floor, the crowd opened up for me, all smiles and goodwill. Clubbers stomped and threw themselves around, waving glow sticks and chewing on dummies. As the breaks hit they pumped fists in the air and screamed, giving it up to the DJ and yelling 'toooon!' The way people were dancing was something else. They didn't give a shit about being cool. There were no self-conscious half efforts, but proper pumping and grinding and going crazy. It looked like a scene from a film, something biblical and about to be destroyed by God's wrath.

The rushes inside me were almost too much. They fired through me like lit gases. All that existed were these feelings and the music and the way it all looked. There was no tomorrow or yesterday or consequences, just the moment and me, alive. The DJ was this pretty blonde woman who was going for it in the booth as much as the clubbers were outside. Iain came over and danced with me.

Then he was trying to whisper in my ear. I couldn't hear him so we moved to the side of the room.

'You want another?' He held out pills to me in a curled hand.

'Okay.'

'How 'bouts we double-drop?'

'Sure.' I'd never double-dropped before but I didn't hesitate. I was already soaring high but I wanted to get monged. I wanted to go out of body. I wanted to end up sitting in the corner dribbling. We banged them down quick as you like with big swallows of water. I burped. 'Beast,' he said, and we both laughed. I grabbed his hand and dragged him back to the middle of the dance floor.

Half an hour later, I came up strong on the two pills and was rushing badly. It made my eyes dart about and I felt dizzy, a bit sick. I sat down and sipped water for a few minutes. The sickness didn't go off, but I didn't want to waste the high feeling that came with it, so I headed back to the action. I tripped and bumped past people on the way back. They didn't seem to mind, but it made me edgy and I wanted my friends. I saw Iain and Merrick dancing and joined them. Merrick was thumping the air and stamping round like a psycho. Iain was more laid back, doing this wide-legged effort where he drifted from place to place but managed to look in time with the wild, mad beats per minute of the sound. It wasn't long before the music absorbed me, too.

I went out of body for a while and when I found my way back into my head, Iain had his arms round me, all loved-up from the pills. I felt the same, full of love for everyone and everything, but especially for Iain, only because he was close and easy to focus on. I reckon I could have fallen in love with a table if I'd sat at it long enough in this state. The whole front of my body ached with pleasure. And it struck me: Iain wasn't one of my clients any more. There was nothing to stop me doing what I liked with him now. So, this time, when he turned and tried to kiss me, I grabbed hold and kissed back, pushing my tongue into his mouth. A minute or two later and we were at the edge of the dance floor somewhere, then away from it altogether, leaning against some wall and all over each other. Iain pushed his hand inside my shorts and I made some token objection, then leaned back against the wall and enjoyed it.

The next thing I knew I was leaving the club with him. It had rained so much that streams of water ran down the streets, the drains unable to cope. It took us a while to find a cab because we were too busy splashing around in the puddles, like kids.

Iain's flat in Wapping was one of those typical yuppie jobs with dark blue walls and huge rooms. He deposited me on the sofa and went to get us both a glass of Coke. There was a pair of curtains behind the settee and I opened them, surprised to see what looked like a wall rather than a window. I pushed my fingers hard against the paintwork, confused and wondering if the drugs were playing tricks with my head. Iain came back carrying the drinks he'd promised and laughed. 'It gets everyone that way.' He placed the glasses on the floor and sat down next to me. Then he leaned in and put his hands on my waist.

My consciousness was doing forward rolls as we lay back on the sofa kissing. Our kisses got softer and softer, till it felt like our lips were melting into each other, slipping and sliding and so juicy you couldn't tell where my mouth stopped and Iain's began. He moved away, sitting back and watching me for half a minute, then laughing. His laughter echoed in my ears.

'You're a mystery,' he said.

I don't know if he meant anything by this, or if he was trying to impress me with his poetic nature. Probably he was just wasted. I couldn't think of anything clever to say back so I just smiled. Mysteriously.

'Tell me something, Frankie. Something you don't usually tell people. You such a secret-keeper, I reckon, tell me something you haven't told anyone we know.'

It crossed my mind that he didn't know me if he thought I did deep and meaningful; I didn't hide my shallows that well. But even as I thought this, I wanted to talk. I wanted to tell him, to be open, to give him a snatch of my soul and hope he loved it, and went with it. I wanted to feel close. Then I was off talking in that way you do on a pill, that random, chopped, fast and frantic, garbled list of a way. 'I was so young, he wasn't much older, and it just didn't work. Neither of us was ready and it ended up being a horrible relationship. We were all wrong for each other . . .' I was going on and on, and could hear it rattle round the room, almost as if I was sitting on the other chair and listening to someone else.

Words kept spewing out of my mouth. But then I noticed Iain's smile getting wider and wider and stopped short. 'What?' I said. 'What's so funny?'

He shook his head. 'Once you get going.' He kissed me, then moved back and examined my face. 'You're so pretty. Do you look more like your mum, or your dad?'

'Don't know.'

'What do people tell you?'

'They don't.'

He paused and looked at me. 'You must have an idea. Like those eyes, unmistakable. Mum or dad?'

'Not Dad. That's about all I know, my mum died when I was three and I don't remember, and don't say you're sorry cos you're not, you didn't know her. I'm not even sorry, I didn't know her either. You can't miss what you haven't had.' I paused for breath.

'You must have seen a picture, though.'

I shook my head. 'I had bad dreams. Dad took the pictures away because he thought it would help.'

'How so?'

I shrugged. I hadn't thought of this as strange before. It was just something that had happened, and I hadn't tested it against external opinion. I hadn't told anyone, not Darren, not even Kate from school, back when we were close and talked about what it might be like when we got our first period.

'You find London hard? A grind?' he asked me then. It was clear from his tone, there in the look on his face, that he did.

'No,' I said. 'But I get lonely. Even in that club tonight. Even out drinking with my mates. Sometimes I get in a cab after a mad night out and the driver doesn't talk and I feel more alone than I thought possible.' I looked at Iain and his eyes were full of what I was saying. He knew exactly what I meant. I thought I might be crying but I couldn't feel my face properly, so I excused myself and went to find the bathroom.

What I saw in the mirror was not pretty. Smudged mascara, chin jutting forward like I'd got some handicap, eyes like almonds cut out from my face. The pores on my skin were visible. I knew that I had gone too far with the drugs tonight. But what did it matter? I had made a connection. I stared at the monster in the glass for a moment. I hadn't been crying after all. I wondered if anything would come of this, of me and Iain. I felt a light inside me switching on. If I'd been sober, I'd probably have panicked at this. But, despite the sight of me, I was filled with a warm glow and I thought – *this could be good. This could be the person who would stop me feeling lonely in those taxis.*

One of Iain's flatmates was waiting for the bathroom when I came out. He leered at me, and I realised my shirt was hanging open, my push-up bra doing its job. I didn't bother covering myself – he could look. I went back into the living room, to the sofa with the fake window. I asked Iain to hold me. We lay there and my head felt mashed up, my eyes darting around in their sockets. I kept catching myself saying things that didn't make sense and doing a double take, pointing out to myself how I'd come undone. I was talking for hours and God knows what other parts of my inner psyche I puked up into the room. Iain squeezed me tight but I wasn't totally inside my body. He finished the job of undressing me and we made love, on the sofa, our eyes locked together. Joining up our bodies felt important, like it added to the bond, but it was a token effort. We were both out of it. I don't remember stopping. I don't remember falling asleep.

---------------------------**4,985.2** ⇧9.0 (0.2%)--------------------------

The next morning Iain brought me a cup of tea and made some excuse about having to go shopping. I asked if he could order me a taxi. I tried to smile but I knew that everything had changed. Iain might not have been a client any more, but he was a trader, and what had happened broke so many promises I'd made to myself.

Shaky Sundays are the worst, and the one that followed, I couldn't sleep it off. I sat round my flat listening to music, ran a bath, but nothing I did stopped my head buzzing with what had happened.

Caustic thoughts ate at my insides. I had said too much. Worst of all there was that light, the one I had felt switch on. The one I deliberately kept set to off and taped down, for my own safety. All that day, every time I let my head slip, thoughts crept in. Something could happen with Iain if I wanted it to. We had connected. Perhaps I should call him, talk some more, at least clear the air. I kept picking up my mobile and bringing up his number, but something stopped me pressing the green button. I composed text messages, then deleted them.

I rang Lorna, but there was no answer. I even rang Kate, in Ilford, though I hadn't spoken to her about anything important for about six years. She wasn't answering her phone either. I was panicking and pacing around the house, and it felt dangerous to stay in. It got so bad, I made my mind up to go see Dad.

It was an orange-coloured day and the light was amazing, like you only get at the beginning of autumn. The rain had stopped, and there were wet leaves everywhere. I was worried they might be the wrong kind and affect the trains; Sunday service was bad enough. There was an Ilford train waiting at the platform in Liverpool Street when I arrived, though. I sat back in the big soft seat and, before I knew it, we'd gone all the way to Ilford, and the doors were opening, and I was grabbing my bag and pulling myself out onto the platform with an effort of will. It always threw me how quick this trip was; Ilford and London were different universes.

I could have rung Dad and asked him for a lift, but I thought the fresh air might shake some of the dizziness from my soul. Ilford never changed. The same old shops sold cheap tat and looked like they were made of cardboard. The shit you could buy on the High Street amazed me. Red nylon G-strings, ornaments made in China rather than from it, those scooters with an engine that were so popular. Seven kinds of crap. It depressed me to look in the shop windows. It hadn't taken long working in the City to make me snobby about things. It went with the territory.

I turned into our estate and walked towards the crescent my dad's house stood on. It was a council estate, but it wasn't that bad. The houses were sturdy brick things, and a lot of people had used their right to buy and looked after their properties. Private buyers had moved in too, so that the area was an interesting mix of people. Most of the gardens were neat and there wasn't rubbish left around except on the odd bad street. It still smelt of estate though, of concrete and people's washing and mud turning over in the gardens.

The door wasn't locked so I let myself in. Dad's house was the way it'd always been. The furniture, the wallpaper (peeling now). Most of the pictures on the wall too, everything was exactly the way it'd been that day in the mid-seventies when my mum passed away and took so much of my dad with her. Everything except the photos of my mum. All that was left of those were very slightly less faded rectangles of wallpaper. Framed ghosts.

I don't know why my dad never redecorated. Maybe he thought there was something left of Mum in the furniture and the fittings. Death is a strange country, possibly stranger than Ilford. He'd told me that a couple of times he'd stopped in the street and been unable to move, thinking he'd seen her. And then the woman came closer, and wasn't my mother, and it was like losing her all over again. This kind of thing didn't happen to me. I only remembered snatches of my mother: a woman with a long patterned skirt and black hair holding out a hand to me; a smile and a packet of Chocolate Buttons, her breath against my cheek as she held me close; a song and the feeling of her chest moving as I fell asleep against its warmth. It was the pattern on that skirt I remembered the best, green and brown curls and commas, paisley I knew now. When I thought of my mother I saw paisley and not much else. I never found myself wishing it was different. But I did wish I'd known my dad before she died.

I could hear the drone of *EastEnders* coming from the front room and all the unease about the night before, all my self-loathing seemed to settle on the house like mist. I hate TV, especially the kind that's more real than life. I walked in and eyed my mother's armchair. I parked myself on the sofa.

'Hello, love,' my dad said, with the barest of glances up from the screen. 'Cuppa tea?'

I said yes, but Dad didn't get up until the break between programmes a few minutes later. I looked around and things seemed to laugh at me; the chintzy three-piece, the clock with the metal spikes that was probably trendy in the seventies when it was bought but had certainly lost its appeal with the years, the electric fire with two out of three bars glowing red. The spiky clock didn't even work any more. It'd stopped at six minutes past twelve one Sunday afternoon and had never been repaired, or taken down. I felt a sudden urge to do a runner but, before I had chance to act on it, Dad was back in the room carrying two cups of tea. He held one out to me. As usual, he'd filled it too full and I spilt the scalding liquid on my hands as I put it down on the coffee table. Dad was busy switching channels on the telly and didn't notice.

'How's the new job, then?' Dad's eyes were intent on the screen again, hypnotised by some advert. When I'd first told him about my interview at LIFFE he went on about what a load of wankers the people were who worked in the City, especially the traders, and how he hoped I wouldn't end up married to one of the knobs. I figured it'd be a waste of my time and energy to go into any detail.

'I start tomorrow.'

He nodded and made some token comment about hoping it went well. The adverts had finished and so did the conversation.

I stayed for two hours, Dad not saying much, me not saying much back. He made tea and I drank it. It was comforting, the drone of the TV and the hot liquid and the easy company. I was glad I'd come. At about six, I'd had enough, though, and made excuses about an early start the next day. Dad made me promise to come for a proper visit the next weekend. I didn't really want to, but I'd been avoiding home and the guilt scratched at my insides like a cat in a bag. He was going for the car keys but I said I'd prefer to walk. It was a lie.

I took the 'scenic' route back to the station, via Darren's. It was one of those things; every step of the way I knew it was a mistake but it was as if an autopilot system set on a crash course took over my body. As I got closer, each street stirred up another memory. Seeing him hand in hand with another girl two months after we'd started seeing each other. The huge row we'd had when I'd said I was going away to university. The way he'd freaked when I'd had my tongue pierced and the time he slapped me hard across the face because he was sure I'd slept with his best mate. None of these things were enough to stop me in my tracks. I doubt even the sight of my dead mother would have rooted me to the spot; I would have just told myself it was someone else. I walked and heard my heels make sharp, short sounds against the pavement to the rhythm of 'a mistake, a mistake'.

As it was, he wasn't home.

Future

1 an exchange-traded contract to buy or sell a commodity at an agreed future date; **2** the time after the present; **3** the life in front of a person; **4** *esp. spoken* the likelihood of success, as in: There's no *future* in this open outcry lark.

Option

1 the right (but not the obligation) to buy or sell a commodity or other asset at a set price (*the strike*) prior to a specific date (*the expiry*); **2** the freedom to choose or something chosen or offered for choice.

------------------------**4,818.1** ⇧12.4 (0.9%)------------------------

'LIFFE' it said on the plaque next to the door, as if everything before had been a rehearsal. The London International Financial Futures and Options Exchange, letters used and missed out conveniently. In theory, I knew most of what I needed for my new job. I'd learnt everything but the hand signals for my SFA exams a few years ago and had used some of it in the brokerage job I'd just left. I'd revised the rest too, and knew all the facts and figures: definitions and specifications, tick values, profit-and-loss profiles, everything about the options and futures that were thrown about on the exchange. I could draw the right diagrams for the trading strategies and explain why a client might want to invest that way. But it still felt like I didn't have a clue – I'd seen it go off right in front of me, and it wasn't as neat and easy as the diagrams and equations in the books.

I pushed my way through the door to the reception area, where men milled around in security uniforms. I walked over to the desk and showed my letter, staring up the escalators. They went on and on and on, upwards, towards my future. They were the longest escalators I'd ever seen, longer than the ones at Holborn tube station or at any of the airports I'd been to. The longest in Europe, someone told me once. I turned back to see the security officer looking me up and down, his attitude just like a bouncer at the wrong kind of club. 'UBF you say? Who's your boss, then?'

'Tom Phillips,' I said, feeling prickles of sweat all over. I tried to pull it together. I knew I'd have to shake Tom's hand when I saw him and I didn't want him to feel my fear, have to wipe it off onto his trousers.

'What's he look like, then? Because there's no note here for me. For all I know you could be a terrorist. Or one-a them anarchy-in-the-City people.' I found myself thinking of answers to his question that I couldn't say out loud. Tom? He was a sexy bloke with thick black hair and eyes that made you think of bed but not sleep.

'Give the girl a break, Bob. She hardly fits the hairy-assed anarchist mould. And they're called the May Day riots for a reason.'

It was Tom's voice, gliding down the escalator ahead of him. I turned and saw him, felt a jolt of desire. 'Hi, babe,' he said. I wiped my hand on my skirt as subtly as I could, but he didn't offer his for a handshake.

'She one-a yours then?' Bob said. A nod from Tom, but

he was looking right at me the entire time. 'You really ought to let us know down here when someone new's coming.'

'Sorry, dude. I'll be sure 'n' let you know next time I fart.' The word fart came out extra loud and surreal, reminding me of people swearing in a foreign language. Tom smiled at Bob and it was pally between them. He turned back to me. 'You made it then. Not changed your mind or decided you'd made a mistake or some shit?'

'Most definitely not.' I heard myself putting on this fake posh accent; I hate it when I do that. I'm not ashamed of where I come from but when I'm talking to people I'm trying to impress my mouth makes strange shapes.

'Good,' Tom said. His eyes were glowing in a way that made it hard for me to look at them. I made sure I bloody well did, though, and I smiled at him. Just the action of smiling made the tension in my body let up.

I stood beside Tom on the escalators and we chatted. I tried hard to be interesting and give more than one-word answers to his comments. We came past TJ's, the café, and then to another reception area. I was taken to a back room and security took my photo. The flash made me blink and left a white mark in my field of vision. They printed out my passes there and then. My three-letter ID was FKS. They gave me a yellow jacket, which I knew I would have to wear for a while, and I wanted a sign to put on it to say I was a trainee not a clerk. I'd have to wait three months before I could do my trader exam and get a proper jacket, and even then I'd have a special newbie badge and get called a blue-button. I was eager to be past all that.

'Did I guess your size right?' Tom said, with a sly smile, staring at my chest.

I felt my face burn but smiled back at him and pulled the jacket across the front of me. 'A wee bit small, I'd say.' We held eye contact for a moment. Then Tom made to go, switching to business mode just like that, as if no flirting had happened. I could have almost believed I'd imagined it.

We walked over to the turnstiles to swipe in. I was headed for the far left, but Tom nudged me aside and went through first. 'That's my lucky turnstile,' he said. I followed him through and decided it could be mine too. I didn't think through the practical implications of us having the same silly superstition. I had no idea it would come to mean anything to me.

Tom marched through to the trading floor, on a mission, and I followed him. I wasn't the only one. The demon eyes of security cameras swept after us all the way in. I could sense their attentions, and it felt like an invasion, like some saddo was trying to look up my skirt. We were walking too fast to talk very much. It was pre-open, so there wasn't much noise, just whispers and a feeling of people waiting. There were a couple of half-hearted chants of 'beaver' as I made my way to the UBF booth. We got there and Tom said something about people to see and he was off, leaving me with this sallow-faced bloke in UBF colours called Jack. Jack didn't say a word to me for ages and I felt like a lemon standing there beside him. I watched while he configured charts and made a few phonecalls, set himself up for the day.

'You up for this?' he said, addressing me at last but hardly making eye contact.

I nodded.

He made a sound I couldn't interpret properly, something between approval and taking the piss. 'You really reckon you can handle it? These big blokes charging round and pushing each other out the way. You know they won't be nicer to you just cos you're a girl?'

'I can handle it.'

'Okay.' I couldn't work out from his tone if he'd accepted what I'd said or was being sarcastic. I could feel that I was frowning, screwing my eyes up at him and giving myself away.

I felt someone come at me from behind and grab my waist, and for a second it took my breath away because I thought it might be Tom. I turned to see a bloke closer to my age, maybe younger. 'Don't let this miserable cunt put you off,' he said. 'You're the best thing what's happened to our team for a long time.' He had an estuary accent, the kind people often mistake for Essex if they're not from the place like I am. I suspected he was from south of the river, Surrey or Kent, somewhere just above the green belt. Even though the bloke was young he wasn't a yellow-jacket, or even a blue-button, but a trader, kitted up in a stripy jacket with a full trading badge. 'Nick,' he said, holding out his hand. I took it and squeezed. 'Good handshake,' he said. 'Tom's fucked off to sort a cross.' I must have looked puzzled because he went on to explain. 'It's a really profitable deal we do from time to time. Line up both sides then bang 'em out in the pit fast as, out loud so you're opening it but quick so's not to get hit on any. You'll see.'

He might as well have been talking Chinese and it sounded close to the rules, but I just nodded along with what he was saying like it was the beat to a ditsy pop tune.

Then began my first trading lesson. Nick showed me some hand signals, being fussy about where I should touch on my arm for different quantities. 'You wanna learn about the easiest way to blow four hundred grand?' he said. 'Yes' seemed the wrong answer, but I made a half-hearted noise of assent. He showed me different ways of signalling to buy a deal. 'This is buy hundred. You gotta hit your forehead.' I copied, feeling like a trained monkey. 'This is buy thousand.' This time his fist moved to hit his forearm. He picked up a telephone handset from the dealer board in front of us and pressed it to his right ear with his left hand. He did both signals again and the difference between them became much subtler. 'Imagine the same thing in a busy room when you're glancing back with the fraction of a second you got to take it in, and the market's moving like wanno against you too. Three hundred and fifty grand I saw lost that way. That kind of shit can put you out of business.'

Nick explained about the 'big figure', the first digits of the price that weren't usually quoted to keep things simple. He pointed at people and told me who they were, what kind of trading they did. It was hard to take it all in, especially as, mostly, people were standing around with papers, or chatting. A couple of times chants went off around the room. When I could make out the words I didn't always get what was meant by them. The fear came that they might be taking the piss out of me. I put it to the back of my mind. This was like being back at school, in the playground.

Just as if it was a school playground, a bell went off for the start of trading and it all changed. It sent Nick diving away from me with no explanation. All the blokes around me turned trader, as if by magic, and the pits filled up. The noise was like engines.

I'd been taken on to work the FTSE futures, not the busiest pit by any means, but the scene in front of me was still hectic. Further away I could see piles of bodies in the

Euribor and Short Sterling pits. I could smell their sweat. Jack was signalling like mad at Nick, and I tried to understand what he was telling him to do, tried to remember all the stuff Nick had shown me. I couldn't – it was too fast.

About an hour after market open, the noise dropped as trading eased off. Play time! A visitor was walking round, one of those typical important-looking types in blue pinstriped suits you see a lot around the City. Someone had made a pair of spurs out of a trade card and stuck them to his trousers and he hadn't noticed. Every so often there was a loud 'yeee-haaa' from a different direction. The traders who yelled out pointed, always away from the pinstriped man. He saw this was going on and laughed at it, clearly unaware it was him who was being lampooned. I felt bad for smiling but I couldn't help it.

On the way to the loo I was 'beavered' again, but in a different way this time. This was a sharp, loud shout just behind my ear. It took an effort of will not to turn to see who it was. Walking back, I saw a bloke take a water pistol from his pocket and squirt it at a yellow-jacket, declaring loudly, 'Ginga's wet himself.' 'Ginga' had that pale skin, like redheads sometimes do, and his face lit up like a fancy lamp, speckled with crimson.

When I got back to the booth, Jack beckoned me over. ''Bout time you made yourself useful. Get me a price for the Vodafone future.'

I was all dizzy with everything going on around me, and preoccupied checking my skirt wasn't wet after the water pistol incident. 'What strike?' I said.

'The future, smart cakes,' Jack snarled.

I laughed. 'Very funny.'

Jack looked at me with raised eyebrows, his face a question mark.

'Don't take the piss,' I said. 'I wasn't born two days ago. There's no such thing as a Vodafone future.'

He didn't smile or break off from what he was doing, but shouted over to Nick. He had to yell and bash the top of one of his monitors to get the young trader's attention. 'Good fucking job I ain't got a client on the phone,' he shouted.

'But you ain't.' Nick gave him two fingers, looked away and whistled through his teeth, then looked back and said, 'What?'

'You better watch yourself, Leeson. This one's so sharp she might cut you up.'

Nick tapped the side of his head, the international sign for madness, and went back to chatting with his mate. It was the first time I'd heard his nickname and it made me laugh out loud. 'He a bit dodgy, then?' I said to Jack. He didn't answer, but gave me this look that said it all – *no shit, Sherlock.*

I'd been expecting to be sent on fools' errands for prices of contracts that didn't exist and people with stupid names so that I'd end up shouting 'I'm looking for Aharte Deeque' or something else suitably embarrassing. Jase and his mates loved telling stories about the things they got up to so I was well warned of these antics. Still, I was pleased I'd not fallen for this one. It felt like passing the first test.

'Might be all right, after all,' Jack said with a curt nod, as if I wasn't standing next to him. Then he gave me a genuine errand to do, ringing back office to check some positions, something that had been a routine task in my last job. I got a stroppy madam on the other end of the line, but nothing I couldn't handle. Then I asked Jack for the client's phone number so I could ring them back. He handed it over and I could tell he was impressed. I could feel his eyes watching me as I picked up the phone.

I could feel something else as well, though. The whisper of something, a dark shadow on the edge of my field of vision. A feeling, instinctual, that something wasn't quite right. I groped around on the back of my jacket and found what I suspect the shadow had put there; a trade card stuck on with tape. With a bit of originality, the note said 'fuck me' rather than 'kick me'. It was hard not to smile but I forced my face straight. Without blinking, I screwed up the card and launched it at the bin.

Tom came over to see me soon after. He brought this dodgy organisational diagram with him, an A4 sheet so thin and worn you could see through it if you held it up to the light. I guessed it'd been used to show many people before me. One of the entries had been crossed out and replaced six times. This was at the bottom of the diagram and the latest name written there in spidery scrawl was mine. Now I knew my place. I also knew the others hadn't lasted.

The FTSE team was UBF's smallest. Tom was officially part of it, as a trader, but he had management responsibilities for a number of teams, represented with dotted lines on the diagram. He told me people had advised him I should work the booth, and what did I think? I said I'd rather be in the thick of it and he smiled. 'I hadda hunch you'd say that,' he said. His smile sent messages over my skin and down my spine. 'They been taking care a you?'

'You could say that.' There was a lump in my throat. I swallowed it, and forced a smile.

Tom's lips twitched, hesitant, as if he was unsure of the correct facial expression for this. 'It's a sign of their affection.'

'Bullshit.'

He laughed so loud it made me start. 'You say what you

mean, girl, don't hold back.' He took the diagram and folded it, placing it in his jacket pocket. 'You wanna grab some lunch?'

I discovered Tom didn't have food in mind when he said 'lunch'. He took me to a pub called The College, a two-minute walk away. Coloured jackets were packed in there so tightly it looked like one of the pits at open. Tom was at the bar, and I ordered a pint of Guinness, triggering him to raise one eyebrow. My drink came and it was thick and heavy. It tasted raw, lined my stomach like oil, and I wished I'd chosen wine or lager. Gossip blew and blustered around me. I didn't know any of the people being talked about. For the first time that day, doubt crept in through some door I'd left open. Had Peter's arrogant shrug been right, and those words, the surprise in his voice? 'Open outcry, huh? They think you can do that?' I headed off to the toilets, feeling like I might puke.

I flicked water on my face then looked up, seeing myself in the mirror and doing a double take at my yellow jacket. I reminded myself that this was what I wanted. I would not let the 'beavers' or the 'fuck me' notes, or any of that shit get to me. And I certainly wasn't going to let that knob Peter and the things he'd said have any effect. I stared myself hard in the face and clenched my jaw. I would not allow it.

I walked back into the bar and the boys were going mad, throwing random numbers at each other and signalling like they were trading. *Pay 36 for 100. Sell 50 at 34.* I knew straight away they were betting on a spread, but the numbers, 34, 36? I processed them as I moved towards the shouting, taking it all in. The winks that passed between them, the odd glance, not even subtle, at my chest.

'Thirty-two,' I said.

Nick laughed. 'You wouldn't say that if you knew what we

was talking about.' He was batting the air in a dismissive way far too near to my head. 'I'll pay 36 for 100.'

'Bad bet, specially when I just told you. Buy low, sell high, Nick,' I said, in as deeply condescending a voice as I could muster. 'Men are so crap at this kind of thing. I'm a 32 D.'

The four blokes stood round me went so quiet that, for a moment, I thought I'd got it all wrong. Then they all laughed, and patted each other on the back, money changing hands.

'I knew it,' Tom said. He was so loud his voice took over the air, drowning out the raucous talk of many groups of traders. 'I took one look into her eyes and I thought – buy 'em!' He made the gesture that went with his words, wrapping one forearm over the other and pulling his fist towards his heart. It looked obscene.

Nick laughed, his voice carrying too, loud and piercing. 'I'll bet you did.' The men around me were in hysterics at this, the noise they made so loud it felt like brain freeze. I didn't care. The doubt had gone. I'd left the door open and the last of my negative feelings were blown away by a good, strong voice.

I was in lust, heels over head in lust.

-------------------------**4,902.9** ⬆54.7 (1.1%)-------------------------

I met Lorna that night at All Bar One. We'd arranged it in advance. I figured I'd need a drink, celebration or commiseration, any which way. As I walked in, it struck me that if she asked me that question, for the first time ever, I would struggle to answer. I considered this for a moment, then settled on celebration, because I was an optimist. I forced the corners of my mouth up and round. Thinking this way made it so and, by the time I found Lorna near the back of the pub, I had a beaming smile raging on my face.

'It went well, then,' Lorna said, before I spoke, kissing me on one cheek, then the other. She smelt like she was fermenting inside. I noticed there was white wine sitting in a chiller on the table and it was more than half empty, making me wonder how long she'd been there. She poured a huge glass for me, and I took a big drink, full of the joys of the day and, boy, did it taste good. Nectar. I smiled wide and said, 'Fucking great day,' and we gave this full-on toast up to the air, without dedicating it to anything or anyone. Nothing existed except the way we felt right then.

'Tell me,' Lorna said, refilling our glasses, once we'd settled from toasting.

I didn't know where to start. There was the teasing and the 'beaver', the 'fuck me' note and the bets about my bra size. I didn't want to get into that. I'd get emotional and it'd spoil the mood. I thought about the other stuff. The way I'd watched traders all day touching the air and turning it into money. You can feel the charge of the cash there, waiting to be earthed.

'It was electric,' I said. It was the only word that would do.

'Go on.' Lorna grabbed an ashtray from the next table and lit up.

'I'm not allowed to trade yet, obviously, but I did a little bit of signalling for Jack in the afternoon, some simple stuff, and I managed to pull it off. Tom said I was exceptional.' I made that last word stretch, proud that he'd used it.

'Was he talking about the trading?'

'Cheeky moo.' I took another huge swallow of wine. I didn't want to talk about this aspect of Tom. I felt uncomfortable and I knew exactly why. I was still determined nothing was going to happen there, yet I felt sick with lust just thinking of him. I pointed out a good-looking bloke standing at the bar. 'Nice arse.'

'How rude,' Lorna said, letting out one of her classy giggles. The heat, and the conversation, was shifted. We did a survey of the bar, checking out the fittest blokes and giving the ugly ones 'bag factor', a measure of how many paper bags you'd need to sleep with them. One bagger meant just one for his head, and two baggers meant you wanted an extra one for you, just in case his fell off. Three or four bags were for real belt-and-braces cases, trolls like Merrick.

Time slipped underneath my feet and, before I knew it, we were well away, and on our third bottle of wine. My glow spread to Lorna, or maybe that was the effects of the wine. We were getting attention because we were so full of it. A couple of men came over and tried to chat us up. Not my type, either of them, typical Essex clerks, wearing Next Directory shirt-and-tie combos. We were polite, but it must have been obvious we weren't interested because they gave up and went off to another group of girls. Younger than us, secretaries or admin types, one of them holding this Chanel handbag that I would have bet on being a fake. These girls were more impressed and Lorna and I pointed and laughed as we saw the lads getting in there.

'Shall we go to Corney's? Better class of Essex boy there,' I said. In truth, it was one particular classy South African who had swayed me in this direction; Iain and I had exchanged texts earlier and he'd said he'd be there. Lorna snatched up the idea of moving because she liked that bar, and we were out of the door and on our way towards Monument like a sneeze.

Corney and Barrow had airs and graces but I wasn't that impressed. It was nothing more than clever marketing. Lorna was into it, though, and performed a little speech for me about how much nicer it was than All Bar One.

Corney's was more expensive, that was about all I knew. It wasn't that I couldn't afford it, but I still had my working-class scruples and didn't like to think I was paying more than I needed to. I probed the room for any sign of Iain. It wasn't busy and he was nowhere to be seen. Lorna and I settled on stools near the bar and I ordered a bottle of champagne. I needed a pick-me-up.

There's that point with alcohol where the experience slips from being all shiny happy and you feel tired and sick, and if you've got anything to be depressed about it bubbles up to the top of your head. That's what happened to me about halfway through our Veuve Clicquot. Lorna was talking away, but I didn't hear a word and was staring into space.

'You all right?' Lorna was saying, and I nodded. She got up to go to the toilet and I wondered if I really was all right. I saw the back of a brown head of hair as a man walked past the other end of the bar and, for a moment, I thought I'd been wrong and that Iain was here after all. Then I saw the man's profile and it wasn't him. I suddenly had an inkling of what my dad must have felt, with his sightings in the street. I'd let in the hope. I'd let myself believe in Iain. I remembered all over again why I didn't do this stuff any more. *I went to bed with my mate and all I got was this lousy text.*

Lorna arrived back and was straight in there, leaning over full of concern. 'What's up?' Closer, more worried. 'Honey, what's wrong?'

'That fucking wanker Iain.'

Lorna hugged me. 'S'okay, honey, you's just had too much.' She was slurring badly. I hadn't noticed how drunk she was.

'He fucking used me. What does he think I am, some slut he can get it on with when and where he fancies? Then not call, and send a crap text that isn't even true. He's probably going round telling everyone I know the gory details of what went on. I'm terminally single.' These words came out in a rush, and I wasn't sure which ones I believed and which ones I was saying to hear them denied by my friend.

'Don't be silly,' Lorna said, but 'silly' came out more like 'shilly' she was so far gone. 'You're wonderful and amazing and you will find the right man.' Wonderfool. Amagshing. These generalities were Lorna's speciality. When a mate had split up with a man, or not got together with a man, or something about a man was depressing them, whatever it was, she had a stock phrase. She had these fucking mantras and I'm sure she thought if she repeated them enough they'd come true.

You'll find the right one.

It'll happen for you soon.

He's out there.

Well, I didn't believe it and I refused to care. Getting a man wasn't my ambition in life. I was perfectly capable of looking after myself and men, I could take them or leave them, shag around the way they did.

Except when I slipped from good pissed to bad.

'Do you miss Darren?' Lorna said.

I said yes and laid my head on her shoulder. Ridiculous, because I didn't miss Darren at all. Far from it. I never wanted to feel that way about anyone again.

'Why'd'you two split anyway?'

I didn't answer her for ages, letting a few tears drip onto her posh jacket. Then I sat up and dried my eyes. 'Fuck, I'm sorry, losing the plot,' I said, and tried to laugh about it.

'You didn't answer, though. Why you split with Darren?' Lorna was like a drunk after an accident, suddenly alert and apparently sober. She wasn't slurring half so much and she was intent on an answer. We were doing the heavy stuff, which was all wrong. I did my best lopsided smile through the haze of tears and said, 'I'm just tired and emotional.' We both collapsed into a fit of giggles.

When we'd stopped laughing, I smiled at Lorna and wiped my damp face with the doily from under my drink. 'What about you and Steven? Are things better now?' I didn't want to talk about her problems much, but it was better than my own: distraction tactics.

'Ach, Steven, he's my baby.' It was a line from a pop song, and there was melancholy in her voice as she said it. She touched her nose and wasn't making eye contact with me. I understood body language well enough, not through some studied analysis, but from playing poker with the boys. I won a lot, and it was mainly because I could tell when people were bluffing. 'He's my rock, you know?' Lorna said, looking right at me. I knew that if I pushed it now, I could get the truth out of her. The tone of her voice invited this interruption. Her body language was shouting 'call me on this'.

I shook my head. 'I don't know what you're talking about, rock.'

'You know, the place I anchor in the storms? The strong thing I cling to. It's one of my mum's theories. Everyone needs a rock.'

'No, don't get it.'

'I'm not that surprised, honey. I don't think you have one. You know, for some people it's their friends, their families. Other people find it in their relationship, like me with Steven. But you, Frankie, I don't know . . .'

'Go on, enlighten me.' She wouldn't have long. They had turned off the sound system and were collecting glasses, and we were the last people there.

'You seem to moor yourself to random things that pass

you by.' She shook her head. 'Sorry, but I worry about you.'

'Rocks schmocks,' I said. Lorna let out a shot of laughter that echoed like music around the quiet bar. It was the end of the conversation, the back end of the night, and soon I would be sitting in a taxi again. We didn't do the deep stuff, Lorna and me. Not if I could help it, anyway. The shallow water was always warmer, and you could see when there were jellyfish there, avoid their sting.

------------------------5,023.8 ⇩22.4 (0.4%)------------------------

Tom took me for lunch at the Imperial City on Friday, to celebrate a successful first week. The restaurant was smart and shiny, in the basement of the Royal Exchange, the building LIFFE had grown out of before it moved to Cannon Bridge. It was a lovely old building, typical City of London with lots of white stone and pillars on its façade. Inside was built large and grand too, even the basement made you think of a ballroom.

'You really are a ballsy one,' Tom said, pouring more Chardonnay into our huge glasses. Right at that moment I didn't feel ballsy. My hand was shaking as I picked up my drink, and I could feel the start of a flush at the bottom of my neck. I cursed myself for fancying my boss. I would have been so much more comfortable with him if I hadn't. 'To women with balls,' he said, slamming down his glass. 'I knew I was making a smart move taking you on, no matter what anyone said.' I tried to smile, and cocked my glass at him, hoping that he couldn't read my thoughts on my face. *What had other people said?* I took a massive swallow of wine and put the glass carefully back on the soap-powder-ad tablecloth.

'I love it, you know, the atmosphere and the shouting and the pushing. It's, like, electric,' I told him, using that word again.

'You betchya sweet ass it is.' He shoved a forkful of fishcake into his mouth but continued to talk. 'It's like anything in life, the floor is, y'know. Where you stand, how you act, how aggressive you are, it's all real important.'

Before I met Tom, I hadn't really thought of Americans as exotic at all, but now I saw they were. I was drawn in by everything about him; his accent, the bad habits at the table, the way he rounded his vowels and sang certain words. I loved the way he called people babe or dude, and the way he used certain English words, like 'lashed' and 'fart', the way those words jumped off his tongue like they didn't belong there.

Tom dug in his inside pocket and pulled out some creased-up paper. He put it on the table and I could see it was a fax from head office over at Canary Wharf. He unfolded and flattened it, then pointed stuff out to me. It was information about various courses they were running over in the Docklands, to do with the Graduate Programme, which I wasn't really part of, but was allowed to go to anyway. 'The way I see it,' Tom said, waving around the paper, then picking up his fork again and using it for emphasis, 'you should go to the lotta them. But if there's anything, and I mean anything, you don't fancy doing then just let me know. I'll tell 'em the floor's going to be too busy that day, make up some bullshit for you, babe.'

I studied the schedule. One of the sessions was a lecture on the first ten years of UBF. 'Well I can tell you already I ain't keen on that one. Sounds a bit long on boredom,' I said, pointing to it on the list.

Tom laughed. 'I hear they put on a live sex show for that.

Keep you awake.' He was smiling through his food and his
eyes were dancing. I felt the flush grow from the back of my
neck then hit my cheeks. Tom was getting the wine down at
a rate and he slammed his empty glass back on the table.
'Listen, babe, being a trainee is crap. You know nada,
everyone hates you, specially if you're a graddie too,
because half the lads on the floor ain't and it's always a sore
spot. You land up on the end of a shitload of resentment.
The only good thing about it is boozy away days doing this
kinda shit.' He waved at the faxes. 'The opportunity to
learn, and network. Make the most of it.'

'All right already,' I said, noticing I was talking the way
he would and cringing inside. 'I said I'd go.'

'Okay, okay, I'm done with the lecture. Talk about long
on boredom,' Tom said. Then he looked me right in the
eyes and said, 'You wanna liven things up?' The first thing
that came to mind was the sex show he'd mentioned. I
raised my eyebrows as I chewed, not willing to risk finding
out if he'd forgive me any bad table manners. 'You wanna
have something a little more serious than this shitty white
wine?' he said.

My new boss was offering me drugs in the middle of the
day. 'Definitely,' I said. He held out his sleeves, showing off
his cufflinks. They were the shape of small, thick buttons,
but made of silver. He flicked at one of them with the nail
of his index finger. I could tell from the noise it made that
it was hollow, but not empty. He undid one cuff and passed
the link to me.

'Frankie, meet charlie,' he said, and the light hit his eyes
so hard they glittered like cut black stones. 'You two wanna
get better acquainted in the rest room?' I looked at what
he'd given me for a few moments, unsure what to do with
it. I looked at Tom. 'Go on, then,' he said, making shooing

signals with his hands. I grabbed my handbag and ran off as instructed.

I stood looking into the toilet bowl for a few minutes. I'd never taken cocaine before and it felt like stepping up a whole league. This was a drug you could OD on, get addicted to. There was definitely part of me that wanted to empty the contents of the cufflink down into the loo and flush it away, go back and pretend I'd had it. But there they were – my working-class scruples again. I knew cocaine was expensive and I couldn't bring myself to waste it. At the same time, there was no way I was going to take it back to Tom. I threw down the toilet seat and sat on top, taking a book out of my bag: my copy of Hull's *Options, Futures and Other Derivative Products*. I'd been carrying the book round with me, reading it every time I got a spare moment. Everyone called it the derivatives bible, which I suppose makes what happened next a kind of sacrilege. I put the book on my knee and emptied the powder on top. I used a credit card to cut white lines.

I felt like a right cliché, wearing my LIFFE jacket and leaning over with a rolled-up tenner towards stripes of cocaine. I sniffed up deep. I breathed out before I moved away and blew a small white cloud into the air. I went for a second snort and hoovered up what I could.

This drug was different to anything I'd taken before because it went to work so fast. I was already glowing as I came back to the table. I could feel my limbs swaying, loose and free, as I sashayed to my chair. Tom was watching me all the way.

'I see you got to know my friend pretty good,' he said. I could tell from the way his eyes flashed that he'd taken the matching cufflink to the gents while I'd been gone. Tom pointed at a spot on his face, near his nose. I watched him, smiling like a fool. He jabbed his finger on the area of skin more insistently and I realised what he was getting at. I wiped at my face to remove whatever had stuck to it. He shook his head, then leant over the table and licked his finger, rubbed my skin hard. 'Mucky pup.' Then he licked his fingers clean.

We didn't go back to the floor that afternoon. Tom phoned Jack and told him we were taking some clients out. I wondered if Jack knew this was bullshit, or if he cared. Tom laughed at my word for what he called 'lunching out'. He told me 'nooners' were okay by him, just so long as there was someone in covering, and you didn't take the piss by doing them too often, or when there were results coming from one of the Blue Chips, the stuff that could send the market crazy. 'Better than coming back in half cut,' he said.

Tom took me to a load of different bars then, all around Lombard Street, then down to Cannon Street. He scored some more drugs off a mate in the City Page and we both had another hit of coke. Everywhere we went, Tom knew people: clients, or ex-clients, or colleagues from previous jobs. I could see as clear as water that Steven had been right when he'd said the City was a small place. I didn't know all the names that featured in their gossip, but I knew some even after the short time I'd worked on the floor. It was a teeny-tiny world, futures and options, but perfect and self-contained nonetheless. So many people I was introduced to had heard about me that I stopped being surprised after a while. Out of the corner of my eye, I caught winks and nudges when I was introduced.

Someone said we should go down to 'the boat', which was the nickname of a pub that floated on the Thames. It wasn't a bad night for it, even though it was September. I don't remember walking there, and I don't remember stepping across the side of the Thames and onto the *Regatta* but that's where I ended up. The sky was mud brown and there was a pinch in the air, but the drugs and booze I'd had wrapped me up snug and warm. Tom pointed out Nick and Diane, sitting on a table alone just a few yards from where we were standing, heads close together.

'He's screwing her. Says what his girlfriend don't know won't hurt her,' Tom whispered in my ear. His breath stroked the skin on my neck. I turned to look at him. His eyes were full of mischief and I knew then he'd told me this titbit of gossip with an agenda. My stomach leapt into my mouth.

The *Regatta* doesn't sail up and down, but has a permanent mooring. What you know, when you come from Essex, is that the Thames is a tidal river. What that means is it's like the sea. You could tell this standing on the boat and the roll of the tide was making me sick and dizzy. The way Tom was looking at me made me feel even worse. The rush I'd had from my last hit of charlie was wearing off, and I was tired. The boat might not have been going anywhere fast, but my head was sailing off into the sunset all by itself.

Tom touched my face, letting his fingers drift down my long, dark hair. 'Your eyes are stunning. You have the second most amazing eyes I've ever seen. They're such a colour.'

I laughed. 'The second most amazing?'

'Hey, it's well up there!'

'What colour are they, though?'

Tom considered this for a couple of moments, screwing up his forehead as he concentrated. 'Like cigar smoke,' he said, and looked pleased with himself. I was less pleased, not sure this was a compliment at all. I considered his eyes, which were amazing too. So dark you could hardly tell the pupil from the iris. They burnt into me, as if they could cut through my skull and open up the deepest parts of my brain, where all my secrets were buried. I looked away, aware of the danger this man could be to me. He kissed my forehead. 'You did good this week,' he said. As he pulled away from me I could feel a spot of heat where his mouth had been. The imprint on my head felt as bright and obvious as lipstick.

'We decided your nickname,' he told me then. All the blokes on the floor had nicknames but I'd been naïve enough to think I'd get away with it. 'You're FKS so we're going to call you Frankie Stein, because turns out you're a freaking monster when you're out.' I giggled at this and swayed, grabbing hold of the table to keep myself upright. Tom held me by the shoulders. Then he kissed me again. It was quick, the kiss, so fast that if I'd blinked I would have missed it. Just a squeeze of lips. I rushed off below deck to the toilets.

I washed my hands and examined my hair in the mirror. It had gone a bit lank and messy so I tried to fluff it up as best I could. I looked closely at my eyes. Cigar smoke? It was too dark down in the bowels of the boat to see much. Was 'second most amazing' good enough, and whose had been better? His wife's? Away from his gaze, the idea that Tom might be dangerous ran down the sink with the soapy water. That was when it struck me; who Tom reminded me of. It had been nagging at me – but I hadn't been able to place his look. I forgot all about the misgivings I had, and rushed back upstairs to tell him.

When I got back outside, Tom was chatting to a woman. She was slightly overweight, from the shape of her face you could tell she'd be getting jowls in a couple of years, and she had a strong Essex accent, the kind that gets to you like chalk scraping. She was standing intimately close to him, and it crossed my mind they might be having an affair. But I dismissed this idea as quick as it'd come into my head. The woman was nowhere near sexy enough for someone like Tom to risk his marriage for her. I bowled right over and touched his shoulder.

'Has anyone ever told you you look like that bloke from *An Officer and a Gentleman*?' I said. 'Younger, I mean, but what's his name? Richard Gere, I think.'

The woman tutted and flicked her hair. 'Yes, they have,' she said. 'A million times.' She looked away with a nasty curl to her lip.

'This is Baby,' said Tom, gesturing at the woman. There was something about his look that was trying to tell me something, warn me, but I couldn't work out what.

'Baby?' I said, aware I was pulling a face, but too mashed on the drugs to be the least bit polite. The only place I'd ever heard this name before was in that film *Dirty Dancing*, and I'd thought it was weird then. *No one puts Baby in the corner*. I remembered the line from the movie and smiled.

'It's short for Babette,' Tom said. He turned to the woman. 'This is Frankie, the new girl on the block.'

'You work with her?' she said, 'her' coming out with eyebrows raised and her nostrils puckered, like it smelt bad to say it. I noticed her eyebrows as she raised them, overplucked and growing back in random directions and I thought, *she should get them waxed properly*. Then I thought how she would never look like a movie star, so what was the point in having Hollywood eyebrows? 'How do you know Tom?' I said.

'I'm Tom's wife,' Baby said. She stressed 'wife', forking her tongue and spitting the word at me. The way she was standing, and how she leaned back before she spoke, it made me think of one of those snakes, a cobra.

71

'His wife,' I said. I could tell by the way she recoiled a little that she could see the shock in my face. It takes a lot to silence me, but this did. I wanted to ask what, how, why, when, all at once. Everything about her was wrong for him; her look, the badly dyed hair, the eyebrows, that godawful accent. It seemed immeasurably unfair that he should have settled for someone this ordinary.

My eyes darted around the tables nearby, trying to think of something to say. Then Baby played her trump card, touching Tom's face with her left hand, the cold metal of her rings harsh against his cheek. It looked like she was using them to put a spell on him. Her rings were the same style as sported by nearly every married woman in the City. Platinum, heavy, simple. So boring and unoriginal and it was wrong, wrong, wrong for him to be with someone who would choose these rings. 'Time to go home,' she said, the wicked witch of Clapham North, stamping her shoes together.

I watched Tom and Baby leave the boat, noticing the way Tom's hand guided his wife over the gangplank, like she was a pet, something he owned. The inside of my skull felt burnt out, and I could hear the echo of Baby's voice. I'm Tom's 'wife', the four-letter word spat at me like venom. I sat down and put my head on the table, all the poisons taking effect.

Next thing I knew I heard Jason's voice. 'Look at you, passed out on the table.' His words sounded like they were coming from miles away. I heard his laugh getting louder as I came back to reality. 'Come on, let's get you home.' I stared up at him, trying to make sense of where I was. He was out of context. 'You been partying with that animal Phillips?'

I was confused for a second, then remembered Phillips was Tom's surname. Typical of Jase to work me out in a breath like that. I could do it to him too; it was like telepathy between us. Cold air hit my face and made me want to throw up.

'You be careful with that one. Animal, he is,' Jase told me. 'C'mon, I'm putting you in a taxi.' He pulled me to my feet.

It was telling that Jase, of all people, had called Tom an animal. It hit me hard in the face; Tom and I had the potential to have too much fun, to take things too far. When there's no voice of reason between two people, that's when real trouble can come along. I clung to Jase as he dragged me off the boat and onto dry land, then along the street to the main road. I gritted my teeth in the hope it would stop the world from spinning round the centre of my brain.

Jase stood with one arm holding me up and another waving madly at the cabs that came by, until one brave driver stopped. Jase opened the door and pushed me onto the seat, holding me in a sitting position for as long as he could.

'You're a nightmare,' he said, and he closed the taxi door. I fell sideways and let my head rest where it landed, against the window.

'It's fifty quid if you soil the cab,' the driver said.

'Buy 'em,' I said, too wasted to follow this up with the appropriate hand signal.

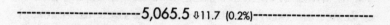

------------------------5,065.5 ⇩11.7 (0.2%)------------------------

My train shuddered and sighed away from London, stopping and starting as if it didn't want to go to Essex. It was right in tune with what I was feeling. Dad had sucked that promise out of me with ease but, now the day had come around, the thought was lead in my stomach. That house again, all my dad's shit. I didn't want to think about it.

Don't get me wrong, I really love my dad. I'll always be grateful for what he gave up for me. He was my hero when I was a little girl. He worked as an electrician at the Ford plant in Dagenham, and I was in awe that he was responsible for bringing to life the huge metal monsters that built the cars. He often had to work weekends and, when I was old enough, he'd take me with him. I remember watching him pull thick cables through ceiling vents and crack them like whips, in charge of the magic that made lights work and sound emerge from speakers. These days the thought of visiting him made my heart scrape against my ribcage, but that wasn't because I loved him any less. Just me, and the love thing.

I sat on the train texting Kate in the hope of forging an escape, at least for a couple of hours. A night out in Ilford wasn't going to rock my world, but it was better than staying in staring at the walls and their spooky rectangles of death. Kate and I used to be close back in middle school, but we'd ended up so different. She was a hairdresser, and it was good to have someone on hand who could give me a decent haircut, but I was finding more and more that our conversation was restricted to the sort of thing that goes on when you're in a salon chair. *You going out this weekend? Where you going on holiday?* Everything short of *Is the water okay?* And these days Kate came as a package with Martina, a single mother who had no interests outside of men and babies. She would even talk about nappies if you let her. It said tons about how different Kate was from me that she chose to spend time with someone like this. When I really thought about it, the only thing we ever had in common was being Catholic, which was why we'd gone to the same school.

Kate replied to say that they had plans to go to The Bell, as usual, but that I was welcome to join them. It was our oldest haunt; the pub we used to go to back when we were young enough to lose the place its licence – and to get some of the blokes we hung round with in proper trouble. Which was the other thing: Darren and his mates would almost certainly be there too. It was his local and the place we'd first met. The other option, though, was a night in with Dad.

I texted straight back to say I'd be there at eight.

I had only a couple of hours at Dad's before I had to head off into town to meet Kate and Martina. It was just as well. He wasn't a conversationalist, my dad. Maybe it was just with me, he didn't know what to say to me any more. I'd grown up so different to how he'd expected. To what he'd wanted. He would have liked me to have had babies by now, I knew that. Give him grandkids and a son-in-law who drove a white van and would talk to him about the Arsenal.

I sat in front of the TV with him until about seven then went upstairs on the pretext of getting ready. When you've hardly slept, being awake is like a vivid dream. Everything echoes, and around your eyes you feel the weight of your world. Your consciousness gets moved to the right of your body, just a little, and you haven't got the strength to stop ideas you shouldn't think about from swimming round your head. I lay on the bed and thought about Dad, the way he loved me but also left me with the distinct impression there was something I'd done wrong. Who was I to judge him, though? He'd only been about my age when he was left on his own with me. I couldn't have handled that. I couldn't have coped with a kid at all, never mind on my own; some screaming, braying monster that'd bleed me dry.

Then I thought about Tom, that kiss, his wife. You'd think she'd at least have had something about her; a wild personality, a special kind of confidence. I tried to picture her again. I wanted to find something worthwhile there, a reason for him to be with her because, otherwise, the only thing I could think was that he'd taken the safe option. For some reason, it unsettled me to think this about Tom. It went against the way I thought of him. And yet, I hardly knew him. What did I really have to go on?

I realised that time had passed and I needed to get ready. I examined my face in the mirror and what I saw wasn't good so I covered my skin with a thick layer of foundation. My hair was okay, not too greasy, which was just as well; Dad had never used his superpowers on the home, to install a shower or anything else that convenient, and the thought of spending any time at all lying down in that manky bath filled me with dread. I changed my clothes and put on loads of deodorant and perfume, hoping that would do. I headed downstairs. My dad eyed the short skirt I was wearing and sighed a couple of times, and I knew what he was thinking but he didn't say it. He asked me what time I'd be getting back and I shrugged, so he told me to make sure I took my key.

I was meeting Kate and Martina down at The Bell, the other side of the town centre, and the walk there was way depressing. It was half-eight and people were already hitting the two-for-one bars. They were mostly young, even younger than me, and they all looked the same. The girls wore jeans with high heels or short skirts with boots and I knew they'd have on black or red G-strings, and that they'd show this off when they bent over. I felt an irrational stab of irritation at this. The blokes were kitted out in hoodies and baseball caps. I saw one lad with a leather mask on, the kind you wear to ride a motorbike, but he was just out on the beers with his mates. It was so trendy to wear clothes that covered your face. It made you think these lads were up to no good, and no doubt some were, but it'd have been nice to be able to tell by looking.

I got to The Bell and went in. Martina and Kate were already there and I hope the shock at the way they looked didn't show on my face. I was wearing a short skirt, but not as short as Kate's, and she was wearing a low-cut top, too. Didn't she know the rules about these things? Martina's jeans were so tight you could see everything, and given that she'd had a baby about six months before, that was not good. It was only of late that I'd noticed the way the pair of them dressed. I hoped I had never been like that, but a taunting voice told me I probably had, when I was young and only had the estate to form my ideas about fashion.

They were sitting there with bottles of some brightly coloured alcopop, in the middle of this big discussion about who was more fanciable in *EastEnders*, Grant or Phil. I said hello and went to buy a drink, hoping the conversation might have moved on by the time I got back from the bar, but ending up disappointed. I came back and sat down, waiting for a few minutes, in the hope they would lay off the telly talk and say something else, anything at all that couldn't have come straight off the pages of *Bella* or *Best*. I realised this wasn't going to happen.

'Grant,' I said. 'No fucking contest. Phil's a short-arsed twat.' Martina and Kate both laughed and then sat back in their seats, visibly more relaxed. Martina leaned over to get something from her handbag and I got a full view of her backside, and the skimpy black G-string that didn't even begin to cover it. The sight made me smile after what I'd been thinking earlier. She was still bent over searching in her bag and looked up at me through her fringe.

'What?' she said.

'Nuffink.' All Essex. I'd never tried to lose my accent but my voice had changed over the years. These days I sounded like someone from North London or Clapham, and when I was with Kate and Martina I could hear this, and I hated it. I wanted to fit in, so I put it on and went all fishwife. Trying too hard, but at least I was trying. They made an effort too, asking me about work, and London, and soon the conversation and the booze were both flowing and I was glad I'd come out.

I was just getting into being the old Frankie with my mates when Darren turned up, some new girl on his arm. It annoyed me that it still stung a little when I saw Darren with a woman. To rub salt and vinegar in, she looked like a model. Darren Matthews always pulled above his weight. Sure, I'd fancied him, but I didn't totally get his universal appeal. He was good-looking, but he was only ever seen out with girls who looked like they'd stepped off the cover of a magazine.

He made straight for our table. There's something about the bloke you first sleep with, like he thinks he's got some hold over you. It's all wrong. Losing your virginity is something you have to do with someone, whoever's around when you're ready. Waiting for someone special is over-rated – the whole thing is best got out the way sooner rather than later. I wish to God I'd done it with some random stranger, not a bloke destined to turn up every time I went out with my friends from school.

'How's stuff?' he said.

'Stuff's good,' I said, wondering how much I could risk

telling him. 'I got a new job on the LIFFE trading floor. It's the real deal.'

'Ever the career girl, my Frankie.' It pissed me off, the way he said 'my Frankie', like I was a belonging he'd never given back. Like I was any kind of belonging. 'How's the love life?' he said then, as if it was the most natural question in the world to ask your ex-girlfriend with your new woman on your arm.

'All right.' Darren's eyes sparkled as he took in everything about the answer. He knew me too well and I hated him for it. He introduced his girl as Sarah. I shook her hand and made some joke about what she had to put up with and Darren played at giving me a thump on the shoulder.

He asked if they could join us and I couldn't bring myself to say no and show that he still bothered me so we all sat at the same table like happy fucking families. Kate bought a round of drinks, but I noticed Martina kept her hands in her pockets. She was always tight that way. I bought about five rounds. But I didn't care. I earned enough and could afford it, and the drinks were two for one anyway. We were all getting pretty bladdered and I was getting louder and louder and making increasingly crude comments. I could hear myself doing it – trying even harder now. Sarah was all life and soul too, making Darren laugh and coo at her. I didn't feel jealous so much as competitive towards her and, when Darren got up to go to the bar, I said I'd help carry the drinks and followed.

The bar was rammed. I stood beside him, way too close, my body pressed right against his. We disappeared into the mass of people vying for the barman's attention. Safely out of view, I brushed my hand across his stomach, then down to the fly of his jeans. He caught my eyes with his, all challenge. I sang to the chart song that was playing. 'I know my ex-boyfriend lies, yeah, he does it all the time.' Darren grinned, taking it lightly, the way it was meant. 'Yeah, yeah, but he's *quite good-looking*,' I sang, changing the words.

'Oi,' he said, giving me a poke under my ribs. He let his hand rest there, then let it drift up the front of me till he was stroking my nipple. 'The song says *drop-dead gorgeous*.'

But I carried on singing and didn't correct myself. He hadn't even tried to catch the barman's eye. I put my mouth right up to his ear, pressing closer still against his body. 'Why don't you take me down the alley and fuck me like a rapist,' I whispered.

He hesitated for a moment. His hand slipped down towards my legs and he rolled his eyes back as he felt bare skin. 'That's got no right to be called a skirt,' he said. Then he closed his eyes and nodded, just like I knew he would.

Five minutes later we were in the alleyway together. Darren was whispering rude nothings in my ear and pulling at my knickers. He pushed me against the wall, grabbed my hair and pushed my face into the brickwork.

We were back in the pub within ten, acting as though nothing had happened. I chatted to Sarah, she told me about her job. I told her about the LIFFE floor. I said I waved my arms about and bought and sold 'stuff', doing an exaggerated demo and ignoring the point in question that I hadn't actually done any trades yet. Everyone laughed. Darren snuggled up to his new woman. I could feel his spunk, wet on the tops of my thighs.

I needed to give myself a break and stop doing this. I might have been casual in my attitude to alcohol and drugs, but it seemed sex with Darren was my only addiction.

'I'm tired out,' I said. 'Been burning it at both ends.' Darren gave me a look that went straight through me, and that was the end of any indecision about staying out. I blew kisses and rushed out of The Bell as fast as I could get through the Saturday night crowd.

Back at Dad's, sleep was elusive. I tossed and turned in my bed, making the sheets come loose and uncovering the itchy fabric of the mattress. This made it even harder, and I had to get out of bed and remake it in the end. I tried to relax all my limbs and muscles but my heart was racing so hard it made my bones vibrate. I worked at making my head go still, but thoughts crept in and made me wakeful. It felt like I was lying watching the ceiling for days. Time gets warped out of shape when you're trying to sleep, it drags and drags. I could hear my heartbeat echoing in my ear, and other stuff too, detritus from the day rattling around my eardrums.

I must have slipped through the delicate skin between awake and asleep because, next thing I knew, I woke with a start. My breathing was all messed up and fast, like I'd been running, and my heart was banging in my chest. My arms and legs hurt, full of blood and adrenalin with nowhere to go. I'd been dreaming; one of the recurring nightmares that have stalked me since childhood. I have several of these and carry them with me everywhere; one where all my teeth fall out and I try to push them back into my gums but it just makes them bleed and the teeth keep coming loose and falling to the floor with blood all over them; another where I float a few feet above the ground, glide from place to place, then I'm flying and getting higher and higher but out of control and too far up and I know I'm going to fall. The one that came tonight is the subtlest, and the scariest. It begins with a feeling in my gut that I've done something wrong. The sense of this grows until it's bad enough to make me shake. The dream cuts, movie style, to me hiding behind a sofa and shaking with fear. I can just see over the top. I turn, and see a woman standing but I can never see who it is because the face is all blurred, as if it has melted.

Often when I have bad dreams, I try to scream but no sound comes out of my mouth. I try to move but it's like pushing against concrete.

When I was little, I'd wake up crying nearly every night and Dad would come running through and cuddle me, rescue me from the monsters in my nightmare. Those nighttime cuddles are some of my very first memories. But you can't keep letting your dad rescue you. You have to grow up and look after yourself.

I got up and went to the bathroom to get a drink of water. I couldn't shake the feeling from the dream, the idea that I'd done something wrong that I couldn't remember. I didn't feel alone in the room. I looked into the mirror, starting as I saw my own reflection. I laughed at how silly I was being. But I still rushed out of the bathroom as quickly as I could.

When I was little and Dad used to come and rescue me from my nightmares, he would tell me that bad dreams were sent for a reason; to move the pain in your head to pain in your body where you could deal with it. But I didn't deal with the pain, did I? Because the dreams kept coming back.

It was 5 a.m. and I knew I wouldn't sleep now. I thought about heading straight to the station, but I knew Dad would worry if he woke up and I'd gone. Besides, it was Sunday and the trains didn't run so early. I got up and made a cup of tea, sat reading a book in the living room. But I couldn't focus on the book either. I looked around the room and felt truly depressed. I knew then I couldn't do this any more, these trips to Dad's. They were bringing me down. It wasn't right; this house, the way things hadn't moved on, and the way Dad virtually ignored me when I came to stay. And I always got bad dreams when I came here. I'd had enough of bad dreams.

I sat on the sofa and stared at one of the patches where a photo used to be. And I made a pact with myself. I would stop putting myself through this. I would stop coming here and visiting Dad, staying in this haunted house.

Volatile

1 *(financial markets)* susceptible to large price moves in either direction over a short period of time; **2** *(liquid)* evaporates easily at room temperature; **3** of unpredictable nature, possibly aggressive or dangerous.

--------------------------5,217.8 ⇩44.3 (0.8%)--------------------------

I went back to London with that promise engraved into the front of my skull. I planned to throw myself into work. This was the way I had always coped; maybe Lorna was wrong when she said I didn't have a 'rock'. I started practising for my trader exam, going along after hours to the mock pit and carrying out fake transactions until the figures and movements were so hard-wired inside my brain I was dreaming about them at night. And that was fine by me if it kept away the nastier things that bothered me in my sleep. After I'd been to a few practice sessions alone, Tom offered to come along and help me. I hesitated, but I did not say no. I would have been a fool to; there was too much he could teach me.

Tom was exactly the kind of trader my dad hoped I wouldn't end up married to. He needn't have worried because Tom was not available for marriage. It was clear he was available for pretty much anything else, though, and resistance wasn't futile, but it was bloody hard. He would look over his shoulder at me and yell, 'What's the delta of the eighty calls?' and I couldn't move my eyes off him to check. The way he said delta, the *e* as clear as a bell ringing, and clearer still when it was the sound on the end of my name, I could have listened to it for hours. Then he would beam, running his fingers through his hair, wiry black curls he wore just a bit longer than most blokes do, looking up at me through his fringe and shooting me that smile, as deadly as a sawn-off at close range. And there I was, a puddle on the floor.

He turned up at one of the after-hours sessions as promised and made straight for me. My heart was pounding so hard I thought it might make a bid for freedom from my chest. He pushed his way through the other people there, a mixed bunch of yellow-jackets, blue-buttons, and people who'd had a few bad days and were trying to sharpen up. They all disappeared into a mist of random colour and noise when I saw Tom, though, and all I could see was him, coming towards me. Then he was there right in front of me, a big slice of American pie. I looked towards the corner of the room, trying not to smile too wide.

'Are ya dancin'?' he said, mockney.

I turned towards him and blushed a little bit, but at least I knew the right answer. 'Are ya askin'?'

'Oh, I'm askin',' he said.

I laughed and suggested we get on with it and we climbed into the pit. It wasn't nearly as busy as it got during peak trading times, but it was still difficult, getting my head and hands around this new language. I made a mistake straight away, buying instead of selling, something that had potential for big losses. But Tom was a good teacher. He didn't lecture, or make me feel bad, he just explained what had happened in calm, neutral tones and made me try again.

I did better the second time. Tom made a big deal out of the words I'd used, though. I'd said 'Buy 200 at 24' and I should have said 'Pay 24 for 200'.

'It sounds petty, but it's real important. There's too much going on and the way you call it out is everything. The fact the price comes first tells the other trader all he needs,' he said. I could have kicked myself, because I'd been around Jack long enough to know that. I wanted the pit to open up and swallow me and I guess that showed, because Tom touched me under my chin, which made me look up at him, and for a moment my stomach jerked as I thought he might kiss me. Of course, he didn't, couldn't, not there and then, on the floor and in front of the cameras, but I felt that he wanted to. 'You're doing real good,' he said. 'Let me show you something, though.'

He slipped behind me and moved my arms around to demonstrate things I wasn't quite getting right. I felt hairs all over my body bristle to attention. The whole thing reminded me of one of those scenes from a film, where the leading man is coaching his love interest in tennis or golf or bowling. There's that intimate moment where they are both enjoying the excuse to get their bodies as close as they can and then they realise, and sometimes they jump apart and sometimes they don't. We didn't.

I heard a catcall and a whistle from behind and it crossed my mind for the first time that none of this was subtle and people would notice. Then a familiar voice and a poke in my ribs. It was only Jason. But I knew it was unlikely he was the only person who'd seen. I was suddenly conscious of the roving eyes of the cameras that spanned the length and width of the building. And of the eyes of the traders too. The latter were sharp, had to be, or their owners would end up bankrupt or sacked.

It was about two days later at pre-open that I got my first inkling of how sharp those eyes were. Jack came back from his habitual morning loo break and put his paper down. He normally read the *Sun*, swearing it was the best indicator of what would happen to the FTSE. His theory was simple: so many of the barrow boys trading on LIFFE read the currant bun that the markets were bound to do whatever its money column said. But today he had a different paper, an industry publication called *Futures and Options World* that was always full of puns like THE RISKS OF PLAYING FTSE or WHAT'S THE FUTURE FOR LIFFE AS WE KNOW IT? I reckon they had a competition to see how many they could fit in each issue. I picked it up and leafed through. There was an article about electronic trading, saying that volumes on the German DTB were picking up, and someone had drawn a ring round this in biro. I smiled at one of the cheesier headlines, then put the paper back down and looked over Jack's shoulder. 'What you doing?'

'Setting up a ticker and charts. Important so I can keep the clients properly informed about all sorts.' He clicked around some more, then looked at me. 'Do anything nice last night?'

'Took the Solomon lot out to that new fish place by Liverpool Street.'

'Any good?'

'Not bad. We got really lashed, though.'

'We got lashed, did we?' Jack stared at the screen and clicked one more time, smiled, then looked up again. 'Lashed?' He gave me this look I didn't like at all.

'What?'

'You know what.' He made a whistling noise behind his teeth.

'Oh God, I'm picking up Americanisms, aren't I? I hate it when people do that as well.' I knew I'd gone red. I could feel the heat coming off my face.

'I think you got more to worry about than that,' Jack said, whistling between his teeth again.

'What d'you mean?'

Jack stopped what he was doing and turned to me, looked me in the eyes. 'The only thing you're getting out of me on the subject of the fucking septic is – be careful. Don't say I didn't warn you.' He stared back at the screen. I grabbed up the copy of *FOW* again and examined it as if I was searching for some secret clause in small print. And I thought – *that's it, they've all decided it's going on.* And I thought – *might as well be, then.*

I was doing so well. Jack and Nick had persisted with the silly initiation games until they got bored, trying to catch me out with errands looking for the keys to the clearing house, or traders called Ate Hurd. They suckered me just once, sending me off to Starbucks to get a half-caff decaff mochita latte with the rest of the order. Let's face it, how was I to know that wasn't actually the name of one of their drinks, given the ponce and ceremony you get at those American-style coffee bars? I came back and called them bastards, but I said it through a smile.

I didn't even let it faze me when I discovered a local who was running a book on who I'd sleep with first. 'Not you,' was my only comment. I could handle the boys and their laddish antics. Diane got to me more; we hadn't had a single proper conversation since I'd joined the team.

Worse, I heard her moan more than once because I wasn't sent to get the coffee as often as she was. I tried to ignore it. I even tried to smile at her, hoping to make inroads, but I was always met with a mask of a face and gave up after a couple of weeks. And that was fine by me, until one Friday at pre-open when hostilities stepped up a level.

It was Jack's fault. I'm sure he lit the fuse and stepped back, well aware of what he was doing, but he was clever enough that there was nothing I could call him on. The room was buzzing that morning. This was partly because England were playing Italy that weekend, and there were flags stuck up on booths, as well as lots of betting going on about the result. Tom had made Batman cloaks for him and Nick from the *FT*, something I saw traders do to that paper a lot more than I saw them read it. Jack didn't smile when they came over singing 'din-ner-din-ner-din-ner-din-ner'. He said something to Tom about the Germans and the Bund future, and they leaned over his screen together looking serious. Tom shrugged. 'Keep your eye on it,' he said, then was off dinner-dinnering again. Jack turned to me with two pages of printout of a client's account, saying the positions needed querying with back office. I could have easily done it myself but it was him who said 'Just chuck it to Diane.' So I did.

She looked at me like I was shit on her shoe. 'Do it yourself.' She turned back towards the trader she'd been chatting with, no doubt her latest candidate for the role of Mr Diane. She never would have said that to Jack or Nick and, although I was a trainee not a full trader yet, I was pretty sure if I'd been a man she would not have spoken to me like that either. Part of me wanted to scurry off and do as I'd been told, but I stood my ground. I'd learnt when I was about five that if you let someone bully you once you'd had it. It took

Diane half a minute to notice I hadn't moved. Then she turned and stared, widening her eyes at me in a vicious way.

I thought about saying that Jack had sent me, but I refused to use his name as back-up. She would do this because I'd told her to. 'Diane, it's your job.'

'Yeah?' She was chewing gum, hard, as if to warn me she'd do the same to my head given half a chance. 'Why the fuck can't you do it? You need to take a long, hard look at the colour of your jacket, girl.'

I didn't respond, just stood where I was, holding out the printed statement Jack had told me to give her. She snatched it out of my hand.

'We all know how you got the plum job,' she said. She was a good-looking woman, but the way her face screwed up all nasty and vicious made her look ugly.

'Care to enlighten me?' Some of the traders around us were making sounds, meows and scratching pussycat noises. Diane turned heel and stormed off, accompanied on her way by catcalls and jeers. I'd won, for the moment, but I knew it wasn't over. Not by a long way. I walked back to the UBF FTSE booth and could feel eyes on me every step I took. It was hard not to turn but I forced myself to hold my head high and look straight ahead.

Jack was yelling at Nick and Tom in the pit when I got back, rubbing his head and shouting 'What's there?' It was looking frantic down where the trading was happening. 'If you had your badge I'd have you in there,' he told me, pointing with a nod of his head. He seemed to be holding five conversations at once and had two phones squeezed against his head. Lights were flashing angry on the dealerboard. I did my best to help out, picking up some calls and giving clients prices, taking orders from them, or queuing them for Jack if they were insistent.

After a while, the phones calmed, the lights going out as if the bulbs had popped. Tom came back to the booth. It had gone well out on the front line, it seemed. His eyes were wet with it and I could almost smell the adrenalin on him.

'You playing FTSE again tonight?' he asked me.

I thought about what Diane had said, and Jack's comments, and the rumours that were obviously going around. And I thought – *fuck the lot of them.* 'You betcha,' I said.

--------------------------5,263.7 ⇧35.2 (0.7%)--------------------------

Once I had time to breathe, it struck me how little I had anticipated what LIFFE would be like. The environment was as harsh as bleach. All I'd seen, from afar, was the bright colours and big money and, with Jase and his mates, the way their eyes lit up when they talked about the place. I hadn't had a clue, not really. It was a case of young Rottweilers at play, the way Tom was fond of saying. Playtime was regular, vicious and loud, and people got mauled. Occasionally, there were proper fights, sleeves rolled up and punches thrown; men holding each other back or pretending to be held.

I remember this French bloke who came on the floor all dapper with designer suit, tie and gelled hair. He got catcalls and kisses blown at him like he was a girl. He tried to tone down his look a few times but it didn't help; I don't think he saw a week out. There were fines for bad behaviour. The idea was to hit the traders in their pockets, because money was what it was all about, making a load of it their reason for coming in every day. The problem was they had enough not to care that much. The numbers got multiplied with further rule breaking, but it took a while before you were talking figures that really bothered the **LIFFE** boys. Shouting or chanting 'beaver', flicking trade cards, all these things were banned but no one really gave a shit.

The bullying left a bad taste in my mouth I have to admit, but, despite this, being on the floor was fun. Not a day went by without my witnessing an incident or hearing a comment that made me laugh, and I mean properly laugh too, the way that involves your lungs and, at its best, leaves an ache in both sides of your mouth and your belly. There was always a game going on. You had to be as sharp as scissors to get anywhere on the exchange, and it helped to own some. Sellotape too, was a valuable commodity. Trade cards were the main props, cut and stuck and modelled into whatever we could imagine; little handbags to wave at anyone who had a strop, shark fins to stick inside collars, 'kick me' on the back of visitors.

A lot of people you'll have heard of came to the exchange – politicians, celebrities, even Tony Blair – and one of the things I liked best is that they were all treated the same. There was no automatic deference to the supposed great and good. Once you stepped onto our territory, you had to earn respect like anyone else. Best of all were the legends like Batesey, nicknamed after Norman of the Hitchcock movie fame, which said it all. When it was quiet he did the 'Wall of Death' in the Short Sterling pit, pretending to ride a motorbike at top speed up on the steps round the edge, all the rest of us watching, cheering, shouting.

I once saw a documentary about cheetahs, about their cubs growing up and the way they learnt from playing. They played rough, jumping on each other, nipping and biting then rolling round on the grass. And it reminded me of work and that made me smile. I thought it was okay. How's the saying go? *It's all fun and games until someone loses an eye.*

It happened one Tuesday morning. I'd been clubbing at the weekend so I wasn't feeling so good. It can get to you like that, and the feeling builds too, if you do Ecstasy a lot. The drug upsets the way your brain works. I'd struggled to get up and into work that morning but I made myself. I hadn't liked what I'd seen in the mirror and it was far too early to get drunk and flirt with someone so they could make me feel more attractive.

The morning went off the way it always did. Jack set up his charts. Tom came in smelling of booze and his hand brushed my arse as he swept by. Diane came with sheets and trade cards. There was betting going on, and some messing around. A bit of a buzz around pre-open. Nothing out of the ordinary, nothing bad. And yet I was over-whelmed by a sense of sadness. Deep down I knew this was just because of the drugs. I rushed off to the toilets.

I locked myself in a cubical and let the tears come. I cried quietly. I didn't want to be heard and end up having someone ask me what was wrong. It was a question I did not have an answer to and any attention to this emotional state would just make it worse. I heard the main door of the ladies open.

'Frankie?' It was Diane. The last person I wanted to talk to. 'Frankie? Are you okay?' She sounded genuinely concerned. She must have noticed me run off, which was a worry. That meant other people would have seen it too.

'I'm fine.'

'You sure?' A pause. 'I'm waiting for you, babe. I want to see that you're okay.'

I licked a tissue and wiped my face. There was no avoiding it. I had to come out and face Diane. At least she didn't seem hostile, for a change. I unlocked the door and walked out.

'Oh, you've been crying.' I felt my face twist again and tried to stop more tears from coming. I didn't succeed. Diane put her arm round me. 'You want to talk about it?'

I walked over to the sink and washed my face. 'It's nothing,' I said. 'I'm just feeling a bit down. You know how it is.'

Diane nodded. 'Hard here sometimes, innit?'

'It's not even that. Not today. Just been burning the candle, you know? Out clubbing most of the weekend and I'm suffering for it now.'

'Fair enough. Just so long as you're okay.' With that, Diane was out of there. It struck me as a quick exit.

I washed my face again, put on a bit of foundation and went back to the booth. I knew something was wrong as soon as I got there. There were snorts, little giggles, whispers. I told myself I was being paranoid, that it was the emotional state I was in. Then it started, with Nick. He opened his mouth wide and wailed like a baby, screwing his hands up and rubbing them into his cheeks. A local who was a mate of his joined in, then Diane; the bitch had told them.

Soon there were five or six people wailing like babies. Jack frowned and didn't join in, but he didn't stop them either. Nick took the abuse up a level, snatches of bitchiness punctuating his wails. 'Oooh, I'm Frankeee, and it's soooo hard for me. I had to go clubbing all weekend and now I just want to cry.' Diane followed suit. All I wanted to do was to run back and lock myself in the toilets again, but I knew that would be the worst reaction. It took all the strength I had to grit my teeth and swallow lump after lump in my throat.

They were going on like this for a good half-hour. I pretended not to hear and got on with my work. Jack gave me a nod. 'You're doing the right thing, love. Just ignore them and they'll get bored.' His kindness almost tipped me over. I was panicking a little and hoping he was right about them getting bored, but it wasn't looking likely. Then Tom swaggered over and they stopped. It wasn't the end of it, though. Nick and Diane carried on all day, whenever Tom was out of hearing range. Wailing and making more comments. Throwing tissues at me when Tom's back was turned. I was boiling inside but didn't react. Then Tom said he was off for an hour or two; he had a meeting and would be back before close. I wanted to beg him to either stay or to take me with him.

As he walked out of the door I felt Diane right next to me, could smell her perfume. I could still see Tom's back as she went off again. 'Aren't you bored yet?' I said.

But Diane wasn't bored. This was her finale, her *pièce de résistance* and the one she hadn't dared risk when Tom was anywhere near. That silly pretence at crying – she was not a good actress – and then the words. 'Oooh, I'm Frankie and it's such a shame for me. I only got my job because the boss wants to shag me and I'll be out on my arse as soon as I've opened my legs.'

Pure instinct took over. I grew up in the kind of place where you learnt it was better to hit first, and hit hard enough that they didn't come back for more. I flew at Diane, grabbing her hair and kicking. I felt people pulling on me but I wasn't letting go. It didn't cross my mind that I would lose my job. Nothing crossed my mind at all. It was no contest. I was a proper estate girl and could handle myself while Diane clearly hadn't had the same kind of hard education. In the end she stopped fighting back, holding her arms in front of her head, trying to minimise the damage. Traders pulled at me, but I was going nowhere except where I could hurt her harder. I couldn't see past the red fury.

Then I heard a voice saying my name. The 'e' sound at the end as clear as a bell ringing. And I let Tom pull me away.

--------------------------5,287.9 ⇧24.2 (0.5%)--------------------------

I was waiting in the same back room where I'd had my interview. Waiting to be sacked. I knew what was coming and that my career would be over; word gets round fast in the City and is taken really seriously. I'd always wondered about the term 'Gross Misconduct' but I didn't any more. I dreaded the sound of the door. It would be Tom, the bloke I not only fancied the arse off, but had huge respect for, coming to tell me to clear my desk and get out of the building. Then the handle turned, and he was in the room, but he was smiling at me. 'Feisty little madame, aintchya?'

I shrugged. I wasn't sure what to say. There was no way I was going to grovel and plead for my job; there was no point. I thought about saying sorry, except I wouldn't have meant it. Sorry didn't cover the way I felt about ruining my career and losing the job I'd had such high hopes for. But I felt no remorse that I'd hurt Diane. The bitch had deserved it.

'This doesn't have to go no further,' he said. It took me a moment to register what he was saying. I had attacked another member of staff. Surely he wasn't going to let me off the hook? I didn't dare believe it, and couldn't speak in case I embarrassed myself. Tom sat down on the edge of the desk in front of me. 'You remember when you came here for interview? When I asked if you were hungry? You remember what you said?'

I nodded. 'I said I was ravenous.'

'Yeah, ya did. And I always believed you, but I never believed it more than this afternoon. You and me, honey, we're from the same cloth.'

I nodded but didn't believe a word of it. I couldn't imagine Tom in a fight. I couldn't imagine him even getting slightly cross he was so laid back. I sniffed. 'But the pit officials, they must've seen it. People from other companies. Surely it's not just up to you.'

Tom laughed. 'Don't worry about it. Dealt with. Like I said in that selfsame conversation, this ain't no normal job, this is the LIFFE trading floor. I sorted it so it won't go no further.'

'Won't Diane complain?'

'Diane's gone home. She won't complain, not if I tell her not to. I can make her life pretty fucking miserable if I choose to. Frankie, take it from me, it's all dealt with. You're not the first trader to get into a fight.' He paused. 'The first girl trader, as far as I'm aware, but not the first trader.' He smiled. Fluffed my hair. 'Let's go have a drink. I think we could both use one.'

My legs were weak as I stood up. I knew there was no way I should have got away with this, that this was too much. What about the company I worked for, UBF? What about pit committee? Tom was protecting me. All I could think was how Diane was right about the reason he had taken me on. More than ever I thought sex with Tom was a terrible idea. Yet, I wanted to have sex with Tom. More than ever.

Tom and I left the building together and headed to join the rest of the team in a pub down Walbrook. We passed the trader statue, and Tom stopped to shove a trade card in its hand, making me smile. We were headed to a Slug and Lettuce. It was a cool enough place, except that it spoilt it for me, knowing it was part of a chain and there were so many places almost exactly the same. I'd noticed a trend for these franchises all over London; Pitcher and Piano, All Bar One, Corney and Barrow, not forgetting Starbucks, Caffé Nero and Costa Coffee. These places were spreading like disease and I could imagine standard-issue high streets where they were the only choices. This was okay in Ilford or Dagenham or Barking, but I was not impressed that it was infecting the lanes and alleys of the City. It was just wrong.

By the time we got to the pub, the scene was carnage. Ties were hanging loose, and there were loads of dead glasses on the table. We arrived to cheers and whistles, and comments about my right hook, as well as those scouser impressions 'Calm down, calm down.' But there were pats on my back too and this was friendly ribbing, not like earlier. Even Nick seemed in good spirits about the whole thing, which surprised me given how friendly he was with Diane. Tom went to the bar and came back with a pitcher of cocktail and several glasses. As we stood necking it, banter turned from bonus size to penis size to the cars people drove. Nick got a ribbing for his crap Porsche. Most people think a Porsche is a Porsche but, in our circles, it was well known that there were good ones and bad ones. Nick had a bad Porsche. It was a 924, and wasn't made by Porsche at all, but Volkswagen. It was a cherry-red colour, with red and black leather seats. Cheesy as Dairylea triangles. Worse than that, Nick wasn't even man enough to drive it, and the Porsche spent most of its time sat in the car park at Swan Lane, around the corner from the exchange.

Tom nudged Jack. 'It's a pussy wagon without the pussy.' The two of them laughed.

'That car sees plenty of action, thank you very much.' Nick batted at the air with his left hand. The way he responded, the small noises he made, ay, ay, oi, it was like some comedy routine he'd rehearsed. He knew how to take stick and I watched, thinking I might be able to learn something from it.

The conversation rolled back then, through penis size to bonus size. I had nothing to add on either subject and got bored after a while. I got up and went to the loo. On the way back I bumped into Nick; neither of us were looking where we were going and we nearly banged heads. We smiled at each other, and he placed his hand on my waist. I wanted to push it away but didn't. Somehow it felt unnecessary; there was only so much he could do standing in the middle of the pub like this. He was playing that game, though, like some men do, pushing his luck to the edge of appropriate. It was close enough to be a move, if I was into him and decided to go for it, but safe enough because he could still act all aggrieved and wounded if challenged, claiming innocence and mere 'friendliness'. It was a game that pissed me off, frankly. I stared at him, then down at his hand. He moved it. 'Thank you,' I said. Then I looked at Nick and realised there was something wrong with his smile.

'You give blow jobs in exchange for toffees to everyone?' he said.

'You what?'

'Is that what it was, a blow job? Or full sex? I mean, just how far do you have to go with boy wonder over there to get away with socking a colleague one?' I realised I'd been naïve not to see through the act he'd been putting on all night. He was always going to come out guns blazing for Diane.

'Sure, whatever, Nick.' I made to walk past but he blocked my way.

'You're not the first, you know. Six or seven he's had like this. Says he's training them up, tells them they'll be a trader. Soon as he's shagged them they're out the door. You're nothing special.'

'Fuck you, Nick.' I pushed past him, heading back towards the others.

'What you doing now, off to have a cry about it?' Nick was shouting after me and his voice carried. I felt my throat contract and knew tears were on the way, which couldn't have been worse under the circumstances. I needed to get out of there. I headed to the door, without saying goodbye or telling anyone I was off.

I marched towards the Poultry without any idea where I might go. It was cold, and the fresh air stung my lungs; the pain of it was cleansing. I heard my name being yelled from some way behind me. The voice was loud and strong; that unmistakable Midwestern twang. Anyone else and I would have carried on walking into the night but Tom coming after me made me stop and turn. I let him catch me up. 'Leeson?' he said.

I breathed that cold air in as hard as I could to stop the tears that were threatening. I nodded. 'Cunt,' I said. This was the cuss of choice for the blokes I worked with but not a word I usually used. It rushed out of my mouth with a surge of hate.

'You filthy girl,' Tom said, grinning at me. I put my hand over my mouth, realising what I'd said. 'It's just a word, Ms Stein. And it's kinda sexy to hear you say it. Gwaan, say it again. For me.'

I looked up at Tom. I still had my hand over my mouth.

'Oh, gwaan, you foul-mouthed little minx.' He put a hand on my waist. I didn't want to push him away, not even a little bit.

I uncovered my mouth. 'Cunt,' I said, this time soft and slow, playing sexy. Tom laughed and pulled me towards him, then kissed me. As his lips touched mine it was like he discharged static into me, and my body jerked.

'You shouldn't've done that,' I said. I stepped back, stunned by the force of the kiss, the way it made me feel. It struck me just how close we were to the pub, how easy it would be for someone to see us from the door, or if they'd followed. Tom read this on my face.

'Hang it, that's what I say,' he said. 'They all think we're having it away anyway, so we might as well.' Then he kissed me again.

Sometimes you fancy someone for a while and when you finally kiss it's a disappointment because you're expecting so much. That wasn't the case with Tom. The second kiss was one of those that go on and on and you lose track of time, and when you've stopped the first thing you want to do is press your lips back again.

I stepped back. 'Sorry. I can't.' I turned and walked off, having to make an effort not to wipe at my mouth with my sleeve. All I knew was I needed to run as far away as I could. The whole situation was making my head spin.

I needed a sensible girlfriend to talk to about it all, to tell me not to let this go any further. A voice of reason. I walked towards the tube and got out my mobile. There was a message from Tom already. My hands shook as I opened it. 'Sorry I offended you.' A second text arrived as I was reading, less apologetic. 'But you're so sexy.' I deleted them both and rang Lorna.

* * *

I'd been to Lorna's flat a few times before, but I'd been drunk every time, so it was a struggle remembering the way from the station. I took the wrong road at first, then remembered almost being knocked down on a railway bridge the last time I'd visited. I found that bridge, and then I recognised a school and knew which way to go.

It was pitch dark when I got to her door. I stood at the main entrance to what had once been a grand old town house. Not any more; it had been split into the smallest possible legally habitable units and sold off. I rang one buzzer after another, because I'd forgotten which number Lorna lived at. Typical London – there was no one at home. Except for Lorna, who was expecting company. I saw her face at a window on the front of the house. She had hung coloured crêpe paper lanterns round the window frame. So pretty; typical Lorna.

She came to the door and we stepped into her flat; two rooms together about the size of a standard-issue council house living room. But it was warm, and welcoming; there were tea lights all over the place, and church candles, decorated vases and table pieces, all these little touches I never would have thought to bother with. All this homemaking made me wonder: did Lorna want to settle down and start making babies? Nappies and breast milk and complications, I couldn't understand why anyone would want to do that. Babies were screaming, pink, wet, shitty-arsed packages of trouble. Worse, you never knew what you were going to get, what they might grow into. Someone was Hitler's mum, and Stalin's and Vlad the Impaler's. Any one of us was capable of bringing that kind of evil into the world.

Lorna was chatting like a pillhead as I walked in, going

on about how the flat was a mess and she was sorry and telling me to sit anywhere I wanted and to dump my coat, asking if red was okay at the same time as opening it. I'd only ever seen Lorna drink red wine at home; it was always white when we were out. She believed the latter got you pissed quicker. I heard the bottle pop, then sigh, as she released the cork, then the music of glasses filling, all this to a percussion of Lorna babbling on. She passed me a glass and paused for breath, taking a big, deep draw on the wine. 'You all right?' I said then, and I had to wait for her to sate herself on the blood-red liquid.

'Mmm,' she said, her lips still covered. I wasn't sure if this was a positive answer to my question, or just appreciation of the wine.

I studied my drink, swilled it in the glass, watching the way it moved, the way the surface tension held and made the liquid cling to the sides of its container. I was no connoisseur, but I could tell really good wine from the way it looked in the glass, and the way it smelt. I looked at the bottle: Châteauneuf-du-Pape. I brought the glass up to my lips. I could almost feel the skin on its surface split as I sipped. The liquid hit my throat, which contracted like it wanted nothing to do with it.

'What's going on then, honey?' Lorna lit a cigarette and relaxed into the other sofa.

I shrugged. 'Not much.'

Lorna studied my face. 'You came over here to talk about something.'

I ran my finger round the edge of my glass. It squeaked and Lorna pulled a face at me. 'What?' I said.

'You aren't going anywhere till you've told me what's the matter. I know you, honey. Always closing up and hiding behind that front of yours. You can't do that to me. I'm not having it.'

But I didn't want to say what had happened today; out loud it would be real. The nastiness of what Diane had done, pretending to be concerned then telling everyone I'd been crying. The fight at work that Tom had sorted, misusing his influence all over the place. And the kisses. Well, those I could talk about.

'I'm in lust. I can't help it, and I don't intend to do anything about it, but there you go, I am in lust with this man.' My throat contracted, the same way it had against the wine.

'Tom?'

I nodded.

'Oh, babe.' She frowned. 'Do you know how he feels?'

'He kissed me today. But I don't think it meant anything. I was pissed off with Nick and things just got out of hand, that's all. I don't think it means anything.'

Lorna sighed. 'It always means something when they kiss you.' She shook her head like I was a lost cause. She looked much older for a moment, and the word that came into my head for her whole demeanour was motherly. I could imagine her with a child latched to each breast. 'What you going to do about it?' she asked me.

'Nothing. I mean, I don't know. I should just leave it, right? I rushed off afterwards and he texted me but I deleted it.' The words were shooting out of me, projectile vomit.

'He's married, and that's that. Surely?'

I nodded again.

'Don't go there, honey.'

I was still nodding, but I knew it was pointless. Even as I nodded, even as I promised Lorna, promised myself, I knew the fight was lost. He wanted me and it was intoxicating. Each time I pushed the wine to my lips I felt his kiss, the warmth of his lips. I felt his tongue, hot in my mouth. It was delicious. Addictive.

Risk Management
An attempt to minimise (usu. financial) risk.

Fuck it
Frankie Cavanagh's attitude to risk management.

---------------------------5,148.8 ⇩77.1 (1.5%)-------------------------

Lorna's mum was big on advice and my friend would repeat this to me like she was chanting at the moon. It was never anything that made me sit up and listen, like how to get on at work or start your own business, but fripperies about men, and dating. The kind of things they talk about in girlie magazines. She'd warned Lorna not to trust a white man with dreadlocks, and never to date a man whose legs were thinner than hers. She'd told her not to get into bed with a man who didn't laugh at her jokes. I often wonder what my mum would have told me if she was still here. Maybe she'd have said not to date your boss, a good rule by anyone's standards. I'd probably have ignored her anyway, the way you do until you're old enough to learn that stuff for yourself, tell it to your kids and watch in agony as they make the same mistakes. It's one sick fucking joke if you think about it.

I wonder if my mum would have told me that sushi is a bad choice for a first date, or any date for that matter, because if you're still using the word 'date' when you meet up you don't know the bloke nearly well enough to eat sushi with him. You shouldn't eat sushi with a fella until he's seen you in dirty underwear.

My first 'date' with Tom was at Moshi-Moshi in Liverpool Street station. It had taken him a couple of weeks to follow through on the kiss. I'd held him off – played it slippery. We were together often, but I was careful to avoid being alone with him, rushing out of rooms and even leaving the pub early a couple of times. Eventually, though, Tom caught me in the admin office. I was trying to sort something out with personnel about my wages and he stood there, quiet, as I talked on the phone. I finished the call but pretended I was still talking for a few minutes, until I realised he wasn't going to go away.

He didn't waste time. 'I want to take you out,' he said. Words that made my breathing faster. 'But, you know that.' He smiled with half his mouth.

Of course, I said 'yes' straight away. He'd gone on to suggest a sushi bar with a voice full of innuendo and I'd said 'yes' to that too.

The décor was clinical and clean. We sat on high stools next to a conveyor belt on which the food floated by. The idea was to grab what you wanted; they worked out the price by counting the empty plates. We ordered sake. Hot wine and cold fish. My dad was alive and well, but I couldn't help thinking this combination would have caused a tailspin in his grave had he had one.

I sat opposite Tom, who was watching me negotiate a salmon nigiri. It kept slipping from the chopsticks, then when I finally got it to my mouth I realised it was too big for a comfortable mouthful. I had a choice: either chomp it down with my mouth too full, or try to bite half off and hold on to the rest, put it back down on my plate and hope I didn't lose my cool by dropping it. I went for the first option, and struggled to keep my mouth closed as I chewed and choked a little. Tom was grinning so hard I thought his face might crack open.

'What?' I said, swallowing and feeling the rice and fish slip down a bit too quick. I coughed. 'What's funny?'

He hesitated. Then he shook his head. 'You are, babe. You don't do things by halves, do ya?'

I swallowed again and smiled back at him, coming over all shy and girly. 'I suppose I don't.'

'There ain't no fucking doubting it,' he said, getting louder mid-sentence, that way he did, something I found so sexy it sent a shock up my throat.

I picked around the plate, looking for some sushi that was sticky, so that when I picked it up the rice wouldn't collapse and spray across the table. Then I decided enough was enough. I put down my chopsticks and picked up a piece with my fingers.

'Good for you. That's how it was designed to be eaten,' Tom said.

I smiled at him. 'Yeah? Well, there you go. It suddenly makes much more sense.' I looked up to find him staring at me. I felt my face flush, the strength of his focus making me shift in my seat.

'Do you like sushi, Frankie Stein?'

'Don't call me that. I hate it.'

'You hate sushi? You seem to be demolishing it pretty darn fast considering.' His face looked ready to be amused, seemed to promise laughter at the first opportunity.

'No. That name!' I gave him a playful smack on his forearm. He faked ducking away from me and I went for a smack again then the laugh came. I loved the way Tom laughed. There was no restraint; it came from the middle of him and exploded into the room.

'Why do you hate your name, honey? You earned that name.'

'Oh, I don't know. I know nothing's meant by it but it sounds like I'm sewn up from dead body parts or something.'

'Take it from me, no one thinks that.' And he glittered at me, this smile on his face that lit up his eyes and made him look naughty. 'C'mon, girl, it's just a play on words. Like Jack is Frosty and Nick is Leeson.'

'Uh huh, and what would you know about that, you fucking septic?'

'That's it. You're getting it now.' Then he gave me this bang-on look, the kind of look that stops a girl dead. 'Your body parts look A-okay to me.' And he grinned like butter wouldn't just melt but boil and then burn. I smiled too but I had to look away.

'Here's a little-known fact for you. In New York harbour, they catch fish and quick freeze it, then ship it to Japan,' he said.

'That's impressive,' I said, hunting down another piece of fish on the platter and taking a bite.

'Ah, you're impressed, are ya?' he said, doing that loud mid-sentence thing again.

I didn't have an answer right away, so I put some more food in my mouth and chewed, bought myself time. 'Yeah, I'm impressed.' I looked at him before continuing, leaving a gap that was just long enough. 'Selling sushi to the Japanese. That's impressive.'

Tom laughed again, and it filled me up, his laughter. I could get used to listening to that sound, I knew it.

We ate up and got the bill, and I insisted on paying half.

As we walked out of the station, I felt drunk. Tom's voice was loud and slightly slurred. We'd guzzled the sake then had beers. The fish made a jelly-like lining in my stomach that was little protection and the alcohol had gone straight to my head.

I looked round Liverpool Street and was suddenly struck at what a madhouse it was. People were everywhere shouting and swaying. A few youngish blokes near platform 3 were braying for a fight. There was mayhem outside a burger place, as pissed people made fusses to get hold of nasty food.

'What line d'you take?' I said to Tom.

'The subway?'

I nodded and didn't correct the Americanism.

He looked distracted. Irritated even. 'Central a stop, then Northern.'

We walked over to the barrier. 'I can go with you to Bank and get a Docklands train,' I said. We slipped through the turnstiles then followed the signs to the platform.

We got off at Bank station and stood there looking at each other. The station was almost as packed as in rush hour, and it was the same work crowd in their suits and shirts, though slightly dishevelled now, slurring and swaying. It gave the impression of people commuting to the pub. It felt like the two of us were completely still, packed in a bubble of our own time, while people dashed past, a blur on all sides. It reminded me of a pop video. I said, 'Well, I'm that way,' and gestured with my thumb over my shoulder.

'Yes,' said Tom. 'And I'm that way.' Pointing in the opposite direction. 'So at least we both know which way we oughta go.' His eyes widened slightly and he glowed at me. 'Let's go for one more little drink.' He touched my hand.

Just a whisper of a brush with his fingertips but it still sent a current through me. I smiled up at him. He set off walking at a pace, towards the Lombard Street exit, and I followed.

We ended up in Swithin's, a wine bar on one of those tiny little streets that are almost alleyways, the sort of streets you only get in old European towns like the City of London. One of Tom's favourite haunts for a quieter drink, he told me. It was pleasant enough, with clean white paintwork, lots of mirrors and an old-fashioned bar. The Italian guy who worked there took my coat as I came in and flirted with me a bit, then Tom and I took some seats in a dark corner. He went off to the bar and brought back two glasses of gin and tonic.

We sat opposite one another, silence stretching so far I felt its stored tension and willed myself to snap it open, yet couldn't. I caught myself staring into my glass, swilling round the bits of lemon with the plastic stirrer. I looked up. Tom was staring at me.

'Your eyes,' he said. He gave me a look that was so intense I thought I'd burst if I didn't look away.

I gazed into my drink again. I looked at the way the lemon had been cut, the way shards were swimming off from it, the half-pip that must have been sliced right through by a scalpel-sharp knife, the cut was so clean.

'I have to say I find myself more than a little offended, Miss Stein,' Tom said, trying and failing at a posh English accent. He sounded more amused than offended.

I looked up. 'What?' Said through a smile.

'You appear to find the contents of that glass more interesting than me.'

My mouth stayed curled, but I couldn't bring myself to look at him again.

'Do I make you nervous?' he said then.

'A little.'

'You make me a little nervous too.' He pushed his hand across the table and rested it on mine. I turned my palm up towards his. I looked at our hands, held together on the table. We touched like that for a while, moving our fingers lightly against each other. It was the most sensual few minutes I'd ever experienced.

A George Michael track came on and broke up the moment. The song was 'Careless Whisper' and it made me feel like someone was watching us, commenting on what we were up to. We looked at each other and smiled, then stood up, banging limbs in that clumsy way of new lovers. He put his arms round me and I rested my head on his shoulder. The music went on, making me feel guilty as it talked about ignorance and how people believed what they wanted to. I listened and thought about Baby, and felt wrong to be where I was, wrapped around her husband like he was mine for the taking. I didn't break off the dance, though.

The music stopped.

'You going to have to leave, lovebirds,' the Italian waiter called over. The way he spoke, it was like he sang the words to us.

'Your place?' Tom said, studying my face. It was almost a cliché of a question, but the second half, the bit he couldn't offer, hung in the air around us like a bad smell.

'Okay.'

We left soon after. It was like the statement of intent would expire if we didn't follow up on it right away. Outside the sky wasn't very dark, more of a muddy grey colour than black, and the moon was huge and bright, wisps of cloud running over it at one edge. We walked along and Tom held my hand, as if this was something romantic, not a seedy encounter. That was how he was good, with the details.

He asked for a glass of water when we came in, and I poured one for him, enjoying the fresh feeling of the spray against my hands. I handed it over and he caught my eyes, took a sip then looked away, put the glass down.

He slid over, slipped his hand on my waist. It fitted perfectly in the hollow just below my ribs. He kissed me. A whisper of a kiss. We both held our mouths just touching and investigated the feeling. Just the once, I told myself, this is fine because it will be just the once. And I wanted to make the most of it, to savour every moment. It seemed he did too.

I took him through to the bedroom and we lay down kissing. He got me undressed, slowly, taking his time over each new part of my body revealed to him. Not touching or stroking or licking, but just leaning back and taking it in. When I was naked he took his clothes off too, all in one go and as quick as he could. Then he cuddled me. He curled up, all foetal, and nudged his head against my breastbone, wrapped his legs round me. I noticed they were thinner than mine. I remembered he was my boss. At least he didn't have dreadlocks, though his hair was no short-back-and-sides. In fact, it fell down round his face in curly clumps, almost ringlets except much wilder, so he wasn't exactly miles off.

At least he laughed at my jokes.

'This ain't something I do, you know,' he said. 'But you're just so damn hot.' His voice went really loud towards the end of the sentence this time, to emphasise the point.

I read somewhere that you absorb chemicals from someone's lips when you kiss them and get addicted to that. I can believe that, just based on this one night. When

I took my lips away from Tom's I got withdrawal symptoms straight away and the only way to relieve them was to get right back on kissing.

After dancing round the point for ages with gentle touches and kisses, Tom made his move. He held me firm and pulled me towards him and kissed me harder than before. As I pulled away my lips felt bruised and swollen. He dragged me on top of him and we smiled at each other. He ran his fingers through my hair.

As soon as Tom was inside me, the energy that had always been there between us came slamming back into the room. It was a change so sudden, so perceptible, that looking back it's like one of those casualty room scenes when they shock the patient back to life. Tom wrapped my hair through his fingers and pulled my head back, sitting up and biting my nipples, then chewing on my neck. I came quick, like my body had been waiting for years.

'I'm gonna have to turn you over,' Tom said. His smile was wicked then and chewed up half his face from the inside. It made me want to do anything he said. I turned onto my stomach.

We had sex again and again until the bed was a mess of spunk and sweat. Tom had left his phone on and it kept ringing. It was a Nokia, and I recognised the ring tone because it was one I'd used for a while called *City Bird*. It wasn't a tune as such, but two tones played in turn, up and down and up again, and sounded like a bird call, hence the name. It rang out over and over again through the night, sounding more desperate each time. It was almost like Baby was in the room with us. Tom didn't answer the phone but he didn't turn it off, either.

We cuddled again, spooned around each other, our limbs loose and heavy. The muscles at the tops of my legs had gone into spasm and wouldn't stop shaking. I tried to relax enough to go to sleep but my heart was pounding. Tom held me like he'd loved me for years. Like he'd known me for ever. He had a talent for that, Tom. For being exactly the way someone else wanted him to be whether it was the truth or phoney as hell.

I didn't sleep much. The *City Bird* call rang out all night and made me edgy. I held on to Tom like I'd never let go.

------------------------4,991.5 ⇩157.3 (3.1%)------------------------

We got up early, not wanting to arrive late together and add fuel to what was already raging. It was a wrench leaving my bed; I'd hardly slept and felt light-headed. I got out the cafetière, almost dropping it, and added several spoons of coffee. I needed a strong boost of caffeine to make the world feel concrete again. I could hear through the wall that Tom had switched on the TV. Then I heard him calling me. I walked through, and could see from his face it was serious.

'The States tanked overnight,' he said.

The coffee was abandoned and we spent two minutes apiece showering. I still felt drunk, but not enough that I felt completely comfortable naked in front of him. I had that morning-after feeling, the sick, seedy one where you realise you don't really know the man you just slept with. I wrapped myself up in my huge, soft bath towel and ran off to my bedroom to get dressed, ringing a cab on the way through and telling it to come in five minutes tops.

To stagger our arrival I got out of the taxi near Bank station and Tom carried on all the way because the team were going to need him. My heart was thumping as I walked up the road towards the exchange; partly it was still racing from too much beer in my blood, but it was also fear about the doors I'd just opened, and about what I might find when I arrived at Cannon Bridge.

I thought about a client who'd rung the day before, buying straddles, a special strategy trade consisting of a couple of different contracts. A straddle was immune to market price and was a trade on volatility. What that meant was this guy expected big market moves. It didn't matter to him if prices went up or down, just as long as they changed some he would make money. Smart guy. I knew he was going to earn on that trade, I could tell from the way Tom had looked at me this morning. I was about to see things really kick off and it sent a thrill through me. It struck me too: I should buy some straddles on my life.

I got there ten minutes of fresh air better off and noticed TJ's was close to empty. I was going to need every second of that extra oxygen. I grabbed a coffee, the vibrations of trains arriving at and leaving Cannon Street below going right through me, making me feel ill. I only managed a few sips before dumping the rest in the bin. I walked onto the trading floor and the buzz was close to unbearable, the psychic equivalent of those high-pitched noises designed to keep people away or drive them out of buildings. I watched Jack set up his charts and moan about Nick not being in yet. The atmosphere felt heavy and thick, as if it was full of dust or spores, and when I breathed in I felt sick to the stomach. Everything inside me was set on edge. It was an animal thing, the hormones making my heart pump and my body get ready to run, for what good that could do here.

There was always a focus, a special buzz at pre-open, but it was more than that today. Brokers and locals flitted from booth to booth taking people aside, having whispered conversations. I felt for the locals, trading their own cash on a day like this. I wouldn't have wanted my own money out there on the table. It didn't matter to us brokers what the prices were, whether the market went up or down. We traded and took commission, rather than buying and selling for our own profits. The only important thing was to be on the ball and not make mistakes because they went on your error account and could really amount to something when the market bounced around. None of us wanted to be responsible for wiping thousands off the bonus pool.

Tom was nowhere to be seen. The options guys stood round checking and rechecking their sheets, the futures blokes fidgeting and talking and pacing. The way the traders were behaving reminded me of being at the dogs, watching the poor animals pushing and fighting against their pens before the rabbit shoots off. None of this behaviour was unusual in itself; there were always a few people twitching over positions on open. But looking around, it struck me what was different. There was no one arsing around for a change; no bets, no books, no dismembered trading cards being used to make fun. Everyone looked deathly serious.

I felt someone dig me in the back and turned to see Tom. 'What'd'ya think, babe?' he asked me, as if it needed saying.

'Going down faster than Diane Cooper's knickers.'

He laughed. 'Faster than Diane's knickers, huh?'

'Faster than Forest last year,' I said.

He looked confused.

'It's football.'

'Soccer?'

I tutted and rolled my eyes. 'No, football.'

'Football then,' he said. 'You be ready, girl, because it's really gonna kick off.'

As if he was commanding it, the buzzer went for the FTSE futures pit. I watched the traders. The locals in the red jackets were the most obvious, playing with their own money and terrified of losing their arses. They were all signalling like mad, arms wide, trying to make out they were after buying, but no one was doing any big deals. They were holding out their big arms like they thought they could hold up the market, Nick Leeson syndrome, but there isn't anyone strong enough. I knew they had long positions they wanted to get rid of, and that really they wanted to sell. I could see desperation in the way they were signalling it so large. They were playing around on the chance they could get the prices up before selling. It didn't work. The prices were dropping and dropping.

Orders started coming in for us, Jack going crazy in the booth. Tom turned trader, and it was like last night had been erased from existence. Nick arrived soon after, and Jack asked him if he'd got the kebabs in on the way, but no one said anything else about it. Nick didn't make any excuses – it wasn't the done thing. He looked worse for wear, and I noticed he was slow on the uptake and had to keep checking what Jack was asking for, which was not good when the prices were changing so fucking fast.

Needs must, and Jack even had me signalling for him to Tom and Nick, and some of the options boys too. The noise was incredible, so loud it hurt my ears. Things were moving by me so fast, my heart was pumping, and there were screams of excitement inside me, rushes that came from nowhere and shook my body up. I no longer felt sick and queasy, or the least bit hungover. An adrenalin cure.

In the pits the boys were manic, and I could see from their hand signals, and the cards Diane brought back from them, that they were doing some volume. It struck me then that a crash was good for business for a brokerage like us. The whole world, his wife and all his mistresses were trading, trying to get out of positions, or profit from going short and then buying back, if they were allowed to. It was the best day we'd had for ages.

When the bell went for the end of the session, it felt like five minutes had passed. The noise dulled, shouting replaced by muffled talking and the rustles, snaps and whistles of trade cards being examined, thrown on the floor, flicked as far as they would go across the room. The close of trading threw me completely. I didn't get what had happened to all those hours, a whole working day; it felt like someone had stolen a chunk of my life. I looked around, dazed and confused, and saw that everyone looked as though they'd been through a trauma: messed-up hair, ties undone, sweat staining their shirts and jackets. No matter where I looked I couldn't get away from the red flash of numbers on screens or displays. It was like someone had sprayed blood all over the room.

The FTSE index had plunged over two hundred points at one stage, rallying a little later on and closing down one-fifty. The futures market had followed it all the way, dragged along by its neck like a puppy tied to a car. People had lost a fortune via their positions on LIFFE but that was just the ice-covered tip of the mountain. The FTSE index represented all of the most important shares in the country and was worth so much money it'd fill up rooms. Millions had been lost on those shares. The money had disappeared into the air, been wiped out of existence, right in front of me. It took my breath away.

It didn't matter to me, though. UBF would get its commission any which way and that would be where my bonus came from. We made our money when the market crashed. We made our money when it rallied too, but that wasn't the point. The room was splattered red and I could smell the sweat and panic still; the blood was fresh all over my hands. We were fucking ambulance chasers.

Jack was famous for crying off home to the wife and kids but even he was in the pub that night. We were so pumped full of it we needed to get out, rave about things that had happened, congratulate and commiserate and just plain analyse it to death. It was complicated. There were whispers about problems in Asia and lots of general talk about a 'correction'.

We went to Drake's on Abchurch Lane. It was dimly lit and slightly damp, so that it reminded me of a cave. I suppose if you were in the wrong mood you could have found it gloomy, but I liked it. Tom and I ordered two shots each of toffee vodka as we came in and we downed them. The drink ripped down my throat, sickly sweet and burning, reminding me of cough medicine. As Tom picked up his second shot, he asked for a jug of vodka Red Bull and two glasses.

The place was packed, no room to sit. I looked out from the bar while we waited and saw everyone standing around in groups, chatting and laughing and shouting. The noise was nearly as loud as it got at the exchange. Tom nudged me and pointed at Jack, then told me he was off to the toilets to powder his nose. I looked over to where Jack was standing, nursing a pint and looking a bit out of place. I picked up the jug and the glasses and headed towards him.

Jack wiped at his brow, smiled. 'Hey, Frankie Stein.' I frowned at the name and struggled with the pitcher of alcohol. There were loads of people standing around and nowhere to put it down so I hugged it to me and put one of the glasses on the floor, poured some drink into the other. 'You got nuff there?' Jack said, and I laughed.

'Not just for me,' I said. I kept hold of the jug and my glass, pouring sips into my mouth with some difficulty and glancing round to see if Tom was on his way. I knew I might as well pour the whole lot out onto the floorboards myself as put it down and wait for someone to knock it over.

'How you feeling?' Jack asked me.

'Good. Really good, actually. It was crazy in there, but we survived, didn't we? We did all right.'

Jack laughed. 'Yes, we did. A good few lads lost their arses though, so don't go waving it around too much that we did well out of it.'

''Course not.'

I sipped some more drink and felt self-conscious, cuddling the pitcher like it was my firstborn child. I looked around at the other traders and yellow-jackets. Some of them were wired but some just looked drawn, like something had sucked the life out of them.

'That's what a crash is like then, is it?' I said.

'Don't get too excited,' Jack said. 'It wasn't nothing compared to what goes off. To be honest, you could only really call it a bump. A parking accident.'

I looked at him and could see the experience etched on his face; it was there in the droop around his eyes. I always thought that wrinkles were fine if they were the kind that came from laughing but Jack had the opposite of smile lines. His face sagged, making him look like he'd spent half his life frowning. I wondered then if I wanted to do this job for ever. I got a kick out of it right now, while I didn't have any kind of commitments that mattered. But would I feel the same when I was forty? When I was fifty? Maybe the key was not to gain the kind of commitments that made you worry so much about the bonus pool.

'What?' Jack said, noticing I was staring and shaking me out of it.

I felt the heat of a flush on my cheeks and was glad we were standing in such a dark, dingy place. 'Just thinking about something,' I said. I felt fingers dig into my waist, and turned to see Nick. This way of saying hello, getting a little too physical, was a habit of his. It was a habit of Tom's too, but I didn't mind that so much. I squirmed away from him and had to work hard not to spill my drink.

'Hey, babes, whassup?' Nick was keeping up the overt friendliness in front of other people on the team and it grated on me, knowing just how full of shit he was.

'We was just talking through today. About how's you was in just in time to get the kebabs in,' Jack said, pursing his lips like an old lady. I realised that was what Jack reminded me of, some disapproving old biddy. He was always the first with the gossip, and I could almost see him, hand on hip, all Les Dawson, talking over the fence to a next-door neighbour. The image tickled me and I laughed out loud.

'You can't seriously find the kebab gag funny. It isn't even the first time he's said it today,' Nick said. I looked at him and said nothing, so he carried on talking, shifting from one leg to another. 'You did all right today, babes,' he said, sounding like he'd found a virgin in a brothel. 'Not bad at all.' He patted me on the bum and I pulled forward before his hand could hit a second time.

'Thanks,' I said.

'Yeah, just that one little mistake but it was fine cos I

closed it out quick enough. Don't you worry, love. It's to be expected. Really Jack shouldn't of had you so involved the way things was, what with you not really being that experienced. It was a couple of grand because of the way the market was moving, but I'm sure Tom'll understand that wasn't your fault.' A half-smile twitched on his face and it was clear what he was getting at.

I didn't respond for a moment, still trying to take in what he was saying, waiting for a punchline or a nudge and a 'nah, only joking'. It didn't come. I stared at Nick. He was seriously trying to pass the blame on to me for some error he had made.

'What?' he said, making a token effort at trying to look innocent but mostly shining with delight at my reaction. I could have smacked him one.

I turned to look at Jack, who shrugged at me. 'So you're going to back him up, are you?'

Jack didn't say anything. I hugged the pitcher closer still and bent down to grab Tom's glass with my one spare hand. Overburdened, I stormed off towards the bar as best I could, slopping liquid everywhere and almost slipping.

'Ooooh, I wonder who the other glass is for,' Nick called after me. I turned, looked towards him. There was a sudden, shocking quiet and I could feel eyes on me from all directions. With every cell of my body I wanted to take the handle of the jug and push it forward, empty its contents all over the cheeky wanker's face. Scratch that; I was murderous and wanted to bring the glass down heavy on his skull and break it. But I didn't. I continued back to the bar where I could put everything down. I felt like one of those dressed-up idiots on *It's a Knockout*, trying to get the coloured water across the obstacles.

Tom came back soon after, and walked over to me at the bar.

'Shall we go and join 'em?' he said, nodding towards Nick and Jack.

'Yeah, happy fucking families,' I said, narrowing my eyes at him.

'What's up?'

I told him what Nick had said and how Jack hadn't contradicted him. My voice broke in my throat as I spoke but I gritted my teeth and refused to cry. I paused and took a deep breath, then mentioned Nick's final dig as I walked off. Tom listened, holding his lips tight together. His eyes were glowing, which made him look mad, but I suspected it was at least in part because of what he'd stuffed up his nose in the toilets. When I'd finished he said nothing to me, but marched over to where Nick and Jack were chatting. But it was Jack he took aside. I figured he was checking up to see what the truth was about the mistake and that made me feel angry. Why didn't he believe me?

Next thing I knew he was squaring up to Nick. They were pacing round each other like men in a boxing ring. A crowd was forming and there was a load of rowdy shouting. I abandoned our drinks on the bar and rushed over, pushed my way through.

'Don't,' I said to Tom, touching the top of his arm. He shrugged me off.

'You were right, babe. This guy really is a wanker.' Tom spat on the floor, and turned to Nick. 'Just fuck off home and we'll talk Monday. In the meantime I'd have a good ole read of your contract, 'specially the words under fraudulent conduct.'

'Oh yeah?' Nick said, putting his face right up to Tom's.

'You really think you got any chance of persuading Rob Jones you ain't one-sided?'

'What the fuck d'you mean by that, asshole?'

There wasn't a person standing around who didn't know what Nick meant. I wondered why Tom was pushing for an answer, given we'd put so much truth in the rumour so recently I was still sore from it. There were a few shouts from the crowd for a 'scrap', but most of us were pulling at the two blokes, trying to get them apart.

'You know exactly what I fucking mean,' Nick said, scowling.

'Do I? Go on then. Say it. Just you fucking say it, Leeson.'

Nick riled at the use of his nickname under the circumstances and had to be held back from hitting out. A couple of blokes pinned his hands to his sides but he stood there looking defiant, chin stuck out and lips slightly parted. He didn't say anything for a moment and I thought he was going to bottle it. Then he said it.

'We all know you're banging her.'

The crowd stepped back as Tom flew at him. There was a huge bloke stood by, a local, still decked up in his red jacket, and I saw him move but it was too late. He grabbed for Tom but missed. The men holding Nick back let go, but not in time for him to get his guard up. There was one fuck of a crack as Tom's fist connected with Nick's jaw. Then Tom was laying into him. They were all over the shop, and it felt loose and dangerous, like any of us could get hurt thanks to the way they were throwing their bodies round the room. The younger bloke staggered about, looking drunk. Then he flung himself at Tom and grabbed him round the chest, clung to him for dear life throwing punches at his body but hugging on too so that Tom couldn't get another proper hit on him. It didn't look like Nick's punches were having much effect. Tom just stood and let Nick hug him for a bit, then he grabbed hold of Nick's hair, like a girl fighting, pulled it back and headbutted him. There was a sound of pure shock from the men around me and a couple waded in to try to stop things.

I'd been wrong about Tom; he could handle himself. It struck me that a foreign accent hid a lot of things. I'd had no idea that Tom came from somewhere you needed to be able to look after yourself. He would have given Darren a run for his money.

Nick was looking battered and Tom backed off. A couple of locals managed to get between the pair of them. Diane came over, eyes full of daggers for me. She grabbed Nick and dabbed at his face with a bar towel. I saw blood as she moved it away. Jack had his arms round Tom, as if he was stopping him from going for Nick again, but it was obvious Tom was allowing this; that he could easily have shook past him and got stuck in again had he wanted to.

'This is your fucking fault,' Diane said, looking up at me.

Tom was straight over to Diane then, his face right in hers and full of menace. 'What the fuck?' She took two steps back, eyes and mouth open like a caricature of the wimpy, girlie victims you get in horror movies. 'I don't want to hear you, or anyone else even fucking suggest that again.' He stood tall, his hands down by his hips but balled up into tense fists, and looked around the room. The blokes in the crowd seemed to shrink. I could hardly breathe for how thrilled and terrified and excited he was making me feel. Diane opened her mouth but thought better of it because of the look Tom was giving her. 'One more word and you're sacked,' he said. And it was clear to all the world he meant it.

He came over to me then, and put his hand firmly on my shoulder, guiding me over to the bar. He poured out the urine-coloured liquid from the pitcher into his glass, then filled mine up. His hands were shaking. We took big swigs of the cocktail. There was blood on his face but I suspected it wasn't his own.

'You all right?' he said.

I nodded. I took another big sip of my drink then said, 'I'm surprised Jack stood up for me.'

He laughed, but it was clear he didn't find anything funny. 'Jack didn't stand up for you. But I knew he was fronting so I called him on it.'

I looked at Tom, who was getting that drink down his gullet. That was when I knew what I'd taken on with this job, how much I had against me. It weighed down heavy in that dark, damp cellar of a pub. I grabbed my drink and swallowed a load more, refilled the glass.

We stayed at Drake's just long enough to get that pitcher down us then made our escape. We ambled to another couple of bars, just the two of us, and then to Fuegos around midnight. A Ricky Martin song came on, and we danced a drunken kind of salsa. Tom was a great dancer. He had natural rhythm and a way of holding himself and he swung his hips so well I would have thought he was gay, except for all the evidence I had piled up against that theory. I smiled up at him as we were dancing, one of those full-of-beer smiles. He took that as a cue to pull me closer, then he kissed me. There was a load of energy in the kiss and I knew right away where we were heading. He hugged me tight. I felt the breath being squeezed out of me.

'Where can we go?' he said as he released his grip, looking at me full of assumptions.

A different question from the previous night. Not my place, not this time, then. And most definitely not his. 'I don't know,' I said.

He looked at me, his eyes begging to be led astray. I stroked his hand, felt the cold metal of his wedding ring. I'd noticed he played with his ring a lot. When we were in meetings, or over lunch, or just standing around waiting for clients to call. He slipped it up and down his finger, sometimes took it off altogether and laid it on the desk or table. I hadn't missed the symbolism in this. Important to note, though, is the way he put the ring back on, always, before standing up and walking away.

I knew the ring should put me off but it didn't. If anything, it made what was happening between us easier to handle. I didn't want to have to deal with the 'love' thing. I didn't want to even think about it. All that crap you get at the beginning of a relationship, waiting for the phone to ring, wondering what he thinks about you. Fuck that. I wanted excitement and I wanted sex. Sorry, but that really is all, folks. My not-so-hidden shallows.

And all that shit of Lorna's about rocks? Well, it fitted here when I thought about it. His boring bit of platinum was a life-ring I could use to keep my head above the waves. Lorna would have said something sensible here about metal not floating and God only knows what her mother would have said.

Fuck it. All this talk about needing rocks or flotation devices is bollocks. You've just got to be comfortable with drowning.

I kissed Tom again, then brought my mouth up to his ear. 'The office?' His head went back and he let out a sound that made my heart beat faster. I knew I'd got the answer right.

UBF had a small office in the Cannon Centre, around the corner from the exchange and about a five-minute walk from Fuegos. It'd been talked about at work, how the place had little to no security, no cameras, and was ideal for certain extra-marital situations. It was Nick I'd heard this from, giving it some about how often he'd used it. At least he'd proved good for something.

The front desk of the Cannon Centre was manned despite the late hour. We showed our passes and were swiped through. If they guessed what we were up to they didn't show any signs of knowing. We took the lift to the tenth floor and made our way along the corridor. Tom entered the code into the panel above the door and it opened, we both walked in.

We all had desks there, except we pretty much never used them. I came to this office once every two or three weeks for meetings, or occasionally when I needed to check back office stuff. We were supposed to come for the APT after-hours trading session, but we didn't. Jack and a couple of the options guys didn't mind covering for everyone and Tom paid them cash in hand for the favour. Jack, Nick and I had cubicles with basic PCs and a phone. Tom had a big office with a state-of-the-art computer system and conference facilities. The whole place had that clear-desk feeling of unoccupied office space. Tom led me into his office and closed the door. The hinges creaked, sounding incredibly loud, paranoia an amplifier. He grabbed me and we kissed. He ran his hands over my body and looked me in the eyes. I held his look without wavering.

'Where?' he said. He still needed me to lead it. It made me think he was expecting to get found out, keeping the excuse on hand that it had all been me and he'd gone along with it because he was weak. I didn't care. He could blame me if that helped him; I had no one to answer to. I took him by the hand and led him over to his desk.

We kissed there for a few minutes. Then I turned my back to him, leaned and steadied myself with my hands on the table top. He made this clicking sound with his tongue, approving of my gesture, and pulled my skirt up, pushing against the back of me so I could feel his dick harden through his trousers. His hands went to my stomach, where he massaged the soft flesh.

'Your belly is just lush,' he said.

I laughed.

'What?' he said.

'It's just a fucking funny thing to compliment me on.'

Tom laughed too. 'Makes a change, I guess? You must've heard shit 'bout your eyes and boobs and legs a million times, and some.'

I smiled and thought how that was true and Tom was clever. I felt him pull my knickers aside.

He pushed me over the desk and fucked me, hard. He came quickly. 'Why are you so sexy?' he said, still bringing blame down on me fast and furious.

I was feeling pretty cheap and then Tom let go of me and walked over to our coats, picked them up. I thought he was making to get out of there already and felt like slapping him. I almost laughed at myself: what was I expecting to do, in the office, cuddle up on the conference room table? But I was underestimating him and forgetting; Tom was clever, and a devil for the details.

He walked away from his desk, to the middle of the room where there was more space, and put our coats on the floor. 'Come here, you,' he said. I walked over and he sat down, pulled me down too. We snuggled into each other on the floor, lying on the coats. He wrapped some of his jacket round me, so I'd keep warm, and held me tight. I tried to relax, but couldn't forget we were in an office, and that the cleaners would be coming around early that morning. Tom must have been much more chilled because only a few minutes had passed before I heard him snoring. I could hear birdsong. We'd stayed out so late it'd got early.

I couldn't believe we were lying on his office floor cuddling up. It made me think a lot of him. Too much. We hadn't even gone our separate ways and I lay awake, wondering how and when we'd be alone together next.

-------------------------4,840.7 ⇩129.5 (2.6%)-------------------------

Those bumps and bruises were our starter for ten. Our team and the markets remained shaky for the rest of the month, the FTSE like a kid with brittle bones: tickling too hard could shatter it inside.

Stress thanks to the tension at work fed my bad dreams and made them thrive. It'd always worked that way. But if you go out all night and don't sleep, you don't dream. If you drink enough and pass out unconscious you don't dream either. The good thing about working in the City was that, if you fancied a mad night out, there would always be someone willing to join you. I'd got used to our team going out together most nights, at least for one or two, everyone except married daddy Jack. That wasn't the case any more. The group had fragmented. But we still went out.

People gave Jack stick when he went home, called him pussy-whipped. But I saw something there, in his movements; a certain satisfaction. Most of the traders wore their jackets as much as they could, as if they were a badge of honour, but Jack was different. He would slip out of his at the end of the day and he would breathe deep, and his shoulders would relax under his shirt. He would say good night, and sometimes take a ribbing for not coming out, and sometimes not. Then he would walk away. He had a bounce in his step as he went. It was different to the way he walked the rest of the day.

Going home could be a powerful thing. The City was full of ghosts and spirits, full of life too, and you needed a break from it. But I lived on the Isle of Dogs, which was hardly better. Besides, there was stuff inside my head that had the ability to spook me just as well as any ghost. They talk about chasing dreams, but I was running away from them.

It was less than a week after the 'parking accident' that I learnt the truth of what Jack was saying about bumps and crashes. I'd managed to sleep the night before, but not until about four in the morning. I woke up late, and stood in the shower with my eyes burning at the onslaught of the water. I missed my usual train, and, as I sat on the next one, I cursed that I was going to miss pre-open. I couldn't believe I'd let that happen, the way things had been. Billions of pounds were being wiped out of existence on a daily basis. I guess I was getting used to crashing; fasten your seatbelt, hold on tight and try not to shit yourself too much.

I went through my lucky turnstile, passing TJ's and smelling the coffee and wanting one so badly. I didn't stop. I rushed to my locker and put on my jacket, then made my way up to the floor. It was busy there, though nothing too far removed from a normal day on open. I couldn't tune in to the mood, work out what was going on and what was likely to happen. I felt blindsided.

Jack made his favourite jibe about the kebabs as I walked over to the booth. Nick was there and wouldn't make eye contact with me, all pretence of friendliness towards me out the window and right down the road at this stage. Tom was talking to some locals a few yards away and seemed relaxed enough. I breathed. I let myself believe this morning would be fine, and picked up the paper, looked at '*Sun* Money'. It said something about Asia but it hurt my eyes to read and I put it down again. Next thing I knew, the phones were going mad.

I didn't see the crash coming and I wasn't braced for it. This time it was like looking down at your car stereo, tuning it in to another channel, cranking up the volume, then looking up just in time to see the back of the car in front of you as you smash right into it.

It was like turning your head forwards just as you walk into a lamppost.

The bell went for open and I couldn't have imagined more phones ringing, but they were. I was answering and trying to get my hands around the orders I was taking, and most of the time I had three or four people on hold for Jack. Some of them waited, some rang off, one or two just got lost in the chaos. From where I was standing, the pit looked like a tub packed with maggots, that way they go crazy, wiggling and struggling but getting nowhere. Tom came back a couple of times, curls sticking to his forehead, his body with us but his eyes elsewhere. Huge sell orders were coming down the phones. I couldn't believe the prices I was seeing. It was like someone had pulled a plug underneath the FTSE and drained its value away. Two hundred points down. Twenty minutes more and four hundred points just gone, gone, gone. Now, this had to be a crash, even by Jack's standards.

Then there came a point when I could see the floor of the FTSE pit again. I noticed a couple of locals running across the room with the *FT* stuck in their collars singing the old-school *Batman* theme tune and Jack was messing with cards and scissors. It was over. I looked at my watch. Only just over an hour had passed; I was expecting it to be much later. Time had its own rules, it seemed, and it played with me a lot, though I gave it a helping hand with the job I did and some of my recreational activities.

Tom came over, his eyes wet, his body moving like he'd had a hit of charlie. Maybe he had; I wouldn't have put it past him, but I don't think it was that. He was just high on the moment. Nick and Tom high-fived each other and Jack bounced away from his place behind the screen to grab them both by the scruff of their necks and plant a sloppy wet kiss on the side of Tom's face. Tom and Nick glowed at each other and, just like that, all the crap was forgotten. And that was good. We needed to get past it and be a team again, couldn't really afford not to.

The market rallied later and the overall fall on the day wasn't that dramatic. But I'll never forget those first few minutes, the dizzy feeling of freefall. The way people's faces looked like fear and the smell of it, like salt in the air near the sea.

The crash had left me with a feeling like concussion and I was desperate to get away. I didn't even want to see Tom. I was worried he might say something about the time I'd made it in, so I left without saying goodbye and phoned Lorna from down the street, telling her 'commiseration' when I got through and switching my phone off once our plans were hatched.

I was trying to describe the day to Lorna but could tell she had one eye on the fact we were running out of wine already. Then I saw Tom, walking up the bar towards us. He waved at me. Then he was on top of us.

'Can I join you?'

I nodded, cursing that no reason to say no came to me quick enough. Lorna had been doing her job as my voice of reason and had made her feelings clear. I was a bad girl and was damaging my karma, which would come back to bite me in the arse, that was, if Tom's wife didn't first.

'This is my friend Lorna,' I said, half gesturing like he could have possibly thought I was talking about anyone else. 'Lorna, this is—'

'Tom. This has to be Tom,' she said. I blushed and Tom did a little bow, the pleasure in being recognised by reputation doing a little dance all over his face.

'Can I get you ladies some more of that fine beverage?' He was Dick Van Dyke-ing out on me again. He pulled the wine from the cooler to check out what it was. 'Why, this is almost gone,' he said, shaking it to show us. He didn't give us the chance to comment but poured what was left into our glasses and walked over to the bar.

'He's tasty,' said Lorna. I watched her eyes following Tom all the way to the bar and back again, checking out his designer suit, then the body underneath, and I was half expecting her to lick her lips.

Tom came back with a fresh bottle of wine and an extra glass. He filled this, and topped up ours, then perched the bottle in the cooler with a flourish. He sat down next to me and put his hand on my knee. It was strange to feel it there, in that context, sitting in All Bar One with Lorna. Like we were going out together in some perfectly acceptable context, not shagging behind his wife's back.

'What's your line of work then, Lorna?' he said. And I thought – *he's a man who remembers names.*

Lorna touched her hair. 'I'm a lawyer,' she said, twirling a blonde curl around her finger. The way she was I could imagine her blowing a kiss to him, Marilyn Monroe style, and even getting on her knees and undoing his zip.

'A lawyer, huh? Good on ya.' He couldn't have sounded more condescending.

I'd seen Lorna crush bigger blokes than Tom for making comments like that but she just fluttered some more and then got up to go to the ladies. I turned to Tom, not sure whether to warn him about Lorna's opinions on our affair. Before I would have thought a lecture a dead cert, but now I was wondering if a threesome was more likely.

'Listen, honey, I gotta warn you, Baby might be coming to join us tonight,' he said, as soon as Lorna was out of earshot.

'Cool.' I was relieved. His wife coming to get him would put an end to this fucked-up situation.

He kissed me then. 'You're cool,' he said as he drew back. He looked at me, all intense. 'So cool.'

Lorna came back and sat down, and we started to make some headway on the wine. Getting the drink down me made me relax, and had the same effect on my companions. Before I knew it, we were chatting about all sorts and refilling our glasses too often. Tom's mobile went off, that birdcall ring tone again. He took his phone out of his pocket and walked away from the table, hand over one ear. Then he left the pub, out into the cold night.

'Lorna Burrows, after all that lecturing now look at you with your tongue on the floor there. You after a bit of Tommy action yourself, now, eh?' I said, but Lorna just laughed.

'Sure, he's sexy, honey, but he's yours. He is totally into you.' She took a drink, then turned her face right towards me and, with a look of complete seriousness, said, 'This could be love.'

That shook me. 'Love?' It was my turn to laugh. 'No, I don't think so. His wife's on her way here. In fact, that's almost certainly who he's talking to now.'

Lorna tipped her glass up, emptying it into her mouth. 'He might be married but he has a big thing for you. I reckon you two are meant for each other.' She waved her glass towards me to stress her point. 'It's funny, because you joked about this, but I think it is kismet, Frankie.'

I looked at Lorna. I sipped more wine. My throat was contracting so hard I thought I might choke.

'I just think you're meant to be together.'

She didn't get a chance to expand on this before charm-school boy was back with us. 'Baby's on her way,' he said. And Lorna winked at me.

We'd finished that bottle and started another before Baby arrived, looking flushed and flustered. I assumed they would be straight off together, but Tom didn't look like moving anywhere. There was nowhere for Baby to sit, and he made no effort to get up and find an extra chair so, in the end, I did. As I went off to get it, I could feel her eyes on me. I thought she might be wondering whether it was me who Tom had spent nights with recently, those times he hadn't come home. I turned with the chair and caught her watching me. It looked like she was checking me out, and she was confused. It struck me, just for an instant, what a smart move Tom was making by inviting her here with us, what a good way it was to blow smoke.

We got more wine soon after that, and a vodka and lemonade for Baby. Nibbles arrived too, though I've no idea who ordered them. There were olives, and curly fries.

I looked at Tom, feeling detached from the action. He wasn't at all self-conscious having his wife and his lover around. He was no different from usual, talking about anything that came up and easily amused, laughing so loud at times that it swallowed your thoughts. If anything, he was feeding off the situation. Lorna was flirting with him, reaching over and touching his arm when he made her laugh. I felt a little jealous, watching her. Not about Tom, I didn't have the right, after all. It was her beautiful private school voice, the gravel at the bottom of it, the proper way she pronounced every word. The perfect laugh she had that sounded like singing.

I could hardly look Baby in the eyes, and thought I must be wearing my guilt like a sign round my neck. I tried to break this by making conversation with her, leaving Tom and Lorna to laugh and flirt and amuse each other. I saw Baby watching their every move. Lorna was dragging her right off the trail.

'What do you do?' I asked her.

'I'm personal assistant to the global head of futures at Barclays,' she said.

'What's that then, a posh way of saying secretary?' I'd met enough PAs to know this was guaranteed to get a rise, *et voilà*, she was off, explaining the differences in terms of specific tasks and random generalities. I heard words but I didn't listen to what she was saying till she was at the end of her lecture and said, 'You know what I mean, though?' in the screechy voice she had. She was not a good advertisement for Essex.

'Yeah,' I said, with no clue what she'd said, never mind what she'd meant. It was tricky then because I'd engaged her. I really wanted to get back into the interesting conversation with Tom and Lorna but it wasn't possible without being rude. Then I had a lucky break because she needed the loo. On her way, she walked past Tom and pecked him on the cheek.

'We got to be at the restaurant by nine-thirty,' she said.

He smiled up at her. 'It'll be cool if we're a bit late though, right?'

I saw her give him a look then, a warning, and he went back to his drink and she was off on her way. The toilets were downstairs and as soon as Baby was out of sight Tom turned to me. 'C'mon. Let's step outside,' he said, sparkling.

I didn't know what to say. How could I 'step outside' with a woman's husband while she nipped to the loo? But something stronger was at work. Something that compelled me to do what he wanted and sneak some time alone together. I looked at Lorna. 'Go!' she said, making shooing signs with her left hand.

'You must think we're terrible,' Tom said to her.

Lorna shrugged and then smiled at me. 'Not at all.'

I hadn't even stood up yet but Tom was gone, heading towards the door. I rushed after him.

We stood in the cold and he lit a fag. He waved it at me. I took it and had a deep drag. It made me cough and I handed it back.

'Am I starting you on a bad habit?' he said, smiling. But I was too busy coughing to answer. Then he wrapped his arms around me and kissed me, hard.

I pushed him away. 'Baby!' I said.

'Where?' he said, playing like he was looking for her all around the front of the pub.

'You know what I mean.'

He kissed me again and I fought it at first, aware that we could so easily get caught, but then the very idea of that danger began to turn me on. I let him kiss me. I ran my hands over the top of his trousers. Then inside the front. He gasped.

Next I knew he was pulling away. And this time Baby was coming out of the doors. I couldn't tell from the look on her face whether she'd seen what had been going on. As she approached, I tried not to wipe at my mouth. It wasn't like there was anything on my lips that would have given me away, but I was so kissed it felt like you'd be able to tell by looking.

'What you two up to?' Baby said. She was smiling and it didn't seem like an accusation.

'Aw, just boring work crap. Something I had to tell Frankie and make sure no one else heard. Confidential,' Tom said. He put his arm around his wife and gave her a kiss on the cheek. 'You all right?'

'Of course. I understand about confidential stuff. I have to deal with it all the time,' she said, her voice brisk and businesslike. I realised her sunny demeanour was a mask. In spite of her smile and friendly words, she was genuinely concerned about what we'd been up to.

Then the two of them were off, hand in hand, into their real lives. As I watched Tom walk away like that, with his wife, I had no clue what to do with myself. I felt bereft.

Lorna's head popped out of the door. 'Babe?' she said. 'She didn't catch you, did she?' She was leaning towards me, all conspiratorial. Her eyes were shining like she was getting a kick out of it all. I shook my head.

'Jesus, she's a boring cow. And she's not nearly as attractive as you'd expect either, is she? No wonder he's gone for you, honey,' she said, touching my arm. I couldn't help thinking that he hadn't gone for me tonight, not really. That he was off doing whatever it was Baby had lined up for him, in a restaurant, by nine-thirty.

Lorna must have caught on to how I was feeling because she hugged me. I could smell the alcohol on her breath. I remembered the wine on the table inside. I remembered the other bottles that were behind the bar waiting for us to buy and drink them. Bottles of Chardonnay and Sauvignon Blanc, of Chablis, sparkling in the fridge lights. Then I knew exactly what to do with myself.

I was going to get very, very drunk.

--------------------------**4,842.3** ⇧40.4 (8.4%)--------------------------

That weekend was the first I pined for Tom. It was not that God-awful proper pining you get with the love thing, but the wonderful pain of infatuation. The kind of pining that feels good, and only happens at the beginning of a relationship. I enjoyed it, and took it with fresh air and a long walk. Then I went for coffee at Starbucks in Canary Wharf. The shopping arcade was dotted with people and, though it still felt lonely, it was significantly busier than it used to be. I wondered how long the peace would last on my island. I could feel something building, feel the place changing. Barclays were in the process of moving their investment bank out here and I had a feeling the rest of London would follow the golden eagle wherever it went. I sat with a latte fast going cold in front of me, trying to think about this, trying to think about the price of my flat going up, up, up the way I was sure it was about to and how this should make me happy. But all I could think about was Tom; his hands on my hips, his mouth on my mouth. And I knew I couldn't spend the rest of the weekend without seeing him, without touching him. I had to spend some time with him, even if it meant spending time with Baby too.

I sent him a text. 'We goin clubbin if u2 wanna cum.' It was an hour before he replied with a 'Yeah I wanna cum.

Where n wen?' I knew he'd respond to the innuendo in my message but I suspected he would bring Baby, despite this. I sent him the details.

We were going out in Old Street, meeting for a drink first then off to a club that had recently opened. I took a long time over getting ready; I kept changing my mind about what to wear and cleaned my make-up right off and reapplied it twice. I wore a tiny skirt without tights, my ego winning the fight with any fears I had over the cold of November nights. I checked myself out in the mirror on my way to the door; I looked good.

I was normally too fashionable to arrive early, but I had to get out of the flat that night before I went insane with nervous energy. Only Merrick was there ahead of me. Jase and Iain arrived soon after, the latter not even making eye contact with me before rushing off to the bar. Jase filled the awkward silence, asking me about work. Merrick had just had a promotion, and went on about that for a while. Jase and I let him, catching each other's eye from time to time and swapping our thoughts on it all without having to say a word.

Iain came back with drinks, finding my eyes for a moment, then jerking his away. I wondered if he was scared of what I might say to him, what I might demand. I hate the politics that come after the sex and wished he'd drop it. I'd rather have discussed intimate details – right there and then with everyone – than second guess what was going through his head. The text alert on my phone went off and my stomach jerked because I thought it was going to be Tom raining off. It was Lorna asking when I was free for a drink. I didn't reply. I was hesitant because I worried that, without Tom's sexual chemistry to protect me, she'd give me the lecture I deserved. As I was putting my phone away,

Tom and Baby walked through the door, smiling at each other, looking like newlyweds, and I wished it had been them cancelling.

Tom shook hands with Jase; they smacked each other on the back. Baby went off towards the ladies and Tom to the bar. Jase pulled a face at me and I knew immediately what he wanted to know. I tried to ignore him, but he slid over and grabbed me by the elbow, pulling me aside.

'Well?' he said, smiling at me and doing that telepathy thing again.

'What?'

'You, him, and his wife,' Jase said, stressing the word 'wife' like it was dirty. His voice was full of pleasure at the drama of the situation.

I blushed. There was no escaping that Jason had worked me out, the way he always did. 'All right, yes, I'm having a bit of a thing with him.'

Jase's head went back as he laughed. 'I knew it was true. You just won me fifty quid.'

I turned and gave him a hard stare. 'You can't say anything,' I said. 'Not to anyone.'

Jase pulled back, faking that he was being hit by me. 'Yes, ma'am.'

Then what he'd said struck me. 'There's a book on it? People are betting?'

Jase just laughed, and I pressed him on it for a while but he wasn't telling.

Tom came back with bright blue bottles, which he handed round. I took one and had a big swig. It was sweet and didn't taste much of alcohol.

'This place we're going to a dance club?' Tom said.

Iain nodded, looking down at the floor as he lit a cigarette. His eyes flicked to me then, looking as if they were asking permission to share a smile. I thought about keeping a straight face and staring him out, showing him none of this was fazing me. But the truth was, I wasn't that much of a ball breaker. I smiled at him, and he smiled back, and blushed slightly and I was suddenly conscious of my breathing.

'Can one of you lot sort me out with a half a square of acid or something then? Or some X. Before the ball and chain comes back cos she don't approve of these things. I can't get into house music without some, well, psychological help,' Tom said.

Jase laughed. 'Nothing like cutting to the punch.' He reached into his pocket and slipped us both pills, embossed with acid house smiley faces. We threw them in our mouths and tipped back our heads, washing them down with the sticky vodka mix like a synchronised event. Baby was coming back from the loos as we did this but, like with the kiss outside All Bar One, it seemed she just missed it.

I was soaring high when we walked into the club, and stood there, tuning straight into the trance music that was pumping out of the speakers. A packed dance floor spread out in front of me like a dark sea, coloured lights and strobes illuminating the arms that were sticking out all over the place; people waving, not drowning. We all stood there; me, Jase, Tom, Iain, Merrick, with our legs spread wide and our arms in the air in appreciation of the sounds. Next to me Jase was shouting, 'Fucking gwaaaaan!' The music sliced into my skin and then the voice, the sample breaking up but it was still clear, strong, good. It scraped through my flesh and against my bones. *I . . . can't . . . get . . . no . . . sle . . . ee . . . e . . . ee . . . ep . . .* It was like the man knew my life, my story. The dreams that were haunting me and keeping me awake. The way nights like this, when I didn't have to think of sleep, when the drugs would take me away from all that, how they were becoming more and more important. And as I held my hands up to the DJ in an act of worship, I looked around and there was everyone else, giving it up to the man in the booth like we were in some kind of church. A surge of power ran out from my heart and to all four corners of my body and held me there, crucified by the music. I looked around at my friends and I knew they could see inside my head. I understood them, they understood me and the world was good, truly and completely good with no doubt that everything was going be all right.

We broke it up and headed off to dance. That's when I noticed Baby had been with us all along. She had been there and, yet, she had not been 'there'. Jase sidled up to me and whispered in my ear, 'That's what I call a giant starfish moment.' I stared at him as he slipped ahead of me, overwhelmed by the power of what he'd said, how bang on the money it'd been and how he knew, he absolutely knew what was going through my head.

I moved onto the dance floor. It was hot and crowded, impossible to move without touching and being touched. I felt the music cover my skin. It built to a crescendo then changed key, broke into a riff that lifted my soul. The beats got to me, made me feel more than alive, like I'd evaporated and was filling the air around me. The synthesised sounds echoed and vibrated through me. I danced on and on, and time slipped, and I forgot the facts and practicalities that haunt us so much of the time; they had gone, gone, gone and so had that sense of me, myself, that lonely feeling of separation. I lost track of where my boundaries were, where I stopped and other people started. We become one.

Later, coming down a little, I became aware of Tom

nearby. Then we were standing so close it would have taken just the twitch of a muscle for us to be in each other's arms. It felt like if I moved, if we touched, something would earth and send us flying.

'You got some front,' I said.

He laughed. 'Yeah I have. How 'bout you? What ya got?' Tom didn't have the post-sex problems with eye contact that had been bothering Iain; he was staring right at me until it was me who turned away. 'You wanna find a quiet corner here and give me a blow job?' he said.

I looked back at him and saw a smile that was infectious and felt my own mouth mirror it straight away. I shook my head. I wasn't saying no, so much as expressing my incredulity at the suggestion.

There weren't many dark corners or hiding places in the club. We found an abandoned bar behind one of the chill-out areas. Couples were lying prone and all over each other nearby and I did wonder if anyone would notice or care if I went ahead and got on my knees out in the open. We snuck behind the counter, though, and I unzipped Tom's flies and had his cock in my mouth just like that. His head went back and he moaned, and was going on about how good it felt. He tangled my hair around his fingers and held on, making sure I wasn't going anywhere.

'Why are you so sexy?' he whispered into the air above my head as he came inside my mouth.

'I don't know,' I said, answering his question this time.

He smiled and pulled my face into his crotch. I nuzzled him there for a minute, then zipped him up. He came down to me and put his arms around me, pulled me right into him under the counter. He kissed me on my face, all over my cheeks, on my nose, on my eyes, kiss, kiss, kiss, kiss, kiss.

'I can't believe this,' he said. 'I've only been married six months. What did you have to come into my life for, eh?' Then he kissed me more, on my face again, then full on my mouth, and it felt like he was shutting me up after what he'd said. The implications of the new information were dancing round my head. The maths wouldn't leave me alone.

We went back to find the others. Baby was there, dancing like something out of the eighties. She looked drunk. She grabbed at her husband's hand and I could see her rings, winking at me through the dark. So simple. So typical and so damn boring. I made my mind up there and then I wasn't ever getting married. I'd never wanted to be someone's wife, but seeing Tom and Baby's six-month-old marriage, that was the final nail in the Y-shaped coffin.

Jase winked at me. A gesture of complicity normally reserved to pass between blokes but I was one of the lads, no doubting it. I beamed at him. I did feel happy. I knew I should feel bad about what I'd just done and I wanted to. I'd worked hard trying to make myself feel guilty over the last few weeks but I was faking it; I felt fucking great that I was getting it on with Tom.

Someone grabbed me from behind. I turned to see Iain. He was smiling wide, all self-consciousness gone together with the brain cells the pills were taking on their way. We hugged each other.

'You found your man,' he said, half nodding over at Tom. Tom who was dancing with his wife of six months. His arms were in the air and she was wiggling, looking wrong next to the music. Looking wrong next to Tom, the way she always did.

I turned back to Iain and the confusion I felt must have been shouting out from my skin. 'She's history,' he said, and I could have sworn I heard him whisper 'kismet', though I can't be certain that wasn't something my head made up. The same word Lorna had used. Then Iain said something else that reminded me of Lorna's reaction. 'Look at her, though. You were bound to happen.'

I couldn't work it out. I'd expected everyone to give me hassle about messing around with a married man, especially when they met his wife. But meeting his wife had made it better not worse, just because of what she looked like.

Kismet. It was a word I hadn't known when Lorna first said it so I'd looked it up. Fate. God's will. People thought Tom and I were supposed to be together, that our seedy little affair fitted into someone's grand plan.

I wasn't so sure. It was fun and we looked right together, even I could see that, but I couldn't get past the idea that a few months before I met him, he felt strongly enough about this silly, drunken Essex woman with the screechy voice and a job as a PA to say 'I do' and promise his life away. It seemed he made this promise lightly, and that bothered me. It was his whole life.

Even Lorna seemed to approve. It annoyed me a little; she had a function in my life and part of it was to call me on these things, to rein in my madness. But she thought I'd end up winning Tom and so didn't see any danger. She thought we should be together because Tom and I, hand in hand, were pleasing to her eye. I figured it went to show it wasn't just me; everyone had their hidden shallows.

Arbitrage

Exploitation of price differences between marketplaces in order to make a risk-free profit. An arbitrageur will buy a security or commodity in one marketplace and sell exactly the same thing in another at a higher price.

DTB

1 Deutsche Termin Bourse; the German equivalent of LIFFE. The DTB listed many identical contracts to the London exchange but on an electronic platform and aggressively targeted the same trading business; **2** them bastard Germans.

--------------------------**4,908.3** ⇧10.9 (0.2%)--------------------------

The months had passed so quickly. My probationary period was over and I had to go to Canary Wharf for an appraisal meeting.

'Rob Jones, Global Head of Derivatives', said the little sign on the desk in front of me. The man that went with the sign was diminutive too, a small man in a big job; a common City phenomenon. Rob Jones was waving around Tom's report about my work, which was glowing to the point of risqué. *Frankie is very eager to please and enthusiastic. She has fit in well and been extremely open to the needs of other team members. It is a pleasure to have her.* It all went over the slightly bald head of Rob Jones, Global Head of Derivatives, who was all smiles and superlatives. He approved the five-grand pay rise Tom had suggested and told him to take me out for a slap-up lunch before going back into the City. Tom didn't need much encouragement.

We went to a restaurant by the dockside and had white wine in glasses like goldfish bowls and bistro food: fat chips with mayo, goat's cheese salad. We sat outside, next to patio heaters, but it was still too cold. We played at being somewhere warmer, taking it in turns to make noises about how it was just too hot, taking off items of clothing and trying not to shiver.

By the time the waitress came to clear away I was bloated, and feeling drunk. The world rocked gently around me and I watched the ripples glisten on the water as it was hit by the winter sun. Tom was slurring, and I knew we were going to make a nooner of that day and not go back to trade. He smiled, and winked at me, then pulled his mobile out his pocket and phoned Jack to tell him exactly what I'd guessed he would. He put down the phone. 'What shall we do now?'

I shrugged, didn't have any suggestions. I had put my jacket back on and was feeling warm again.

'Let's do a runner.'

That made me jerk awake. 'You what?'

'You heard me!' The waitress was hovering around, and the power in Tom's voice made her jump. She recovered herself.

'Can I get you anything else?' she asked.

'Just the check,' Tom said. She was walking away. 'Gwaaan. Now,' he whispered to me.

I'd left my bag in my locker at the exchange and travelled light – just my underground ticket and my debit card. I took one look at Tom. It was clear he'd spotted my tendency to have 'fuck it' moments and my weakness at the challenge of a dare. We got up from the table and walked casually away from the restaurant. We hadn't gone far before I heard a voice calling after us, the waitress's distinctive Kiwi accent. 'Excuse me.' We carried on as if we didn't have a clue it was us she was talking to. 'Excuse me. Sir. Madam?' Louder but still polite. We kept on walking, swapping glances but not stepping up the pace. 'Excuse me!' She was shouting now. I felt guilty for a second, thinking she might have one of those bad managers who'd make her pay for any losses on her shift. I shook off my conscience; those bosses were urban myths.

I looked at Tom. 'Shall we run?' Everything inside me fluttered.

He shrugged. 'Maybe.'

We both turned to see whether we were being pursued. The waitress was sprinting after us. We didn't discuss it any further, but were off, running towards the steps that led up to the main part of the Wharf. I followed Tom, taking the stairs three at once, tripping a couple of times. I was breathing fast, and worried I might fall over. We both made it to the top, though, and flew off fast towards the shopping arcade.

We were still wearing our LIFFE jackets and must have stood out a mile, running through the shoppers in the arcade. I had a full stomach and bad stitch. Tom was ahead of me, and I glanced back. The waitress was gaining on us. She was fit, a good strong build. Tom was halfway up the escalators to the DLR and I reached for the first step, stumbling a little but regaining my balance. I got a spurt on then, bounding up towards the trains. We were on the wrong platform, the one going out of town. We ran right through the Beckton service and onto the platform the other side. In front of me was the Bank train; its doors beeping ready to set off. Tom flew right on and collided with this bloke in a suit who was reading the paper. The man tutted, then bounced back to how he'd been standing before. Tom laughed as I collided with him and sent him into the man a second time. I collapsed, choking on my laughter and out of breath from running.

The waitress made it up near the doors but not until they were closed. She stood there looking at us, leaning forward and holding on to her legs. I watched her breathing hard as the train pulled out. Tom put his thumb on his nose and wiggled his fingers at her, stuck out his tongue. The adrenalin had sent me flying and I lost it at this point, collapsed into a fit of giggles. This infected Tom and he was gone too, and we both pissed ourselves, bent double with how funny it was.

I'd been planning to go to the after-hours trading practice session that night, but by the time it came around I was too wasted. Tom shrugged and said it didn't matter, that what I'd learnt helping on the booth during those bumpy weeks should be enough, and I realised he was right. Things had changed for me at work. The way we'd had to pull together as a team had brought us together and I'd been accepted by the men. Not by Diane, of course, but she didn't matter, not that much. As each day passed I felt less like the new kid everyone picked on and more like one of the gang.

Someone rang Tom inviting him for a drink in Drake's so we went there. I drank so many toffee vodka shots I thought I might melt my throat off. I remember thinking it felt late, based on my level of intoxication and the lighting, but I had no idea what the time was. That was the thing about Drake's, it being in the bowels of the City under Abchurch Lane, there wasn't any natural light. You'd come up for air, especially in the summer, and the sun would send you dizzy. I'd grown to like this about the place, its removal from the space–time continuum.

We were having such a laugh, me and Tom and a few of the other lads I didn't know so well. Tom was getting less and less careful who knew about me and him. Not that he came out and said anything, or kissed me openly, nothing that obvious. Little touches gave him away, though. This is what it's like to have an affair; the little things give you away when you're not looking. The lads were talking about the World Cup next year, and whether we had a chance. Tom was making fun, saying how he just didn't get 'British' sports. I tried to explain cricket to him. I was doing all right, using empty shot glasses to demonstrate wickets and the players. But when he asked how long the games went on, and I told him Test matches lasted five days, we both lost it and I gave up trying.

We'd just ordered another round of shots and were downing them, and Tom turned to me, his eyes wet and face glowing with the fun we were having. He touched my arm and we were all shouting and laughing about who'd got the shot down fastest, when Baby walked in. The sight of her stopped my drink on its way to my mouth. Tom had his faults but he had always been reliable in warning me when his wife was going to turn up somewhere. I turned to look at him, and I could see it was a surprise to him as well. That was when it struck me – *she knows. She knows and she is learning our haunts and hunting us down, smoking out the affair.*

'Thought I might find you here,' she said to Tom, and she smiled at me. 'How are you, Frankie?' Said as if there was nothing she should worry about at all, her husband out and looking so close to his young female employee. The way she handled it summed up how different Baby was from me. I would have just got to the point, screamed my head off at my husband and his tart, thrown myself at her and pulled her hair. But Baby didn't do any of these things. It was like she was playing 'Let's pretend'. We were signed right up to that one. Adultery: a game for adults, 3 players or more, 18+.

'You getting your wife a drink then?' Baby said, casting spells with her magic rings. We got proper drinks in then, vodka and lemonade for Baby, but Tom and I had gin and tonic, and the lads all had pints. Some of them had vodka shots too, and either chased them or bombed them in their beers. I had begun to notice Tom always choosing the same drink as me. I don't know why he did it, but it made me feel good. Another symptom of having an affair, to notice and cling to these tiny little things.

The pub was crammed. I felt great, enjoying that powerful boost you get from a certain level of alcohol in your blood if your life is going well. Mine couldn't have been better. I had the perfect job and had just had a glowing appraisal and a pay rise. I had a sexy, crazy lover in my life who was a few feet away and looking edible, and I had just the right amount of drink in me. For a cherry on top, Tom and I managed to collide in a space that was hidden by the crowd. We stood and looked at each other and it was like the rest of the pub did not exist.

'Fuck me in the toilets,' I said.

He stared me out, his eyes dancing a little and his lips twitching. 'Ladies or gents?'

I didn't have to think about it. 'Ladies.' It was more of a challenge.

'Okay. I'll give you a nod and you get up there, wait for me.'

We went back to drinking then, and we were drinking with intent. Baby was looking flushed and troubled. The rest of us were raucous and loud. We were standing round chatting and laughing for about another half-hour when Tom sent me the signal he'd promised. I guess he thought it was subtle, but I saw a couple of the lads clock it. I didn't dare look at Baby. I put down my drink and headed upstairs.

I waited in the ladies, playing with my hair in front of the mirror. My eyes stared out at me, cracks of red blemishing the whites. I smoothed the skin underneath them, wondering if it was true that drinking lots of gin made you age. So far it didn't seem to have had much of an effect, but I'd been drinking much more of the stuff recently. The door opened, almost into me, and then I saw Tom's black curls behind me in the mirror. He smiled at me through the glass, and I smiled back. He came right into the tiny room, closing the door, and grabbed me, kissing me hard and manoeuvring me into one of the two tiny cubicles.

He pulled at the buttons on my shirt, making it spring open, and he grabbed at my tits. 'Your body's been fighting with that top all day long.' He kissed me again. We heard the main door to the ladies open, and we both froze. Tom climbed on top of the toilet seat, crouching there so no one would be able to see his feet. He made a shushing gesture with a finger over his mouth. I couldn't help but let out a giggle, so Tom grabbed me and put his hand over my mouth. We heard a woman clear her throat and then I knew it wasn't Baby. People's voices are there even in the way they cough or throw up and how they breathe, so subtle you almost don't dare rely on it, particularly when you're half naked in a toilet cubical with someone else's husband. The woman used the other toilet, washed her hands and dried them, then left. Tom let out a big sigh and let go of me.

He got down and I stifled another giggle. He kissed me to shut us both up. He moved back and looked at me. 'You're such a badass,' he said. 'With such a nice ass.' Grabbing at my bum. He took hold of my hair and used it to pull me around and bend me over the toilet, pushing me forward so hard I had to grab the cistern to keep from falling. I wasn't wearing tights and he ran one hand up and down the inside of my bare leg, making me gasp and want him badly.

'Do it,' I said. And he pulled up my skirt and fucked me, just like I'd asked him to.

He left first, told me to wait a few minutes before following. By the time I got back, Tom and Baby were on their way out, on the stairs up towards the surface. The lads virtually stopped talking when I joined them, and I could tell they knew exactly what we'd been up to. And I saw Tom, going off into his real life again, and I could hardly bear it. I rushed to the stairs.

'Goodbye!' I threw my voice after them. 'I came to say goodbye.' Tom turned, looking surprised. Baby turned too. She looked down at me and, for a moment, the act got dropped. She didn't look angry so much as bewildered; completely at a loss for how to respond. Then she regained her composure and smiled.

'Have a great weekend,' she said. And there was nothing I could do or say. They went off into the world again, leaving me under the strip lights of the basement bar, a place outside time, where nothing was real.

* * *

I went over to Lorna's after that. I wanted to hear her mantras, to be told it was all for the best. To hear about fate and how everything happens for a reason, get motherly advice, even if I thought it was a load of crap.

My mate came to the door holding a huge glass of red wine. I followed her to the sitting area, where she poured the dregs from the bottle into a glass for me. She smelt like she'd had the rest by herself, at home that evening. I sat down on the sofa, made myself comfy. Then I couldn't talk. I realised what she'd think of me if I told her what had happened and fear struck me dumb.

I grasped for something to say, making some random comment about the football, even though I knew Lorna wouldn't give a shit. She made the noises of someone not listening as she opened a second bottle of wine and topped up my glass. She dropped into the chair opposite me with a sigh. 'What's eating you, honey? You sounded distressed on the phone.'

'Just fancied some company. Everyone was crying off.' I could hear the false cheer in my own voice.

Lorna frowned at me. 'You're doing this too often, Francesca.' She took a big swallow of wine then firmly placed her glass down so I knew she was serious. 'Right, I'm waiting. We are staying here until you tell me what's going on.' She sounded like a teacher at school after something has gone missing. She folded her arms.

'It's Iain. He's still being weird with me and it's driving me mad. I think he's really hung up on what happened.' It was a worry how quickly this slipped from my tongue. It wasn't a lie, as such. Iain was exactly like that and I did regret that lust had led us to a place where our friendship couldn't exist. But in some fundamental way, I was being dishonest.

157

'You've just got to talk to him, hon,' Lorna said. 'And maybe think twice before you sleep with some random bloke next time.' She was almost wagging her finger at me and I had to stop myself from laughing at how full of shit it all was. Why did I come to this girl when I needed advice? All she was good at was stating the bleeding obvious. My interactions with Lorna were starting to get boring and repetitive. I'd feel bad and want to talk, go over, but by the time I got there all I wanted was to get drunk. Talk about a pattern.

'You still seeing Tom?'

A cold sweat hit me and I knew I couldn't talk about him, not even to admit there was still something happening. 'Not really.'

Lorna's eyebrows both arched. 'What the hell is that supposed to mean?'

'Nothing. It's just, there's no point, is there? With Tom.' Her expression did not change. Diversion tactics were called for, and fast. 'What about Steven? I can't work out what's going on with you two these days.'

She looked back at me, her eyes flashing. 'Shame about Tom. I liked him. For once.'

'And you lecture me about clamming up.'

She went quiet, then sighed. 'I want a baby.'

This was no surprise to me but I had no idea what to say about it. I couldn't even begin to appreciate how she felt. Girls are supposed to be good at empathy but that one was beyond my powers.

'Steven doesn't. He says kids are the end of your life.'

Now I could empathise. I couldn't have agreed with him more but I didn't tell her that. I let her ramble on instead, about her nieces and nephews and how she loved them so much and how when she saw them she wanted to hold them so tight she had to be careful not to squeeze the breath out of them. I thought it all sounded wrong; her need was too physical, too violent.

I just didn't get it. Apart from getting fat, getting ripped apart by labour, stretch marks, sagging tits and shitty nappies, as if that wasn't enough, there were so many other things. I just didn't want to do it, bring some poor little sod into the world, give them this fucked-up sick joke of a gift called life that wilts and dies. Leave them stuck on a ride where they can't get off and the only possible outcome is pain and death at the end. I sat there, making noises like I was listening but I didn't hear anything for ages until Lorna said, 'What do you think?'

I looked back at her and it was clear as glass I hadn't been listening.

'You know, I think you'd be a lot better off if you didn't take so many drugs,' she said.

'How so?' I narrowed my eyes and could feel my throat tighten.

'You're tired all the time, you can't concentrate. You keep having sex with people you don't want, or can't have.'

Good follow-up. I was so glad I hadn't told her the events of the evening because there was no way she would have got it. At the same time, I was tempted to do it now, just to see her face. *I fucked him in the toilets while his wife was downstairs and then I ran up the stairs after the pair of them as fast as his spunk ran down my thigh.* My brain went on with this line of thought, without my permission, into places I didn't want to go. *I watched them walk off into the night and I wanted to run after Tom and grab him, tell him to come home with me instead.* And I was glad I'd not started saying anything because I don't think I could have stopped.

Lorna was right on the money that I was tired. I was out

all the time, staying up all night when I could. When I went to bed, disturbing dreams came to visit. I hadn't had a decent night's sleep for months. But I could concentrate fine. I did it every day, at work. She didn't know what she was talking about. And I was struck by the hypocrisy of it all. I took pills, and cocaine once in a while, but I was no junkie. And there was Lorna, pouring more wine into the big bowl she called a glass.

I thought about putting her straight. She smiled at me, nervous of the silence, her lips stained red like some vampire queen. And I just couldn't be arsed.

'You could be right,' I said. I took the wine and poured more into my own glass. 'Let's just get drunk.' We had to; it was our only common point of understanding.

Lorna smiled and clinked her glass against mine. It was a conspiracy.

------------------------**4,898.6** ⇩87.2 (1.7%)------------------------

The morning of my trader exam I woke up covered in sweat. I'd had a dream. This one was new.

I was floating in a museum, in front of some kind of scientific exhibit and there were cabinets all around me. Behind the glass were rows and rows of jars, each containing an animal, dead, swimming in formaldehyde. Their faces were squashed against the sides of the jars like screams. In the centre of the room was the biggest display. I walked over to it. The specimens here were human foetuses at different stages of development. There were labels on the jars; 24 weeks, 20 weeks, 18, 16, 8 weeks. As they got smaller, they were less like babies to look at, more like an alien life form. I stared at the smallest one. It had hard black bullets for eyes, and I felt a sharp pain as I looked into them and saw that it was moving. It broke through the glass like a snake on the strike and opened its jaw wide, screaming. Its mouth was full of gunk and half-formed teeth and it reminded me of *Alien*, making me wonder what those films were about.

'Go the fuck away,' I screamed at the vision. And it did. The cabinet and the babies in formaldehyde dissolved, then I woke up, wet, cold and with pains in my arms and legs.

It took a while for the room to form around me properly, for me to work out my surroundings as separate from my dream. I looked my alarm clock and saw it was early, five-thirty, but not too early to get up, so I did.

I'd only been in bed a few hours, after a late drinking session the previous evening with Tom and Jason. It had been a mad night, and it had felt like the two of them were competing to be the funniest, to be the wildest. I had some snatched memories of kissing Tom in an alleyway. I didn't really remember getting home. I pulled myself out of bed, feeling light-headed. My breath was heavy with stale alcohol.

As I showered, all I could think about was the dream. I couldn't get the faces of the half-formed babies out of my mind, especially the evil leer of the one that launched itself at me. I wondered where these disturbing images had come from, what they were about. There were no obvious explanations. I'd never had an abortion or even a pregnancy scare. I'd always been so careful and, when I hadn't been careful, I'd been lucky. Unless there was something I was repressing. I smiled to myself. I didn't believe in repression. It was something people invented to make their lives seem more interesting.

I drank coffee but could not face food so I brushed my teeth and pulled on some clothes. At least I'd have time to sober up before the exam, which wouldn't be until after close of business. I thought about ordering a cab, but decided the fresh air on the way to the DLR would be good for me. I had a monster of a hangover; throbbing head, waves of nausea and the works.

I made sure I went through my lucky turnstile that morning. I didn't really believe in all that crap, but you could never be too sure and other people I knew swore by it. I headed to TJ's and smelt hot bacon, which set me off dry heaving. I knew the hangover wasn't the only reason for this – I was stressed about the test. Maybe that was even what had caused the dream. It wasn't that I was expecting to fail; I've never failed anything in my entire life, and the multi-choice on the computer held no fear for me. I reckon I could have done that in the state I'd been in the night before, at least, at the stage before my vision started going and I couldn't focus on anything any more. I was stressed about the practical, though, filling orders in a mock pit. Physical tests are so much harder. When I did my driving test, my foot shook so hard on the clutch there was an illusion of stillness and I managed to hold biting point at its average position. My trader exam had the same kind of effect on me except my whole body was infused with the stress of it.

I walked over to the booth feeling light-headed and queasy, though I'd stopped wanting to throw up. Tom and Jack were crowded around one of the computer monitors, talking in low voices and whistling between their teeth like a pair of Hackney plumbers. It struck me there'd been a good deal of this kind of behaviour of late. I peeked over Tom's shoulder. They had up some Bloomberg screens with data for futures volumes on two exchanges, LIFFE and the DTB. The DTB had set up and listed a number of contracts competitively, including the future on the German Government bond, or Bund, but as far as I was aware they were no threat. I looked at the figures now, though, and saw that the volume of trades going through LIFFE and the DTB were close to the same. The Germans were well on the way to stealing the contract.

'That's unbelievable,' I whispered. But even as I said it, I knew how it had happened. Jigsaw pieces slotted together in my head, little factoids that had hardly gone in, but now combined to give me a full picture. Like something Jase had said months ago, how he was making a fortune from the arbitrage opportunities now that the same contract was doing business on another exchange.

'Believe it, baby,' Tom said. He'd stepped back so I could see better and his body was pressed against my back, pinning me to the edge of the booth desk. 'It's the barrow boys here, can't resist a cheap profit. Wham bang thank you ma'am, and to hell with the consequences.' He paused and all I could hear was his breathing. 'You can't blame 'em. There's shitloads of arbing going on and it's driven the German volumes right up.' He touched my hip. 'It'll be fifty–fifty soon. Then, well, who knows?'

I turned to look at Tom. His top lip was twitching. There seemed to be some subtext to what he was saying, but I couldn't work it out. Maybe it was because, next to what I'd just learned, the whole Tom and me thing, it didn't matter. It was one of those rare moments when clarity hits you like lightning, road to Damascus stuff. Everything I held dear was at risk; the school playground that was the LIFFE exchange. I'd fallen for the place and that crystallised for me then, appeared before my eyes as solid as the desk I was leaning against. Maybe I did do the love thing, after all.

My hangover, the growl of my empty stomach and the stress about my exam combined with the shock of what I'd just worked out to weaken me. I only remained standing because I was trapped between Tom and the desk. I turned and wriggled out, fell into a nearby chair. My skin crawled with fear.

'You okay?' Tom said.

I nodded and looked up at him. 'What do you think will happen?' But he just shrugged. I sat and stared at him, at the screen, and all I could think was *How could I have missed all this?*

The trader exam turned out to be much easier than I'd expected. My hands had been shaking all day, and people noticed when I was adding details to trade cards, so that I was asked more than once if I was using an 'electric pencil'. But as soon as I got going with the test, I felt at home, felt like a trader, and I never looked like coming anywhere near failing.

I got my result a few days later, which only confirmed what I knew already; I had passed. Of course, everyone was out that evening to celebrate. As Jason put it, wouldn't want to get too much blood in the alcohol stream. I invited the people I wanted and they all came, except Iain, who was now positively avoiding me. Everyone else was there, though. Even Lorna's Steven, his presence, unusual on a group outing, giving Lorna a special glow. Baby didn't come to meet Tom or try to hunt him out because she had to work. That put glitter all over my evening. Special offer, one night only, Tom was mine.

My friends were the loudest group in the pub by far. We bought jugs of vodka Red Bull and were getting through them. Every time I forgot about my little victory someone would remind me by proposing a toast to it. Warm hits of pride rushed through me each time I remembered I would be wearing a proper trader's jacket so soon. My badge would have a blue dot to indicate I was still a trainee, or blue-button, and I'd have to be supervised for a while when I actually carried out trades, but I'd be wearing UBF's blue and gold stripes at last. And I had earned them.

By chucking-out time, we were all pretty messy. Jase suggested a Ruby down Brick Lane. I used to love going there, deciding which of the neon palm trees was calling on a particular night. The food was always tasty and you could take your own booze. But Tom gave me a look. 'Eating is cheating,' he said, a real drinker's theory about diluting alcohol with food. The others were hungry for bad fatty food, though, and left with that in mind. Tom and I went hunting for a late bar. We ended up in Fuegos.

It wasn't very busy and we got a table. 'Vodka Red Bull?' Tom asked. I nodded. 'And perhaps a little something from here?' He held out a cuff to me. My dad always told me you should never turn down a gift of love from a child. Tom was not a child, though he threw me that cheeky smile he had and looked boyish, despite his age, and I felt it was a gift of love. Yes siree, because Tom loved that fine, white powder, no doubt about it.

At silly o'clock sometime the next morning, Tom and I were out on the street messing around, shouting and playing tag as we crossed London Bridge. My face ached from how much I'd smiled and laughed that night. Tom's mobile started going off; Baby's birdcall. She could never leave him alone, and he could never switch off the fucking phone. I needed a distraction. I did my Kylie impression for Tom, bellowing out a tuneless version of 'I Should be so Lucky' and skipping down the road. We came past a

Starbucks coffee house and I karate kicked the door. It swung open. I hadn't kicked it hard enough to have broken anything: it must have been unlocked. Tom and I both stopped walking and our eyes met. His mobile was still ringing on and on and on. I could tell what he was thinking.

We walked right into the dark, empty coffee house. I sat down on a sofa and curled up, said something about how comfortable it was. Tom laughed. It was his loud laugh, the one that drowns out the sound around it. As that noise faded, I could hear something more subtle, getting gradually louder. It was the alarm. I sprang off the sofa and to my feet, moving on instinct to get out of the building and leg it down the road.

Tom grabbed my arm. 'Stay.' He put a hand on each shoulder, as if to calm me.

'How long?'

'Long enough to put these,' he gestured at the furniture around us, 'in there,' he nodded over at the disabled toilet.

I laughed and pulled away from him. 'There'll never be time.' But I didn't make for the door.

What came next could have come straight out of a TV challenge show. I hadn't done anything so silly since I was a student. We filled the disabled cubical with the standard-issue furniture – all those purple velvet chairs and chessboard tables. I showed Tom the trick of locking it from the outside, but he knew it already. Cut from the same cloth. Therein lay the danger, I knew that.

As we walked out onto the street, there was still no sign of the police, or anyone else, reacting to the alarm. It must have been going off for a full half-hour, getting louder all the time. This was the City, though, and there was no neighbourhood watch because, outside of office hours, there was no neighbourhood. Other than the muffled sound of the alarm and the first morning birds, the streets were so quiet you could hear the dead whisper. You can, in the City, on certain nights.

Tom and I walked away, hand in hand. Whenever my pace sped up, Tom squeezed my fingers so hard it hurt, like that game 'mercy' at school. There was no mercy until my pace slowed right down again. That was another danger with the pair of us. One of us was forever ready to make it more risky, to push things that bit further. I felt it strongly; there would be a point of no return to all this.

As I walked into the exchange the next Monday, a smile spread across my face that nothing could have wiped away. The streets of London were paved with gold and I could prove it. I could pick it up and wave it at anyone who said otherwise. I was about to, because I was a LIFFE trader, fully qualified to get down and dirty in the pit and bring the precious stuff out with me. I didn't know how long Tom would leave it before he'd have me doing just that.

He answered that question for me later that day, coming over and flashing me plenty of white teeth. 'Having fun?'

I shrugged. 'I just wanna get stuck in, now.' I meant it, but felt flutters all over as soon as I heard it out loud.

'No problem, keeno. We'll have you do a trade this afternoon. I'm all for in at the deep end.'

I said nothing, staring at him and waiting for a laugh or a nudge, some indication that he wasn't serious.

'That okay? You sure you're ready?'

''Course,' I said, wishing I'd never opened my big mouth. And I rushed off to the toilets to throw up.

In the ladies, I studied my reflection, searching for traces of vomit on my clothes. I held my hand in front of me and watched it shake, willed it to stop, then splashed water on my face, running it through my hair with my fingers. Catching sight of the blue and gold jacket in the mirror, I did a double take, surprised to see how real I looked, how serious. I practised hand signals to the mirror, praying to the God I no longer believed in that Diane or one of her mates did not walk in. I took one last look at myself. It was time to go through the looking glass and be the trader I could see in front of me.

I came out of the toilets, then through another door, then hard into the sound of busy pits. I walked over to Jack in the booth, who yelled, 'Where the fuck you been?' Then he looked at me full on and I understood him; he was good at communicating without words and I was picking up this skill like a natural. *Don't fuck this up.* I turned away from the sunken pit full of lads in bright jackets. They were all shouting. The noise and colour merged into one mess, a pool of chaos. I stood on its edge, shitting bricks, for what felt like ages. Then I held my breath and took a dive.

There was loads of whistling and clapping as I merged with the craziness of the pit. Everyone knew me and they knew it was my first time, too. I felt someone pinch my arse but I ignored it, pushed my way in deeper. I looked around for Gerard, the local who'd been assigned to supervise me if none of my team were available. I couldn't do the trade without him. I was surrounded then, and drowning. It was too bright, too loud, too fucking everything. It reminded me of when I was little, jumping in the deep end of the swimming pool and feeling the water fill my throat, fast followed by panic until my dad scooped me out by the armpits and I coughed for about an hour. I could see Jack standing up and screaming from the booth. I couldn't hear what he was saying but I could read his lips and see his hands going crazy. He waved his arms at me like a madman, but I was dead still, letting the water cover me, calm as Ophelia. Jack stopped shouting and made some comment to Nick. They both laughed. Then I felt a hand on my back, ready to pull me up, save me just the way my dad had. I turned. It was Tom.

'Did you think I'd let you down? Leave you on your lonesome, here, like this?'

'No.' And I realised I hadn't. I'd been waiting for him.

I jerked into action like I'd been on freeze-frame and someone had just pressed play. I placed the order and glanced at Jack, saw him relax. He sent me a thumbs-up across the room. A tall bloke in a Barclays jacket stamped on my foot, his golden eagle flapping in my face. I breathed out and pushed for the surface. 'Twelve at twenty,' I yelled, screaming and waving my arms like I was raving.

'Buy 'em!' It was a local I vaguely knew, lifting my offer. I had traded. I felt different, it was like the action defined me in some way; I had traded therefore I was a trader.

I signalled the fill to Jack. I could see a smile on his face as he picked up the phone to get back to the client. My whole body was buzzing now, not shaking. I filled in the details on the ticket with a steady hand but I felt removed, like I was watching from above.

Nick met me as I walked back, flinging his arms around me. He planted a wet kiss on my cheek. 'Popped your cherry,' he said, but I could hardly hear. Crédit Lyonnais had sent a trader into the FTSE pit and everything was drowned by singing.

'If yer smell like Grimsby Harbour then you must be fucking French!' Fifty or so men screamed the words, sounding like a football crowd and, as I walked back to Jack, it was all I could do not to dance to the tune.

Texas Hold 'Em

Texas Hold 'Em is a popular version of the game poker. In Hold 'Em, each player is dealt two cards. Two players clockwise from the dealer must bet blind on their hands, putting in cash or chips (the *blinds*) before they see their cards. At this point, all players examine their own hands and a round of betting occurs.

After each round of betting, the *dealer* places a number of common cards face-up in the middle of the table. First comes the *flop*, three consecutive cards dealt in one go. A second round of betting ensues. After this the dealer adds two more cards one at a time, the *turn* and then the *river*. Between each there is a round of betting. Each player may use any or all of these shared cards to make a winning hand.

In order from bottom up, hands that can be created are: *high card, pair, two pair, three of a kind, straight, flush, full house, four of a kind, straight flush* and *royal flush*. Higher cards in equivalent hands always win, e.g. a pair of kings would beat a pair of twos. A full house made up of threes and eights would lose to one with kings and queens.

Magic Mushrooms

1 the general name for a number of fungal hallucinogens, often drunk in tea or added to prepared foods; **2** a drug that can open doors; **3** not recommended for those with mental health issues.

On 11 December, UBF had a whole company get-together to celebrate Christmas. Those magic words 'office party' conjure up all sorts of sitcom clichés about silly string, wine on the carpet and a drunk sat giggling on the photocopier as the light scans his arse. This is not how it's done in the City. Every December, special companies set up for a month or two just to cater the season, competing for business by offering increasingly outrageous attraction packages. Our party this year was to be held on Battersea Common in a network of marquees. All the drink and food and entertainment was laid on for free and there was just one rule: no partners. That suited me and Tom.

That day was arsed up from the moment Tom and I left the building for a liquid lunch in the Cannon. We came out of LIFFE and into the harsh winter daylight and that wasn't the only thing waiting to surprise me there. Darren Matthews, leaning against the wall, smoking. He threw his fag down and stubbed it out. He walked towards us and I could see from the way his face changed that he'd guessed everything about what was going on between me and Tom. The ways I could handle this situation raced through my head. I went for the option where I would pretend I hadn't seen him.

Darren walked straight across the front of us. 'You can't just fucking ignore me.'

'I think I just did.' I continued to walk.

Tom turned to look at me, then back at Darren. 'Who the fuck is this loser?' But his body language made like Darren didn't exist.

'Your dad is fucking worried sick about you,' Darren said, following Tom's lead and acting like the other bloke wasn't there either.

'You wanna talk with this meathead?' Tom said.

I shook my head. Darren began to lose it, waving his arms around and raising his voice. 'No fucking way are you gonna ignore me, you little bitch. He's going spare worrying about you. He thought you might be lying dead in a ditch somewhere, but I told him it'd just be you arsing around again. For fuck's sake, what's wrong with you?'

I tried to pass him but he sidestepped to block my way, then a second time, as if he was marking me in a game of basketball.

'You heard the girl, asshole. She doesn't wanna talk with you.' Tom pushed his way between us. The two of them were facing off. The last thing I wanted was a fight between Darren and Tom; that would have been vicious and could cause someone real damage.

My ex's face shot up from behind Tom's shoulder. 'You can't be that fucking heartless. I know you're screwed in the head but you can't be that big a cunt, surely? Your dad's been through enough down to you. He fucking loves you. Worships the ground you walk on.'

Darren knew where to shoot and my legs weakened at his comments. I wanted to tell him to go back to Dad and say I was all right, and that I was sorry for not ringing. But I was struck dumb. Darren leaned forward, eyeballing me. Then he turned to Tom. 'Serious, man, you watch yourself with this one.' He tapped the side of his head. 'Nut job. Believe me, I have been there. Play with your head, she will. Drag you round by the balls, just wait and see.' Then he walked off.

Tom and I stood watching as Darren headed for the tube, then he seemed to change his mind. He turned back to face us and yelled at Tom, walking backwards, 'I hope she's told you that she don't do the love thing. Not no more.' He grinned, showing where half of one of his front teeth was missing, and disappeared into the station.

Tom turned to me. 'What was that all about?'

I shook my head. 'Just my psycho ex-boyfriend.'

'You wanna talk about any of that shit?'

I almost laughed. For a man who had seen me naked so many times he knew so little about me. 'I just want to get a drink,' I said.

So we did.

I was going to the pub and then on to the party straight from work and had brought clothes and make-up with me. I got ready in the toilets. I was the master of the three-minute face job: dabs of concealer, dark eyeshadow smudged just above my lashes and a subtle lipstick applied in one movement. No messing. It was important to look good, but it was also important to look like you didn't give a shit. I pulled on a strappy red dress that fell about six inches above my knee. I sprayed on perfume: Jean-Paul Gautier Pour Femme. Tom had introduced me to this scent, buying me some and telling me it was sex in a bottle. He wasn't wrong. I had really noticed how readily men responded to it.

I put my make-up and perfume away and zipped the bag shut. Glancing up, I caught sight of myself in the mirror. I looked good and it took me by surprise. I did not feel good. Darren's little visit at lunchtime had shaken me up. I'd never made a conscious decision not to ring my dad, except that every time I picked up the phone to dial his number something had stopped me. A black dread about speaking to him lay heavy on my stomach, like cheap stout. Of course I wasn't a bitch and Darren knew that too. I couldn't help thinking that he probably took up the task of coming to see me readily, jumped at the chance to march into my world all self-righteous and have a big go. He'd always enjoyed the drama between us.

And something else had struck me now I'd had time to think, about what must have been going on between Darren and my dad. The pair of them had bonded, I knew that, over the football and a few beers and, I suppose, the idea that they might end up related. It was a shock to me, though, that they'd stayed in touch since our nasty, messy break-up. Why would my father do that? And what was this 'enough' that he'd been through down to me? A picture formed in my head and I couldn't get rid of it: the two of them in the pub, heads together and slagging me off, grinning as they finished off pint after pint. Darren, slurring and putting his arm around my father and calling him 'Dad'.

I breathed. I took out the Jean-Paul Gautier again and gave it one last spray, like I thought the beautiful scent could mask the crap. And it did. For the moment.

I walked across the road to join the guys in All Bar One. They were near the back of the pub and had already got the champagne in. Jack was there, and Nick, but not Diane, who had gone home to get changed. They were standing with colleagues from other firms who wouldn't be joining us for the party. The rest of the room was quiet, but that lot were a bubbling pot of conversation that boiled over with hot laughter more than once as I approached them. Almost none of them noticed me arrive, they were too wrapped up in the fun they were having.

Except Tom. He noticed me as soon as I walked in the door, as if he'd been watching for me. Maybe he smelt me coming, wearing his favourite scent. He stood in the middle of the raucous lot of them and, at the same time, he was completely separate. He looked like a swan in a pond of ducks, standing tall and elegant above the other men, and turned away from them, looking at me.

I walked towards Tom in a cloud of the beautiful smell he'd introduced me to, glowing in the knowledge that I looked good. Tom split from the crowd and walked towards me. And the scene around me changed, my brain cutting and editing all the background crap I didn't need to know. The noise of people drinking and chatting and laughing was muffled, like my head was underwater. I could hear Tom's shoes against the spit and sawdust of the floor. As he got closer, I could hear his voice. These noises, the ones Tom made, were as clear as they would have been in a silent room. 'I love you,' he said, popping a finger into the bubble around me and making the world flip back to normal.

I smiled at him but said nothing in return. I didn't believe him, not for a second. I knew what Tom and I had and it wasn't love. There was no way I was going to pass back the L-word and there was nothing else I could say that wouldn't sound like a put-down. He kissed me, only on the cheek, but it still made me burn. His breath stank of champagne.

There were a couple of whistles and catcalls from the group. I couldn't work out if these were because of the kiss, or my glamorous get-up. I did a few twirls to make light of it and got more whistles and shouts about not recognising me, and cleaning up good.

We were steaming by the time we got to Battersea. The party encampment was the size of a small town. It made you think how much it must have all cost and how much good these companies could do if they gave the money to charity instead of spending it on their staff like this. That wasn't going to happen, though, and the best thing to do was to lie back and enjoy it.

Inside the marquees you forgot quickly that you were in a tent. The theme was robotics and the place was full of struggling actors in costume, faces spray-painted silver and serious. Some had on skates or rollerblades; others were stood on four long stilts, arms and legs, giving the impression of a human spider. Free bars were dotted around the place, and there was a casino. Madness had been booked to play a set later in the evening and there were proper DJs in the dance tent. Dinner had been served at eight sharp but we'd missed that; eating is cheating.

Put a bunch of traders in a room and they'll seek and find at sixty paces somewhere they can put a bet on. We headed straight for the casino. It wasn't the real deal, where you bought chips and could play for money. I guess they would have needed a licence for that and, besides, UBF could be slightly coy when it came to cold hard cash, calling our wage rises and bonus figures 'compensation packages', for example. Instead, you were given a pile of chips to play with and whoever could amass the most won a holiday for two to Nice. I was determined it would be mine.

I played roulette for a while, enjoying acting the part and having a puff on a cigar that Tom passed me. I knew, though, that roulette, craps and all those games of chance were for losers. The only casino games worth playing were blackjack and poker. If you knew what you were doing, you could clean up. Blackjack, though, relied on the other players also getting it, and you could get shafted by the dealer if one idiot didn't know basic strategy. So I made for the poker table.

Tom had got there a few hands ahead of me and was already building a wall with his chips. Nick's pile was looking depleted and I suspected these two facts were not entirely unrelated. Tom loved poker as much as I did. We played often together, when we spent evenings at my flat. We had invented our own version of the game, the bastard child of strip poker and spin the bottle, which was loads of fun and helped hone the skills I'd learned over years, playing with the lads. It was pretty much only Tom I played with these days, though.

As I sat down, Nick rubbed his hands together and made some comment about winning his chips back. A bloke I didn't know asked if we could change the game to the strip version. All eyes around the table settled on me then, to see my reaction. I studied the cards I'd been dealt, then put them back down on the table. I fiddled with one of the little red straps on my dress, playing it coy for a moment, then flipping that mood on its head, leaning forward and giving him a violent two-finger salute. It moved him in his seat.

Tom laughed so loud it made Nick start, then leaned over towards our new friend, all conspiratorial. 'She may look like a young lady, but she's one of the LIFFE boys underneath that awful pretty skin.' It was a description that made me sit up in my chair. It was so right, so spot on, and it felt like a compliment at the same time. The man's lips curled a little, but it didn't look much like a smile. I winked at him. He looked around at the other guys for a clue about how to react but they didn't help him. The bloke was pale, with ginger hair, and a flush built quick and pink on his cheeks. A word danced near my tongue: Ginga! But we weren't on the floor now. We were in the civilised world, at a party, and a UBF party at that. School playground antics would not be tolerated here.

We were playing Hold 'Em, the version I was used to. The croupier dealt a fresh hand and everyone looked at their cards. Nick pulled a face as he put his cards down, then picked them up for a second look. I clocked this, and knew he would play this hand. He scratched his ear. Was this a tell? Probably. I would have to wait and see.

It helps if you're intuitive when you play poker, and if you can look at the people around you and notice the little things that give them away. The way they look at their cards twice, or even three times, if they have something but just once when they don't, or the way their eyes widen slightly or they mouth words to trigger their memory into action as they take in decent cards. I'm sure I have my own tells but I'm careful to do the same things in the same order every hand, to eliminate this as much as possible. I take one look at the cards and commit them to memory, then put them face down on the table, where they remain for the duration. I never pick up or count my chips before it's my turn to bet.

The most important quality you need to be a decent poker player, though, is patience. It can be the right time to bet for all sorts of reasons and the hand you get dealt is just one of those. But you have to wait. You don't bet until you believe. Tom's biggest weakness as a player was how he'd go in impulsive sometimes just because he hadn't bet in a while. He'd ended up naked and at my mercy a load of times, just because of this. Me, I was patient. After I sat down at that table that night, I folded seven hands before I saw a flop.

Then I got dealt two tens, my favourite hand. It was a good hand, worth betting on if things didn't go mad, but there were much stronger and you could lose your arse on it. But for me, for some reason, this was like my lucky turnstile at work; I always won on two tens. The betting ticked around the table with most people staying in and calling the blinds. Then it came to Nick, who went all in. I shoved too, and everyone else dropped out. We turned our cards up. I let out a sound as I saw Nick's: a pair of twos. He looked away from the table with a poker face.

I watched as the flop came down. There was another ten, giving me trips and a really good chance of winning the hand. Nick was managing the cold, hard face still, but I knew that this must have got to him. Things had been better between us of late, but I knew he'd still hate to lose to me. I stuck out my tongue at him and played with the piercing. But he wasn't seeing the funny side. The dealer put down the turn, which was a two. It wasn't over yet. The odds were still way in my favour; anything but a two on the river and I'd won.

The dealer paused. Tom made a drumroll noise. Then everyone went quiet and I wanted to laugh because it was so overdramatic, like a scene out of a spaghetti western. The dealer turned the final card and dropped it on the baize. It was a ten, combining with the rest of my hand to blow Nick's to pieces. He flung down his cards and left the table.

'Oooh,' said Tom. 'Lady's lost her lemons.' I had no idea what he was talking about but it still made me laugh. Nick was stomping off, a distance from the table.

I took off then. With so many chips it was easy to dominate and I played hard against the men. I began to build up a pile of chips and quite an audience. Tom dropped out and left the table for a while. By the time he came back I had doubled my haul.

'You got enough, babe. C'mon. Let's go have some fun,' he said.

'I wanna win.'

'You did already.'

I wasn't totally up for being dragged away from the table; I reckon I could have doubled my chips again easily. I did want to spend some time with Tom though, on one of the few nights we could be out and count on Baby not tracking us down.

'You can have my chips too. To make sure,' Tom said. This offer clinched it and I climbed down from the stool. Between us we took our winnings to the competition desk, where we exchanged them for a raffle ticket and the woman counted them, recording the figure in a book. The look on her face said it all – I was easily winning at this stage and so far ahead it looked unlikely I'd get caught.

Tom said there was someone he'd like me to meet, but the way he said it I could tell his tongue was firmly in his cheek. He led me towards the dance tent. There was a banner swinging over the entrance announcing IT'S ALL GONE PETE TONG. It made me smile because underneath it said 'Sponsored by Deutsche Termin Bourse', the very same DTB that was squeezing its hands tight round LIFFE's scrawny neck, so that I couldn't have agreed more with the sentiment. I felt bile and proper anger towards the German exchange, more like it was an ex-lover still trying to get at me than a corporate entity. I was so much a LIFFE trader by then, my existence punctuated by the rhythms of the exchange rather than those of my body, marked by the expiry of contracts: Sep97, then Dec97, then Mar98.

Inside, the dance tent was adorned with sparkles and tassles. The evening dresses and smart suits looked totally out of synch with the tunes, especially as many of the dancers were obviously drunk. It was a waste to have someone like Tong DJing here. I couldn't get into the music, didn't have the right chemicals inside me. Tom guided me across to the far side of the room and a bloke who was sitting against the canvas holding a flask. The scene was all a bit granny's outing.

'I'd like some more of your fine tea,' Tom said. 'And my girlfriend here would like some too.'

I was so intrigued to hear Tom call me his girlfriend I didn't stop to work out what was going on. His girlfriend? Did he mean that in the English or American sense? He'd put on an English accent when he said it but did that mean anything? A plastic cup was thrust into my hand and I took a sip, Tom looking at me like this was the most interesting thing I could possibly do. The liquid tasted like iron filings. I pulled a face and passed the cup back. Tom put his hand in the way. 'Drink it, Frankie. Let's just say it has certain, urm, medicinal qualities.'

And all at once I knew what the tea was. I looked down at the cup in my hand and saw it in a different way. *Drink me*, it whispered. *Go on, I dare you.* And of course, I did. I felt like I'd been invited to the Mad Hatter's party. I'd never taken a full-on hallucinogen before, though probably the main reason was that I'd never been offered one. I swallowed then passed the cup back to Tom, who refilled from the flask then downed it like it quenched his thirst. He grinned at me, moisture shiny in the corners of his lips.

I wanted to see Madness play, but Tom vetoed it. Instead, we went to the dodgem ride, hogging a car and crashing it loads until they asked us to leave. We approached random groups of people and introduced ourselves, hanging around and chatting if we found them interesting. Meanwhile, the world changed. It was a slow process, and not nearly as dramatic as I'd been expecting. Everything I'd heard and read about acid and magic mushrooms had given me the impression I'd see goblins and fairies and chat to people who weren't there, but it was more subtle than that and marked by confusion. Tom's head seemed bigger than it should be. My feet looked the wrong size too, a whole set of toes too small. The spiky-legged robot men gave me the creeps and, as they swept by, I thought I saw insect faces. When people leaned in too close they turned into demons. This sounds frightening, but it wasn't. It was just there. The world around me took on the aspect of Michael Jackson's *Thriller* but I watched it in the same way, with interest and amusement, and I was not scared. It wasn't a bad trip. It wasn't even really a trip at all, just the edge of one.

As the feeling grew, I knew it was time to find Pete Tong again. I grabbed Tom's hand and dragged him to the dance tent. The music sounded better now, dripping onto my skin like honeyed rain. It wasn't the same kind of change you get with pills but it was good enough. It was like I could see the music, taste it, hold it in my mouth. The sounds invaded all my senses. 'Café del Mar' came on, a track I loved. The way it built, it was like a creeping plant growing around me, holding me upright. It went on and on and on, and I forgot myself, and I forgot Tom and I forgot where I was and just danced.

Tom said he was tripping out badly and wanted to go back to my place. I couldn't think of anything I'd rather do. I didn't feel the cold as we came out onto the common. There were lights everywhere, it seemed, and they sparkled and glittered and winked at me. We walked through the London streets and it was like being in a fairy grotto, a magical world where I might actually see an elf or a pixie, although I didn't. I did see a yellow light, though, and it was attached to the top of a taxi. I flagged the vehicle down and we both climbed in.

When the cab pulled up outside my apartment block, I

was at a loss. I could not remember how these taxi things worked. Tom was having a laugh all by himself, sat deep in the leather seat and moving nowhere. I had a feeling we were supposed to get out but I couldn't quite remember. I tried to focus. Money, that was it, that was what the driver was waiting for. I got out and gave him a twenty, telling him to keep the change. Tom was still sitting inside, laughing his (slightly oversized) head off. I opened the door next to him and encouraged him to leave the car.

I tucked my arm under Tom's and we walked towards the building. The dock glistened, its oily nastiness responsible for the sheen. It was easy to look at the surface and forget how dirty the water was, how many people had thrown in rubbish, or shopping trolleys, how many companies poured their waste into the Thames before it flowed here and stagnated. How it was grease and motor oil that was making it shine, that the bubbles glinting under the lights were chemical scum. In fact, it looked inviting. I had a sudden flash of invincibility. I felt assured that I could jump in the dock, or in front of a car, even a lorry, jump from a building and that I would never die. I shivered and upped my pace. Deep in some logical place that I could still just grab hold of, but only just, I knew that my state of mind was getting dangerous. The best place for me was inside, with doors and windows tightly shut.

In the flat, we put on a chill-out album and draped ourselves over the furniture. The music felt like fat, warm drops of rain. It felt like lounging in a hot bath. I told Tom this and he jumped out of his seat and left the room. I was too relaxed to wonder what he was doing. My arms fell limp over the sides of my armchair. I couldn't imagine ever needing to move from this place again. I heard Tom moving around in the hallway. If I'd been on a pill this would have made me edgy, wanting him to come back and relax, desperate to be 'us' again instead of 'me'. But I didn't feel that way. I was happy to sit and watch as the electricity in my head did its little dances, as it leapt and skipped and played from neuron to neuron and made things happen that normally did not.

My eyes half closed, colours flicked through my head. I thought about life, and how we were put together, the physical stuff that went with being human. I touched my belly button, thinking how it all starts there. How we grow around that spot, cell upon cell, until we become another person. How we do that, generation on generation, so that we never really die. My skin felt like plastic and I could smell rubber. Phlegm rattled on my chest and I guessed this was the source of the smell. The tinny flavour of the tea was repeating on me too. My empty stomach growled in protest but the thought of putting food inside my mouth appalled me, the idea of chewing, of the mashed-up bolus being propelled down the tubes inside me, all of these facts I'd learnt in GCSE biology bounced around my head and made me feel sick.

The music came to a dead stop, mid-track. I opened my eyes. Tom had come in and switched off the stereo. 'I gotta surprise. Something I made for you.' He offered me a hand and I took it. He pulled me up to standing and led me through the apartment to the bathroom, where he flung open the door. 'Da da!'

The bathroom light was switched off and tea lights winked from every available surface. The air smelt of cotton candy. Tom must have hunted down bath salts and elixirs from all over the flat. He'd put the stereo on in my bedroom and turned it up loud. A Beatles song was playing: 'Norwegian Wood'. I turned to him. 'No one's ever made me anything like this before.' I swallowed, more of that nasty bubbling phlegm moving in my throat.

'I meant it. What I said in the pub.'

I looked at him, ready to give up the fight. I was all set to hand myself on a plate to this man, the person who'd made me such a beautiful gift and told me he loved me. I was ready to give him my soul and fuck the consequences.

I wanted to tell him I loved him right back but I was scared, and walked over to the bath to stall for time. I was about to step in when it happened. It was as if lightning struck the room and lit up what was really there, hidden by the dark mask of time. A woman was sitting in the bath, looking up at me, but it wasn't my brand-new bath in my brand-new Docklands home, but the horrid old tub from my dad's house. She was looking up at me and there were words: *Don't you dare.*

It flashed up and then it was gone. Count and wait for the thunder, one hundred, two hundred. I looked at the bubbles, popping and hissing on the top of the water. I wanted nothing to do with that bath or that picture. I didn't know if it was a memory, or something created by my brain, under the influence of the mushrooms. What I did know, however, and this was a shock to me, was that the woman was my mum. Turns out I did know what she looked like, after all.

Some drugs, like acid or mushrooms, they open doors. Some doors are best left shut and barred with furniture. I rushed out of the bathroom, pushing past Tom, and to my bedroom. I threw myself on my bed. My heart was beating like crazy. I could feel another chemical in my blood, one I was used to and recognised straight away. A chemical I usually enjoyed: adrenalin. But, this time, it did not feel good.

------------------------5,035.9 ⇩94.8 (1.8%)------------------------

Tom was gone from the office a few days after the party and was not due back until the New Year. He was at home, doing family things, with Baby, and had not been in touch. Being the newbie, my holiday didn't begin until end of play Christmas Eve. I didn't mind; it was a quiet time, we were able to relax and have a laugh. And it wasn't like I had any big plans of my own until New Year, when I'd managed to get the long weekend off. Jase was having a party and I planned to have one helluva blow-out and knew I'd need time to recover.

I was annoyed that Tom hadn't been in touch. I hadn't tried to contact him, that's true enough, but he was the married one. He was the one who knew when it was safe to talk, and so I waited. This is what it's like to have an affair, you wait. Jase was a real mate during all this, working hard to distract me from the Tom issue. He took me out drinking and clubbing, gave me drugs and hung around my flat so there was someone there in the morning. I wished it was him I was involved with, rather than Tom. It crossed my mind that maybe it could be that way but I was way too wrapped up in Tom to take this seriously.

Of course, I had my own family stuff to do too. Darren Matthews was right: I wasn't 'that fucking heartless' and I did break my promise about spending time in Ilford for the occasion of Christmas. I couldn't bear the thought of staying over at that house, or even spending an entire day there, so I booked taxis to take me to and from with just enough time in between to have dinner and ignore the Queen's Speech.

It was cold enough that the ground had frosted over. The

cab driver had his heaters switched on too high, which made my skin itch. I opened a window and heard the sound of sucking teeth from the seat in front. I ignored it, staring out as I sailed through the quiet streets. The driver lit a cigarette. I coughed but didn't complain. He made no move to stub it out and I decided he'd lost his tip. We passed through the City. It was always a ghost town on weekends and holidays but today it seemed more thoroughly deserted. Even those who haunted the streets had gone home for Christmas.

I remembered the vision that had been haunting me, the picture that I saw the night of the UBF party. I was no nearer to working out what it meant or where it had come from. It had joined the foetus jars in the invasion of my dreams. The same scene, my mother in the bath, ending on the same words: *Don't you dare.* It had crossed my mind to ask Dad about all this. I was sure he'd be able to explain it to me, that or help me dismiss it as a hallucination. He would be able to tell me the truth. There were so many reasons not to ask him, and that was one of them.

I stopped thinking for a while, found that quiet state of mind I only manage when I'm being driven somewhere and the motion sends me into a trance. I stared out of the window and the scenes passed me by and I didn't connect with any of them. When we pulled up outside Dad's house, I was startled to find the journey over, and had to hunt for my purse, eliciting further teeth-sucking from the driver. I gave him some cash and waited for every penny of my change. Then I scrambled up and out of my seat, onto the pavement, feeling like I'd been woken up, disturbed from sleep in a deep part of the cycle.

I opened the front door and was hit by the watery stench of overcooked vegetables. I called out to say I'd arrived.

Dad came, giving me a kiss on the cheek and a glass of fizzy wine.

'Happy Christmas, chick,' he said.

'Hey, Dad. Happy Christmas.'

I walked into the living room and the scene there made cracks in my soul. He'd brought out the table from the corner and put it in the middle of the room. It was properly laid for dinner and there was an open bottle of red wine, pride of place. There were even a couple of candles and a box of crackers. The telly was asleep in the corner, the standby light on, giving the appearance the set was keeping a beady eye on its territory. Music was playing; something classical. My throat tightened and words came out, whispered. 'Oh it's lovely, Dad.' I turned and saw him smiling at me. Caught my breath. Just for a second I had the strangest feeling, a conviction almost, that this would be the last time I saw him. And there it is – right there – the problem with the love thing. No one and nothing is for ever.

We swapped presents. I'd got Dad some expensive men's scent. He shrugged and put it down, and I realised that of course he would never wear it. He'd got me a silver jewellery box. It was covered in ornate patterns and really very beautiful and delicate, but Dad seemed to have overlooked the fact I never wore jewellery, aside from the stud in my tongue. We exchanged thanks and kisses.

Dad served up dinner, turkey and all the trimmings, followed by Christmas pudding with proper brandy sauce and we both drank a lot of wine. I would have been enjoying myself if I hadn't felt the weight of how it would soon be over, pushing down and suffocating every happy moment. I was on my second cognac when the doorbell rang. My taxi home. And my dad didn't need to say a thing, I could see it in the way his mouth moved a little, his eyebrows shook; so soon, so soon, so soon.

I almost sent the taxi driver away. But then I looked around me and imagined spending the rest of the day here. The telly would resume its usual dominance of the living room soon. The wallpaper was still peeling and the clock was still stopped and she was still there, wailing from every corner: the ghost of my mother.

And I remembered Darren, the way he'd come to the exchange to yell at me about how I'd not been in touch with my dad. How everything he'd said had made me realise they'd stayed in touch, been meeting the whole time, behind my back. I imagined them together, plotting against me, working out a plan between them to tie me down with Darren and his white van, his less than white Essex associates. That was enough to move my feet over to the door, and help my arms open it.

'Goodbye, Dad.' And, again, it felt so final.

I got into the cab. My whole body was like the side of your face after an anaesthetic at the dentist, frozen in places, so dead in others you have to poke with a finger to check it's still there. I thought I heard the door shut and turned to look, but I was wrong. My dad was still standing there. He watched my cab all the way down the street and did not go inside. He was still there as we turned the corner, and the house disappeared from view.

On New Year's Eve I went up West to buy something new to wear out that night, and stopped outside Vidal Sassoon. I wasn't expecting them to have an appointment, not on New Year's Eve, but some force pushed me in through the door.

'You lucked out, gal, I just had a cancellation,' the receptionist told me. She had a broad Essex accent, which reminded me of Kate, making me feel guilty for not having called her for such a long time. The woman took my coat and put a gown around my shoulders, tied it at the front. Then she waved me towards the sink.

The shampooist was pretty and looked French. Her hair was cropped short and layered around her ears. It suited her. She asked if the water was okay, in English but her strong accent was a giveaway, so I answered her in French. She let out a squeal of delight and began talking at me at quite a speed. I hadn't spoken French in a while, but I could understood what she was saying. Then she stopped chattering and I sat back and enjoyed the feeling of her hands in my hair. She rubbed my head and neck, sending soft, sensual messages over the entire surface of my skin. It was worth the expensive salon's rate just for the massage. I'd pay for this kind of intimacy any day of the week. My anxieties over Tom, and the crap with my dad, and Darren, all of my worries, melted away into her fingers.

As she deposited me in the salon chair, I caught sight of her hair again in the mirror. I thought it was the best haircut I'd ever seen. When the stylist came over I told him I wanted the same cut.

'Gosh, that's very short.' He was as camp as a pink silk tent. 'You sure this is what you want, cos I think you can take it, love, you got the face for it, but I don't want you to come back and sue me if you don't like it.' He was a man who spoke without punctuation.

'I'm sure,' I told him. 'I need a change.'

'Okay then.' And he was off. Once he got going, he was not the kind of hairdresser who had time for chatting and I was glad of that. He focused on me, and my hair, and didn't care about the weather or my plans for going out, or any holidays I might have booked. Then he got a razor out and began hacking away. 'Oooh, now this is fun,' he said. I could tell he meant it. He was dancing around as he sliced at my hair. I watched the floor, rather than the mirror. Big thick lengths of black hit the ground and lay there like oil slicks. I felt a strange sense of release.

As he continued with the chopping, the bits of hair falling onto the floor became smaller, lighter, and blew away in the stream of air conditioning. I looked at the mirror. A new person stared back at me. I realised that the hair on the floor was the last of the hair that Darren had touched. The cut was short enough that what was left attached had never been mauled by his sweaty paws. And that felt good.

'Look how pretty you are and you've been hiding that face behind that mop all this time, I mean, that bone structure.' The stylist stepped back to admire me. 'I can't believe you've been hiding behind all that hair for so long, look at yourself.'

And I looked.

Jason had recently bought a place in Crossharbour; it felt like the whole world was moving out my way all of a sudden. Everyone who was anyone in our circles was going to his party, well, except Iain, who'd gone home to South Africa for the holiday. I was quite glad because things were still a bit awkward there, at least until he got a lot of beer or a couple of pills inside him.

I could walk to Crossharbour in a matter of minutes, so I didn't start getting ready until half nine. I put on a small black dress, knee-length boots and the right perfume: Jean-Paul Gautier of course. The smell reminded me of Tom, though, trailing me with melancholy. I checked my phone, again. Still nothing. I stared at the screen, as if I was expecting something to flash up there and then in front of me. I threw the thing on my bed. I would not take it with me. Looking at its stupid blank face had the potential to ruin my night. I turned to the mirror to do my make-up, surprised by the stranger I saw there. I still hadn't decided whether I liked my hair short.

I headed out without a coat on. I had just enough wine inside me to get away with this, and didn't feel the cold as I walked. I came past a group of lads and noticed one guy staring. Then there were giggles as the daft arse walked straight into a lamppost. I turned and smiled at him and his friends, who were in bits all the way down the street.

Jase opened the door and handed me a glass of Kir Royale. The fizz of champagne and sour blackcurrants against my tongue was almost painful. He looked at me, then shook his head, the smile on his face barely contained.

'What?' I asked him.

'Nothing.'

I stared him out, widening my eyes. 'Tell me!'

'It's just your hair. You look, I mean, well, you look amazing.'

There was something about this compliment that bothered me. The way he spoke, his face, everything, it seemed without restraint. I tried hard to smile back, because it's important to do that when you're paid a compliment, but I couldn't look at his face for long. Iain came to mind for some reason. The way he used to tell me things like that all the time and now I never see him. I made good my escape to the bathroom.

I walked in and my reflection took me by surprise. Jase was quite right. The hairstyle fitted my face so well it was scary. Together with the tiny amount of strategically placed make-up, it highlighted my cheekbones and my almond-shaped eyes. I returned to the living room with a swing in my step, realising Jason was just telling the truth, not trying to get into my knickers.

The brand-new flat was open-plan and minimal. There was wooden flooring throughout, and steel fittings in the kitchen and bathrooms. It looked like something out of a magazine: absolute perfection. The main room was filling up with a real mix of people and there was nowhere to sit down. Jason made a beeline for me and handed me a couple of pills. There were bags of cocaine sat on tables and people were helping themselves, cutting lines and snorting them where they sat. The music was so loud the walls were moving. I felt a sudden rush of excitement. It was New Year's Eve and I couldn't have been in a better place to celebrate. I curled my hand round the pills and gave Jason a hug. He squeezed me hard.

An hour or so later and the world was a different place. A projector had been set up to cast simple shapes onto the main wall and make them dance. There were both fairy lights and disco lights flashing in the room. I let this hypnotise me as I listened to the music.

Now this was a party. The apartment was packed full, and the wooden floor was rammed with sweaty dancers. I got up and joined them. Jase came too, dancing close. Merrick waved to me from across the room, his usual massive gurn on. He turned away from me and I saw hair coming out of the collar of his shirt. What was he, the missing link? I didn't miss my phone and its empty fucking inbox. I don't think I would have cared if I had brought it with me, but it made me smile to imagine it at home, out of reach and unable to ruin my night no matter what it tried.

A pill and a half later and the year turned. 1998. I couldn't believe it was here already. We were so close to the turn of the millennium. I remember thinking about the year 2000 when I was little, calculating that I would be twenty-eight and thinking how that was ancient. And here I was two years away. It did not seem possible. I still felt like that little girl in so many ways as we stood, our arms crossed, singing 'Auld Lang Syne'. Everyone kissed and hugged. I let Jason peck me on the lips and I didn't even flinch when Merrick leaned in. It's funny, that few moments after midnight that one time a year, when you'll kiss anyone and it doesn't matter.

After that, the party got messy. Quite a lot of people coupled up, lying down where they wanted and getting it on. Everyone stayed more or less dressed but, other than this little detail, the scene in the living room brought to mind frescos of Roman orgies. I got ridiculously high and hours slipped underneath my feet. I dropped more pills and did a couple of lines and danced and talked the heads off people I knew really well and people I hardly knew at all. Jase and I had a fight with shaving foam, each armed with a can, and everyone crowded round, shouting 'scrap' and clapping and getting really excited. We ended up on the floor wrestling with each other. I did a body lock on him that Darren had taught me, where you twist your legs around the other person, then straighten up, making their legs bend in all sorts of directions and causing considerable pain. There were whistles and shouts from the crowd. I'd forgotten how sexual that move looked, but I didn't care. I was too high.

Then Jason flipped me over and pinned me to the floor. His face was right in front of mine, our lips almost touching. Our eyes met and we stayed like that for just slightly too long. Then he got up and walked away. I sat up and pulled my dress back down. What was happening here?

I stood up, my head rolling like crazy. I felt sick and faint. Merrick saw me wobble and grabbed my arm, pulling me down onto the sofa and sitting beside me. I put my head in my hands, then looked up. I opened my mouth and sounds came out, but nothing I said made sense. I could see Merrick looking at me, amused, but I couldn't make myself understood and it was frightening. I stared at him. He met my gaze with a big wet soppy smile that reminded me of a mate's old Labrador. He grabbed for me, and tried to kiss me. I turned my face and he put his sloppy chops all over me. It was disgusting, like when a dog you don't know licks you on the face and you think about all the other places that tongue has been. Merrick wasn't put off through.

'C'mon, babe.' He pulled my face around again, trying to get my lips with his slobber. I was fighting him off and turning away. One of his hands was wandering up my skirt.

'Fuck off, Merrick.'

But he didn't listen. He just kept mauling at me. Then he pulled back sharp and I didn't really know what had happened until I got myself back together and saw that Jase had hold of him.

'You heard the girl, she said no,' Jase told him, pulling him right off the chair and onto the floor. Merrick picked himself up and looked at both of us with heavy-lidded eyes, his face all lopsided and mangled by the number of pills he'd had. He seemed confused, then looked away. Jase turned to me. 'You okay?'

I nodded.

'Out the flat, cunt face,' Jase said to Merrick.

Merrick gurned at him. Someone made a comment about it being New Year, and the guy was wasted and to have a heart, but Jase was having none of it. He pulled Merrick to his feet and had someone call a cab. Merrick was so out of it he didn't seem to register what was happening, never mind care.

Jase saw Merrick out the door, then came back over. 'You wanna go somewhere quiet?'

I ran fingers through what was left of my hair. It felt good, shorn and easy. I nodded.

He took me to his room. He had a bar in there, stocked with optics and bottles of mixers.

'Ha! Typical bachelor stuff,' I said.

Jase laughed and held up both hands. 'Guilty as charged.'

There was a cocktail shaker and I filled it with random liquids: gin, Malibu and vodka with limeade and fresh orange. Jason was watching me and sitting on the bed.

'What you gonna call that one then?'

'A wanker. After my friend Merrick,' I told him.

Jason laughed a lot at this. 'Don't hold it against him, though, Frankie. He was out of his box.'

I poured the strange mixture into glasses, then walked over to the bed with the drinks and gave one to him. 'I know and I won't. But I'm still calling the drink wanker in his honour. It's fair enough.'

Jase agreed it was and took a sip. He sprayed it out of his mouth straight away. 'Oh good God, that's grim.'

'Don't be ridiculous,' I said, taking a big swig then doing the same. It was sour and nasty. We were both laughing, and Jason was spilling his share of the evil concoction all over the bed. I put my glass on the floor and put my arms around him. My heart felt good about being there with him. I knew Jason wouldn't take advantage of this situation, wouldn't try to jump my bones or touch me where I didn't want him to. He was perfect.

'Can I stay here tonight?' I said.

Jase smiled, and the little wrinkles it made round his eyes seemed to light up his face. ''Course.' He made an amused sound. 'Well, you can stay as long as you like, but it ain't nighttime no more.' The window was above the bed and he pulled the curtain open, just a little. A slice of light cut into the room.

I giggled. 'Well, doesn't time fly?'

We lay there, touching each other's hair. My head rolled and rolled and my consciousness spiralled in on itself in time to the music, which was muffled in the bedroom but still quite loud. The room spun, but not in the way it does when you're drunk and about to throw up or pass out. It spun around us, like we were the centre of the universe. I got some visuals. They came like a slideshow behind my eyes, lighting up and dropping out; fields of irises, a meadow in summer, grass so green I could smell it around my eyes like I was lying in it.

I woke up on Jason's bed many hours later, fully clothed and outside of the covers. Jase was fast gone and snoring beside me. The bit of exposed window was black with night now.

I got up and went into the living area. There were sleeping people in every possible place. There was even a man on the kitchen floor and I tried not to wake him as I climbed over to get a glass of water. I thought about going home. I wanted to know if Tom had bothered to get in touch to say Happy New Year. I didn't want to know if he hadn't.

I turned to see Jason stood behind me rubbing his eyes. 'You going, babe?'

'I don't think so.'

'Wanna do a line?' He was still rubbing at his eyes.

It didn't seem like a very sensible idea. I loved it. There were still plenty of half-full baggies lying around. Between us we gathered them and took them over to the coffee table.

I did more coke with Jase in the next few hours than I'd ever done before, even with Tom. We were shockingly hedonistic. We went for a walk. The air was crisp and dry and even, the stars and the moon shone in the murky dock water. We came back in and put the music back on and woke everyone up and the dancing resumed. People were soon up and popping pills, trying to get hold of the remnants from the bags of coke, licking them clean and fighting each other for what was left, but in a good-hearted way. Lots of joints were lit, and passed around.

It was the third of January when I made it home, with a gasping thirst and skin as dry as paper. I drank straight from the bathroom tap and pushed water through my hair. I examined my face in the mirror; not pretty. I smothered myself in moisturiser and rubbed the hinge of my jaw. It was clenched tight.

I filled a glass with water and took it with me to bed. Of course, I found my phone there. It needed recharging so I plugged it in beside the bed, telling myself to leave it, to sleep and let it charge. But I needed to know if he'd thought about me at all, if he'd bothered to say Happy New Year. No messages came through at first, but I knew it sometimes took a few moments. I lay my head back on my pillow and let the phone drop beside me. Then I felt it vibrating and grabbed it back up.

Message after message hit my screen, much faster than I could open them. Five or so were telling me I had voicemail, but mostly they were text messages from Tom. They started all casual. *Drop me a call. Ring me back. Hey, babe, what's going on with you, ring me!* Then, at five minutes past midnight, *happy new year hope you're having fun babe xxx.* As time progressed they got slightly paranoid. *Have I done something wrong? Did I upset you?* Then apologetic. *I should have been in touch. I know I was crap, Please forgive me and give me a ring.* When I rang to get the voicemails, three out of the five were from Tom too.

This was more like it. I'd never been one for games before, never felt that kick in the ribs that is the thrill of someone losing it over you. I'm not saying this is some noble way to live your life, but it felt fucking great. I decided there and then I would have my mobile on less, be much slower to return calls and text messages, be careless with my phone, leave it places and not charge it consistently. I would be less accessible.

I wrote a reply to him and was about to send it. Then I thought, no, and saved it to drafts. He could wait a little longer. Just then, the phone started ringing. The name of my lover flashed on the screen. I let it go to voicemail, then switched off the phone and lay down to sleep.

EUREX

1 a European derivatives exchange created upon the merger of the German Deutsche Termin Bourse (DTB) and the Swiss Options and Financial Futures Exchange (SOFFEX); **2** them bastard Germans.

-------------------------5,262.6 ⇧69.0 (1.3%)-------------------------

When I went back to work after New Year I was nervous about seeing Tom again. It's bullshit what they say about absence and the heart. I could hardly picture his face.

I put on my blue and gold stripes again. If the novelty of seeing myself kitted up this way was ever going to wear off, it hadn't happened yet. There was a letter waiting for me when I arrived at work. It confirmed something I'd been told might happen; I'd been approved in record time by pit committee. Tom had told me that it was being discussed and his bet was that they'd push my approval through because, and I quote, 'They're gagging for it and you're sexy.' I didn't really see what that had to do with my trading ability, but I didn't care that much either. All that mattered was that I was no longer a blue-button. I had a full trading badge.

Seated at the booth, I was reading my letter a third time and feeling pleased with myself when Tom came along. He peeked at me from below his fringe. I tried to smile but it felt forced.

'Good vacation?' he said.

'Great.' I showed him my letter and he congratulated me. Jack arrived and budged me over so he could set up charts. Tom picked up a copy of the *Sun* and opened it, raising his eyebrows as he flicked past page 3. I couldn't think of anything to say and picked at a broken nail. Nick arrived, full of it about his New Year celebrations and talking like a Madchester reject about how hardcore it'd all been. Then Diane was there too, in a skirt that was too tight and short for work. I switched off while they went on and on about New Year.

I was staring into space and half noticed Diane sit down next to me. She'd been there a few minutes and I was minding my own business when I felt a pull on my jacket and saw she had hold of my badge. She brought it right up in front of her eyes, like an old man who's forgotten his reading glasses. 'That's fucking quick. For pit committee.'

Everyone turned round, Tom, Jack, Nick, even some of the team in the next-door booth were staring over to see what was going on. Of course, everyone knew how badly Diane and I got on and no doubt there were still books running about when next the two of us would get physical. I shrugged and said nothing, not wanting to give anyone their morning's entertainment. Diane pulled a face like she'd just drunk sour milk. 'I guess the question's not so much who, as how many,' she said.

Tom's eyes widened for second, like he was staring into the headlights of a car. Diane had almost certainly been aiming for damage and she'd hit her target. Then he pulled himself out from that trance and stepped in.

'For fuck's sake, Diane, Happy New Year to you too. Why don't you fuck off for a bit and get some fresh air? I'm sure we can do without you for a while. Go to TJ's and have a good ole think about life,' he said.

She looked at him with a tight face. Then she grabbed her handbag and stormed off. Tom turned to me. 'We're going to take a trip. A friend of mine's trading down the road on the DTB screens and I'd like to see what's happening. It'll be very useful for you to come see.'

I had a feeling it was just an excuse to get me alone, but I wasn't arguing with that. And I wanted to see these trading screens anyway. He was right: I did need to learn about it.

Tom's mate worked on Lombard Street, which was quite a walk from Cannon Bridge. We hadn't gone far when Tom pushed me into a doorway set back at the side of the street. He pulled me close and inhaled. 'I've missed you. Let me take a look at you.' He drew me back then planted a kiss on my lips. 'You look amazing. I love the new look.' More kisses, all over my face, and another deep breath, and then, 'There ain't no truth in what Diane was getting at, is there?'

''Course not. I'm not the office bike, you know.'

'Oh God, I do. She got to me, for a goddamn second the petty little bitch got to me, you know?' I did. I had seen it in his eyes. 'You got plans tonight?'

'Yeah, I'm going round to Lorna's. She's having some boyfriend problems.' This was a lie. In truth, her and Steven were going from strength to strength again and, me, I was avoiding the pair of them.

'Aw shucks,' he said. 'Maybe tomorrow?'

'Maybe.' His face was sagging at this and I couldn't keep it up. I wanted to see him too. 'You know, actually, I'm pretty sure I'm free then.' He gave me such a big smile it nearly knocked me over. I wanted him badly, there and then, and was regretting my lie about tonight. It was so much easier to play games over the phone.

Tom visibly relaxed now he'd had a chance to wrap me up in his arms and breathe me in. The bounce was back in his step, together with the cocky, arrogant edge to his face. As we walked up Cannon Street, he talked about his holiday, how much he'd missed me, and how he wished I was easier to get hold of on the phone, what with his circumstances and all that. I nodded in all the right places but had no intention of reverting to my old habit of availability.

We arrived at the Lombard Street Mees Pierson building and signed in. Tom's friend Mark came up to get him and they shared a manly handshake, slapping each other hard on the back. I was introduced and had my hand shaken too, only this time I could see Mark was undressing me in his head at the same time.

We went down into the basement of the building. The room smelt of old socks, beer and farts, a bit like the inside of a football ground. There were lots of comments and even a couple of catcalls from the men there. I recognised some faces, though I wasn't sure if it was from nights out or the floor. Mark gave us a bit of a tour. There were a number of trading systems. The most basic were the green and black screens provided by the exchange, which looked something like the old technology you see on low-budget sci-fi. They were clunky and I couldn't see how this was faster or slicker or better in any way than standing face to face and agreeing a deal.

In contrast, some of the trading software was whizz-bang. It listed the bid offer spread and market depth. You could double-click to trade, or even set it up for one-click trading if you wanted. The whole thing was a little too Space Invaders for me and even Tom was shocked at how easy it was to trade. It's all very well, but if it's that easy to carry out a transaction, then it's that easy to make a mistake too. Single click? You'd have to be crazy.

This Hugh Grant lookalike with blond floppy hair came running out of an office shouting something about the server being down. Everyone groaned, and someone shouted, 'Not a-fucking-gain.' There was a scramble as people phoned the exchange to make sure positions had been pulled. I thought they were all crazy, trading this way. How could this possibly be better? With LIFFE you stood in front of each other and came to an agreement and everyone knew where they stood. I wasn't into this point–click–trade nonsense and I didn't like the panic in the room when the technology had let them down. Anyway, this place was too smelly. I couldn't work out how the DTB had taken as much business off us as they had, if this was typical.

On the way back, Jack phoned to say it was busy, and we didn't have time to go to the pub or anything, so we nipped into Sainsbury's. I was standing with Tom, staring into the fridges, a bit overwhelmed by the choice of sandwiches, when I had a sudden naughty impulse.

'Steal something,' I whispered.

Tom looked at me. 'Shut up,' he said, but all sarky rather than abrupt.

'Gwaan,' I said.

He looked back at me then, eyes shining, responding to those words with the same kind of *fuck-it* I might. 'You really shouldn't suggest things like that.' He looked at the shelves in front of him. 'Nah, it has to be better than this if I'm gonna bother.' He walked off to another aisle and I followed. Beers, wines and spirits; what else? Keeping his eyes on me all the time, he slipped a bottle of whisky into his inside pocket and headed for the door. He walked straight through, and out onto Bishopsgate. My heart was beating fast just watching him. Nobody followed.

I wanted to leave too, run right out of there after him, but I knew that would not look cool. I stood looking at the bottles of wine, not sure what to do next, when I got a text message. It was from Tom – 'ur turn'. A thrill shot through me. I looked along the shelf. Tom was right, it had to be something worth having. I settled on gin, quality stuff in a blue bottle.

My career would have been over if I'd got caught. You had to be cleaner than Daz whites or the SFA, our regulators, chucked you out. My legs itched to run, but I resisted. I knew that would be stupid. What I did instead was walk over to the checkout, pick up a bar of chocolate, buy it, and head towards the exit. Everything was burning brighter, as adrenalin hit me in waves. I made a point of walking slowly towards the door. I could see Tom, a short distance away, watching me with a smile on his face. Then I was out of the door, and stood in the street with the bottle in my pocket. My back itched with the idea of the security guard's arm, reaching over, touching my shoulder and ordering me to stop right there. My head echoed with the idea of someone calling me back.

And then, just like that, there was someone calling me back. 'Excuse me.' The deep voice of a young, black man.

It felt like everything had stopped for a second. Nothing existed, there was just that voice. I turned. It was the security guard, and he was talking to me. I didn't panic. I looked him in the eyes and smiled, charm-school style, thinking – *I'm fucked* – but not actually quite believing this was happening. I was considering whether to bolt. My brain focused on the bloke, and the sounds around me were muffled so that all I could hear was his voice.

'Hey, love,' he said. He smiled and everything was out of kilter with what I was expecting. He was holding his hand out to me. 'You forgot your change.' And the other sounds came back, just like I'd popped my head up from the bath. The sound of the traffic on Bishopsgate, and of people walking-talking-jostling in that rowdy-busy City lunchtime way.

'Thanks.' I took the coins from him and walked, calm as you like, across the road to Tom. The security guard headed back inside. As soon as he'd gone the two of us rushed away down the road. We broke into a jog, even though that drew attention to us. We were laughing as we ran, which felt weird and was harder than it sounds.

When we finally stopped I couldn't talk I was breathing so fast. I stood there, bent double with a stitch and with laughter, my breathing so heavy it was all I could hear. I was gone; laughing so hard I couldn't speak. Tom kept saying, 'What, what, what?' but I couldn't tell him.

We walked back to the LIFFE building hardly speaking. Every so often one of us would look at the other, and the eye contact, the memory of what had just happened, would give me a rush. I smiled, realising that the thrill we'd shared had blown away the absence, made things seem normal again. About halfway down Cannon Street Tom stopped walking. I turned and gave him a look. 'What?'

He smiled. 'My turn to be the bad influence.' He beckoned me to the side of the pavement, right beside an office intercom system, and I had to concentrate not to lean back and ring someone's bell. He turned me to stand so I hid him from the pavement and dug into a pocket, held out his hand. There were two little pills sitting in his palm. I looked him in the eye.

I grabbed one of the pills and put it straight in my mouth. I pulled a face as I tried to open the bottle of gin, and struggled, the taste of the pill making me want to spit it out. Tom got the whisky open and we used that. The pill did not go down easy and I had to flood the back of my mouth with liquid. I retched a little, but it had gone. The liquid burned my throat and made me burp.

'Charming,' Tom said.

An hour or so later we were well into the afternoon trading session and both rolling like mad on the pills. They were knock-your-head-off strong. I could feel I was grinding my teeth, and it was a real effort to concentrate on what Jack was signalling, but it was the biggest buzz ever.

That day was pretty special. There was this trader who turned his hand to magic tricks in his spare time, and that day he'd brought balloons with him, and was using them to make sausage dogs and poodles. He'd even made some swords, and some of the guys paired up to duel with their new toys. He made something for everyone. Jack got an icicle, and Nick 'Leeson' the bars for his cell window. I was expecting something like a bolt to put through my head. I begged him to tell me what he was making but he wouldn't say a word. He held a finger over his mouth in an exaggerated gesture. The whole way he made out he took the act so seriously, well, it destroyed the rest of us and all I could hear was laughing. The sides of my mouth were hurting with the strain of it all.

I watched him as he worked, making something that resembled those life preservers you see on the side of the docks. I had no idea what it was supposed to be and looked blank as he handed it to me. To give me a clue, he got down on one knee and mimed a proposal. It was an oversized engagement ring. I took the ring and blew a kiss to him as I walked back to the booth. Tom met me on the way, his eyes glowing. He grabbed the balloon off me and threw it on the floor, jumping on it to burst it.

The fun was over and we went back to trading but I was still off my head. It was busy, and I made a mistake but luckily I was able to trade out in a second at the same price. High as I was, it struck me that our dares were getting more serious. We were risking our jobs and our reputations. We were risking getting arrested. Yet somewhere inside I suspected this was just the start.

--------------------------5,595.8 ⇩17.0 (0.3%)--------------------------

The Christmas separation and my New Year's resolution to make myself less available were soon forgotten. If anything, I was seeing more of Tom than before the holidays. We went out, drank, took pills and cocaine, went back to mine and shagged. Occasionally he stayed all night, but usually he didn't. Sometimes he would come over all romantic; I think he thought he had to but I didn't care. Like when he made a fuss about doing something the afternoon of Valentine's Day. I went for a quick drink with him and let him buy; it seemed to make him feel better. Then I went home and ate greasy Chinese and refused to think about what he might be doing with his wife. I would not be that kind of mistress because, that stuff, well, it could eat you up. I would be the kind of mistress who knew what it was like to fuck on cocaine.

I was getting good at that, and becoming a half-decent trader to boot. I was careful and clear with my hand signals, and fast, and I didn't make many mistakes. It wasn't easy for me in the rough and tumble of the futures pit but I could do it. I did do it and Tom was pleased. I was having fun but it felt fast, loose, unsafe. The feeling reminded me of one of my recurring nightmares. I'd been floating above the ground for a long time but now I was flying high, too far up, and fear that I would lose control and fall to earth haunted me. I tried to ignore it. I tried my 'fuck it' spell but it didn't always work.

There were whispers, rumours about what might happen next with the exchange. It was already clear we would lose the Bund contract to the DTB. The traded volumes were consistently rising there and falling on LIFFE. It was too late to win that particular battle; all that was possible was damage limitation to stop anything happening to the rest of our business. People reckoned LIFFE would get an electronic trading platform up and running to compete, and there were even resignations by those who wanted to get in and set up a business ahead of the game. Most people scoffed at them, though. They talked about liquidity and clung to the complexities around some of the contracts we still controlled.

Me? I did what I do when I don't want to know about something. I stuck my fingers firmly in my ears and shouted 'I'm not listening' like a five-year-old. I did it with the DTB and I did it with other things too. Mostly, it worked, though it left me feeling edgy. The ground underneath me was soggy, and set to slide, I could feel it. And what was happening with Tom compounded this. Not just the sex but the other dangerous things we did. I knew it was just a matter of time before we'd risk our lives, just for the thrill of it.

It was a Wednesday or Thursday night when it happened. We'd been drinking in the West End. We were both roaring drunk, and Tom had been sick and carried straight on with another cocktail, saying it was like falling off a horse. We left the bar, planning to head to my place. As we walked out, I was struck by the feeling I'd left something behind, my bag or my purse, and I went back. Inside, I remembered I hadn't brought those things. Although I was sure I was right, it was confusing because I was struck with some clarity that there was something I had forgotten. This had been happening to me a lot recently. I guessed it was all the drugs I'd been doing, some effect on my short-term memory.

We walked along the Embankment hand in hand. The river was strung with coloured lights that winked and glittered in its surface and in the sky. The place seemed huge and built for cars, not pedestrians, like one of those American retail parks. It wasn't long before we came to an underpass with a big round sign showing a walking man with a line through it. I looked for the pedestrian route. It was a long way round. Tom started off in that direction anyway.

'Oi, mister,' I said. He turned back to me. I pointed into the traffic-only underpass. 'Let's go that way.'

Despite the sign, there was a slither of pavement for us to stand on inside the tunnel but we were both in such a state, it might as well have been a tightrope. Cars flew past at sixty. One of two of them sent us long, protracted beeps, warning us we weren't supposed to be there. Tom giggled and fell off the pavement. I grabbed at him, pulled him back. A car came by so close that I was left with the impression of it glancing his jacket. A thrill went up inside me, a fix of the chemicals I was getting addicted to. 'Let's run,' I said.

It was impossible to stay on the tiny pavement and run, and we both fell onto the road several times. Cars came by.

God knows where they were going at this time of night. One had to swerve into the other lane to avoid us, and it was lucky there was nothing overtaking or we would have had it.

Tom's face was shining. He stepped onto the road, then carried on walking but with his eyes closed and arms held out in front of him like a sleepwalker. My heart was banging in my chest and I closed my eyes too. I heard the loud whistle of cars coming by. I heard the huge sound of someone holding down their car horn for ages and, for all the thrill of it, I couldn't keep my eyes closed.

A car was heading right at Tom. There was a lorry in the fast lane and nowhere for this car to go except right through him. And it wasn't braking. I stood frozen as the car headed faster and faster towards him. It looked like the driver had put his foot down, trying to make a point. Tom just kept walking. It felt like being in one of those dreams when you want to scream but you can't make any noise. I wished it was a nightmare, and willed myself to wake up and see my bedroom, but that wasn't happening.

The car was yards away and he didn't stand a chance. I closed my eyes again. I didn't want to see him hit hard, bouncing against the windscreen, flying up into the air then onto the road to get hit a second time.

When I forced myself to look, I saw Tom on the pavement and the relief surged through me in such a rush that I forgot all the fear. He was laughing his stupid head off and completely unharmed. How the fuck he'd managed to get out of the way in time was a mystery.

As we came out of the tunnel, we were dancing. Waltzing down Lower Thames Street like it was a fucking ballroom. I could hear music in my head. It felt like there were bubbles all around me, holding me up, making every move easier. It felt like the air was thinner somehow.

--------------------------5,582.3 ⇧29.8 (0.5%)--------------------------

The DTB merged with another exchange and rebranded itself as EUREX. They continued to eat away at the Bund contract, not dropping below 50 per cent of traded business again. LIFFE was a scary place to be all of a sudden and there were a lot of people pulled in by the crisis. Plans were being made to fight back and there was definitely going to be an electronic trading system at the exchange. It hadn't been announced yet, but the news had leaked and we all knew about it.

Jason was trying to ignore all of this too, except he was a Bund trader and much nearer to the heart of the problem than I was. He couldn't afford to stick his fingers in his ears. I realised how serious his problem was one morning when I saw him in TJ's. At first, I was encouraged because he looked happier than he'd been for ages. He was sitting at a table with his feet up, eating a bacon sarnie. It had so much HP on it I could smell him before I saw him.

'Yo, girlfriend,' he said, in a silly voice.

'Yo, heart attack waiting to happen.'

He shrugged. 'Tastes good though.'

I pushed his legs over and made some room so I could sit on the table.

'I can see up your skirt from here,' Jase told me.

I crossed my legs then uncrossed them, *Basic Instinct* style. 'No you can't.'

He looked up at me, smiling so broadly I could see chewed-up bacon. 'All right so I can't. Pity, though.'

I sat there for a few minutes, chatting with him about the possibility of going to a Boy George night at the Ministry in a few weeks' time. He was full of it about what a banging night it'd be and I said I'd think about it but I wasn't properly listening. As we chatted, I felt something claw at my stomach. He was mid-flow about how good a DJ George had turned out to be when I just had to stop him.

'Jason, do you have a plan yet?'

The expression dropped off his face. 'About the Boy George night?'

'For fuck's sake, no. About your livelihood. Your life.'

He took a bite of sandwich. He didn't let it stop him talking and I had to look away because the sight was making me queasy. 'Nah, I'm not bothered. I got a feeling things'll turn around here. I think it's just a matter of days before we're back in control, this new system coming along and everything.'

It was one of those moments where a casual statement illuminates the whole silly world. I could see clearly and suddenly that LIFFE was a hotbed of delusion, with all of the comments flying around about liquidity in certain contracts, and strategy trades, and all sorts of reasons why we wouldn't get put out of business for good. Jase was right there with a few others in the core of this and it was a dangerous place to be. Like the eye of a hurricane. I knew I couldn't handle this. But I knew a man who could. I made my excuses and ran off to find Tom.

My boss was chatting to a local over near the FTSE pit. They were nudging each other and having a laugh. I interrupted and Tom smiled at me, was easy to drag away. I saw the red-jacket making some inappropriate gesture about me to Tom, just on the edge of my field of vision. I ignored him.

'Can you speak to Jason? Help sort him out with that place down the road we went to, or something, anything. He's going off the rails.'

Tom knew what I meant. He'd seen more of it than I had. A friend of his had walked into the woods and blown his own head off. The pressure could be enormous and people lost it, they just did. Usually it was over mistakes, cleaning out the bonus pool. Even a little cock-up and the way people looked at you could send you into a depression. The loudest, brashest personalities could take a nosedive when something bigger happened.

'I don't know, babe. He's been blanking me lately. Ain't got a clue what I've done, but he ain't happy with me.'

'For fuck's sake, Tom. He's been funny with everyone. Take him in hand, or get someone else to. Please. For me.'

Tom looked a little startled. 'Bolshy young Frankie asking for help? From anyone? Christ, don't tell me there's shit the girl cares about.'

'Fuck off, Tom, Will you help me or not?'

He chewed on his lip. 'Is something going on with you and this guy?'

It hadn't even crossed my mind he might come to that conclusion. I felt a pang of guilt about my relationship with Jason. It was definitely more complicated than friendship. But who the fuck was Tom to demand anything of me? He didn't have the right to ask, coming from the place he was, with a wife in Clapham and all that deadly dull platinum gluing them to each other. 'For fuck's sake, no. You really must think I'm some kind of slapper.'

He looked slightly ashamed then and I thought – *too right.* He chewed his lip some more. 'I have a mate who can do this. I'll get him over here this afternoon.'

* * *

Tom's mate did the job, taking Jason aside, telling him the truth and almost insisting he sign up for a seat at Lombard Street, that smelly, dark place I'd visited. Jase had been up to hearing the truth, but it took a lot out of him. I took him for a drink after work to try to cheer him up, and we met up with Steven and Lorna in the City Page. I'd never seen Jason looking so beat. He was the kind of bloke who always had a smile on his face, the sort of person who, when you think about them, it makes you smile. He was the bloke I'd hunt down or invite out when I was feeling low because he'd always perk me up. As he sat opposite me nursing a pint he looked older. The lines that usually got killed by his smile were left etched and on display. Lorna was chatting away like silence could kill someone, talking crap to drown out the mood. Steven was puffing on a cigar and trying to talk about what had happened with the Bund, even though it was the worst possible subject. He didn't take the hint. He was desperate to get in his *I told you so*.

Jase looked up at him and lit a fag, but didn't say anything. Lorna said something about how everything would come out in the wash, and that Jase would realise this had been sent to teach him something. No one was listening to her platitudes, least of all Jason. Steven blew a smoke ring and smiled. 'I did tell you, though, honey.' He wagged his cigar at me. 'It's the beginning of the end for open outcry, you mark my words. It's old-fashioned and too expensive.' He might as well have called Jason's mother a whore.

'What would you know about it, old man?' Jase asked him. He stubbed out one cigarette and lit another. He looked at Steven through narrowed eyes, his mouth tight and mean. I felt like I was sitting opposite a stranger who happened to look like my friend. Lorna escaped, off to buy more wine.

The expression on Steven's face did not change. He'd worked in the City far too long to be intimidated by some twenty-something trader type, no matter how much money the bloke might be worth or how hard he could have hit him if he'd chosen to. Steven took another drag on his cigar, this crappy little Hamlet he kept sucking on like it was a dummy. 'I'd know a lot more than you'd think.'

Jase nodded his head upwards – *go on.*

Steven sucked on the Hamlet some more. In no rush. 'It was all planned. Surely you know that? You can't think this kind of thing just happens, overnight. Systems like that, they take months to set up.'

My face must have been a right picture at this point, because I'd cottoned on to why Steven had always been so smug on this subject. Jase looked at me and I saw add-ups going on behind his eyes.

'Who d'you work for?' he said, washing down smoke with a big swig of beer.

Steven raised his eyebrows and smiled. I knew what was coming because I knew fine well who Steven worked for. He flicked ash off the end of his cigar and spat out the name of a big German bank. 'Best laid plans and all that.' The allusion didn't even make sense.

I thought Steven was going to get a smack at this point but Jase didn't move. He shrugged. 'Fuck ya,' he said to Steven. 'Fuck the lot of you.' He pushed his beer over on the table. He didn't throw it, didn't aim the liquid at anyone, he just pushed it over with a cruel curl on his lip. Then he grabbed his fags and made to leave the bar. Lorna came back with white wine in a cooler. She looked confused as she placed it down.

I was off after Jason without turning to look at Steven. I couldn't bear to see the look on his face – it would make me want to spit in his eyes, or punch him, anything to wipe that expression clean off, I knew it.

Outside the pub I could see Jase marching off ahead, on a mission to get away from the crappy day. I called after him. He didn't stop so I ran to catch him up. I grabbed at his arm. He turned and I thought he was going to smack me one. Then I saw that the look I'd mistaken for anger was something else. Jase was crying.

I put my arms around him and he collapsed against me. After a while he stopped crying but I didn't let go. He was bent over, and nuzzled his forehead against mine. We looked each other right in the eyes, way up close. 'Don't you ever fucking tell anyone about this, Frankie.' I still didn't speak. It went without saying. I kissed him, gently on one eye then the other, cleaning them of tears. Then I held his hand and saw him to the tube.

I remember the rest of the Bund story taking about a week to play out, though it was probably longer. It's a blur for me after that. I just remember coming in one day soon after and the Bund pit was empty. A gaping hole in the floor that had been sucked dry.

Jase moved into Lombard Street and claimed he was loving it, but I wasn't convinced. I went to visit him there. Jase and his mates looked wrong seated at desks, too big somehow. The way some men look like bouncers when they put on a suit. The brokers who were there still used hand signals to communicate even though it wasn't noisy and they didn't need to. People still told each other buy 'em and sell 'em in conversation and made the signals to match, trying to hold on to what they'd lost. Some of the traders had their LIFFE jackets and badges, and kept them on the back of their chairs. Souvenirs. Things to remember with.

Acid

1 of pH less than 7; **2** a corrosive substance; **3** an early form of house music originating in Chicago in the late 1980s; **4** a hallucinogenic drug; **5** not recommended for those with mental health issues.

----------------------------**5,767.3** ⇧2.5 (0.04%)----------------------------

It was at a party in Clapham when it all went wrong; Tom's birthday. He should never have invited me.

It wasn't Tom's actual birthday, nor the day before or after. In fact, it turns out that Tom was one of those 29 February people. It was typical of him; you couldn't even pin him down to a birthday except every four years. The light was fading fast and the air smelt green as I came out from Clapham North tube. As I walked, I was again nagged by the idea I had forgotten something important. This paranoia was beginning to get to me. It was almost constant, and unsettling, and made me feel sick.

We were meeting at a pub near Tom's house, this place called the Bread and Roses. Tom called the Bread his local and said it was his favourite pub in London. It was strange that he should feel that way. The name of the pub was from some lefty quote and inside it was done out with a deliberate lack of chic: bare wood, basic tables and chairs, and an attitude as red as a bunch of Labour roses. There were posters for demonstrations against capitalism, for campaigns to send aid to Romania, for Amnesty International. But the clientele, well, they were all like Tom. Typical Clapham yuppies come from a break from their twenty-something, thirty-something conversion flats: split-level, high ceilings, picture windows and all mod cons. People who worked for City or media firms or over west for the BBC. Couples with six-figure combined incomes and direct debits set up to send ten pounds a month to their favourite charity. Talk about champagne socialism.

I arrived and made a beeline for Tom, giving Baby a wave as I came past. Her eyes met mine but she turned away and pretended she hadn't seen me. Tom said hello and kissed me on the cheek, then walked off to speak to someone else. Jack and his wife were there, but I knew no one else so I stood chatting with those two while Tom did the rounds. There are some people in your life, not just lovers, but friends too, where you feel so close to them that you can't imagine you don't know them inside out, that you don't know everything about their lives. With these people, it always comes as a surprise that they have friends you've never met. For me, Lorna came into this category, and Jason. And so did Tom. But looking around at the sheer weight of strangeness in the room, the plain and simple number of people I'd never met before, it took my breath away. I felt like one of those wives who discover their husband has another family somewhere, a whole separate life.

I got chatting to different groups of people and walked away and on, each time my spirits sinking to a new low. No one knew who I was. They asked my name, how I knew Tom, polite questions. I wasn't expecting any of them to turn around and say, 'Ah, so *you're* his mistress,' or anything like that. But with his mates, even his close friends, I looked for that spark of recognition you get. That little 'ah-ha' you see in people's eyes when they do the add-ups. It wasn't there.

Tom had told none of his friends about me. It wasn't just that Tom had a separate life I wasn't part of, it was like he lived on a different planet. In a similar London but a parallel universe.

He came to find me, about an hour after I'd arrived. He touched my waist. I was polite, and there was banter, but I was cool with him.

'You wanna creep off to the toilets?' he said. He gave me that smile, the one that worked tricks on me. This time, though, I just thought it looked cheesy.

'I don't think that's a good idea,' I said.

'Aw, gwaaan, babe,' he said, grabbing a sneaky feel of my arse. But I shook my head. His charm was not going to work tonight. Tom didn't push it. He walked off, his face telling the story of a man who was used to getting his own way. It didn't knock him off his stride for long, though. I saw him, minutes later, sat in the corner, with Baby and her mates. The girls, looking up at him like he had all the answers. Like he was the king of the world. I was talking to Glenn, who told me he was Tom's best mate. I had never heard of him. He knew so little about me, about who I was to Tom, that he was chatting me up. This Glenn bloke looked over at Tom, holding court to his ladies in the corner. 'That thing he does, it works. It really works.' He shook his head and smiled in appreciation of his mate's skills.

I stood there, staring at Tom. Glenn asked if I was all right. I nodded. I thought about turning and shoving my tongue down his throat, just for badness. I thought about taking him home with me and showing him the time of his life, just so Tom could hear the lurid details of what I'd done first hand. I thought about how good it would make me feel, this man all over me. How he would tell me I was gorgeous and sexy and mean it. I thought about how I would look, reflected in Glenn's big blue eyes.

I told myself, no, said I wouldn't be that girl any more. I made my excuses and left the pub, planning to visit Lorna for some gin and sympathy. I scrolled through my 'calls made' list for ages before I came to her number. The list said Tom, Tom, Tom, Tom for a long way down. I opened up my text messages, sent and received. Tom, Tom, Tom, Tom, Tom. I was way too involved with this man. This married man. Did everyone except me know this? It was such a shock to me that bile shot up into my throat.

I went back to Glenn and invited him to my place. Maybe I would always be that girl. *Fuck it*, there were plenty of men the same. Tom didn't ring or text to find out where I'd gone, how I was. It wasn't that he didn't care, I knew that. It was much worse.

I did not exist.

-------------------------5,733.1 ⇓74.6 (1.3%)-------------------------

I renewed my resolution to cool things with Tom after that and tried to ignore his calls and messages, avoid being alone with him at work. I couldn't keep it up for long, though, and a week later I ended up out with him and a bunch of LIFFE people, in Fuegos. I could feel things slipping back to normal between us too quickly, but I was determined not to forget his party, how it had felt. I tried to grit my teeth and hold on to that feeling, and it worked, more or less. It didn't stop me in my tracks the way it should have, though.

The place was quiet, for a Friday, but Nick and Diane were there and they were winding me up, as usual. I could see them, whispering stuff to each other, then looking at me and Tom. They couldn't have been less subtle about it. Tom told me not to worry about them and jangled one of his famous cufflinks. I took it off him and headed to the toilets. When I came back, Tom's eyes were shining too. We went outside for some fresh air and he was angling to take me down an alleyway somewhere, but I wanted to go back and dance.

As we walked back in I noticed Nick had left the keys to his crap Porsche on the table. I thought about his car, its black and red leather interior and VW engine. The machine was as cheesy as the music the DJ was playing. Its keys winked at me from the table. I went over and grabbed them, then sidled back over to Tom.

'Look what I got,' I said, opening my hand a little to show him.

He put a hand on my waist, singing the lyrics to 'Vogue' and half dancing. He moved his eyes closer to focus on the keys.

'You bought a Porsche-a?' he said, that way the Americans pronounce it.

'They're Nick's.'

'And?' He was moving to the music and looking around the room but bent his head in my direction.

'Let's steal it.'

Tom stopped dancing and looked straight at me. 'No,' he said. 'That's too much, man.'

'Nick won't notice. He's out on the beers and it'll get left at Swan Lane again. You watch.'

Tom looked at me and I could see he was thinking about it. 'We've been drinking.'

'Don't you got the balls, dude?' I said, doing this really crap imitation of his accent.

He was on the way out of the club before I'd finished the sentence.

The Porsche tyres screamed as we tore out of the Swan Lane car park. I was at the wheel because Tom said he didn't know how to drive a 'stick shift'. I made a joke about him wussing out, and told him he'd have to take a turn later, and he shrugged. The car handled better than reputation gave it credit for, that much Nick was right about. We fair flew down Lower Thames Street, then along the Embankment, under the tunnel where Tom had nearly got himself killed.

'Where you taking us?' Tom said.

'Just hold on tight for Frankie Stein's tour of London.'

'Monster.'

There was a bite in the air that night, but we put the top down on the car anyway. We could handle getting a bit of cold. The car's acceleration was sweet. You pressed down the pedal and it roared like a jet engine and the car took off. It wasn't a vehicle for the faint-hearted, even if it was a crap Porsche.

I did a tour of London, like I'd promised, taking in Buckingham Palace, then the Houses of Parliament, then back up to St Paul's and through the City to the Docklands. Once I hit the City again, I drove the way you'd expect someone to after a couple of hits of coke, treating the highway like it was Le Mans, cornering at speed and crossing to the other side of the road with little regard for other traffic. The place was deserted, though, and the only other car we did see moved fast out of my way. Neither of us was wearing a seatbelt.

We came onto the Isle of Dogs near Canary Wharf, past a road island that had a sculpture on top of it; a huge metal tree made of a load of old traffic lights. I'd seen the sculpture before and it had made me smile, but I'd never driven past it. The lights changed as I came towards it, red to amber to green to red in random sequences. I couldn't work out what was up and what was down, whether I had to start, stop or put down my foot. I stopped the car and giggled. The combination of the coke and the random traffic lights made me lose it for a while, and I sat there on the give way line, bent double laughing, with Tom just going, 'What, what, what?'

I made my way over the roundabout eventually then found a quiet street on the island and practised handbrake turns, making the car squeal and the tyres burn. I stopped the engine and got out, walking round to the passenger door and opening it. The smell of rubber was strong in the air.

I opened Tom's door. 'Your turn.' He hesitated, and said something about the stick shift again. 'Get in the fucking driver's seat, pussy.' He rolled his eyes and climbed over the gear stick to the other seat. I got in the passenger side and put on my seatbelt.

'Now who's the pussy?'

'Not really,' I said. 'You're going to crash it.'

'Love your faith in me, babe.'

'No, I mean you're going to crash it deliberately. Either that or I'll call you Tom-no-balls from now until I die.'

He stared at me. He let out one of his speciality loud laughs. 'That won't be long the rate you're going.' He shook his head and laughed again. 'You're nuts, but I don't half love you.' There he was again, using the L-word.

I frowned. 'Come on then,' I said. He kissed me, then put on his seatbelt and started up the engine.

Tom hadn't been bullshitting about his abilities with a

manual car, and I had to teach him about the clutch and biting point after he'd kangarooed the poor red thing along for a couple of blocks. He got it right eventually, and took us smooth and fast around the island a couple of times. He had started whistling. I turned up the car stereo and he shook his head and smiled.

'Where you thinking I should trash this thing, then?' he said. I didn't answer.

'Where?' He was shouting now.

'That silly traffic lights island.'

Tom's laugh was so loud it ripped into my ears. I turned the stereo up again and Tom revved the car. Off we flew.

Tom drove fast down the tiny streets. I held on tight and squealed like I was on a fairground ride. The more I screamed the faster he went, just like the pikeys at the fair. As he took corners, I saw how close the wheels skated to the kerb. A sliver closer and we could have clipped the concrete edge and the car would have turned over. The roof was down. I knew I might die and it made me burn brighter. It made me horny too. It was the same feeling I get when I stand on a high balcony or platform, the feeling of nerves sparking and causing trouble right at the centre of me and the unsettling idea that I might just jump playing with my head.

I looked at Tom. He was grinning fit to split his cheeks and his mouth was wide open. Loving every minute of it, just like me. As we came to the roundabout with the sculpture he let out an amused yell, catching on what had cracked me up before. He didn't look to see if anything was coming, but turned to me instead, and put his foot down harder, heading straight across the middle of the island instead of around it.

We hit the lights hard, bending one branch of the traffic light tree. I heard the scrape of metal and I could smell petrol fumes. Then all I could hear was Tom screaming.

I turned towards him expecting to see blood everywhere and his leg chopped in two, or the steering wheel rammed in his chest. There was none of this. The airbag had inflated and he was burying his head in it.

'Shit, what's wrong, Tom?' He kept screaming into the airbag. I undid my seatbelt. 'What the fuck's wrong?' I tried to get up out of my seat and banged my head.

I got out of the car and went round to Tom's side. The Porsche didn't seem too damaged. The bonnet at the front was bent and the engine was steaming, but the car had held together. The sculpture hadn't come off so well. The branch we'd hit had bent right over and all the traffic lights had gone out. I pulled on Tom's door and it opened with no effort. I bent down to try to find out what was wrong with him.

His head shot out of the car towards me. He had a massive smile plastered across his face.

'Gotchya,' he said. 'Hook, line and fucking sinker.'

'You bastard.' I was walking away.

I heard the car door close and then shouting behind me. 'Aw c'mon, Frankie Stein, don't lose your sense of humour.'

I turned to face him, fully meaning to scream in his face after what he'd done. He really did get me hook, line and the rest. I'd had visions of him on crutches, minus half his left leg.

I turned and saw the silly look all over his face, and the half-destroyed traffic light tree with a crap Porsche sticking out of it and I couldn't stay mad. I burst out laughing and Tom ran towards me, grabbed hold of me and pulled me close. Kissed me hard.

We walked away as if we'd just got off the tube rather than crashed a stolen car. It was an unwritten rule between the two of us now, another little pissing contest. You only ran if you had to.

There are loads of side-effects of adrenalin that make sense, but one that doesn't is the way it makes you want to fuck. By the time we got back to my place, Tom and I were ready to devour one another.

I came in the door my usual bad and dirty self, unzipping his flies and getting down on my knees, but Tom stopped me. He pulled me up to standing in the doorway and kissed me. He said he wanted to kiss me every step towards the bedroom. I don't know if being scared for his safety had messed with my head, but I melted a little and conceded. I giggled all the way, though, refused to be serious about it.

'I love you,' he said, by the bedroom door. I didn't even pull a face. I took his hand and led him to the bed. He undressed me slowly, kissing my shoulder, then my belly. 'I love you,' he said again. He waited. I guess he wanted me to say it back but I hadn't thawed that much. 'You're a hard-hearted, bitch. But I don't blame you. Under the circumstances.'

'Damn right. You gonna fuck me, or what?'

He smiled and shook his head. 'No. I ain't gonna fuck you. I'm gonna make love to you, you fucker.'

He did just that, mooning like a fool into my eyes the whole time. Forget all the daft risks we took, the silliness under bridges and crashed cars; this was the most dangerous thing he'd done by a distance. I was good at keeping it together but I was only human and there was part of me I couldn't control.

A good half-hour later, the bed destroyed around us, we lay in each other's arms. Tom was whispering stuff in my ear. Dangerous ideas. Half plans he had about us running away. We could go to Australia and work for a software firm. We could get floor trading jobs in the States. A new life together. He went on about this for about fifteen minutes like a man with a death wish.

He stopped talking and pulled me close. We lay together all spooned up, Tom kissing my back, and I forgot we weren't a normal couple. I fell asleep.

I woke up and Tom was beside the bed getting dressed.

'Where you going?' I said.

'Sorry, babe, I gotta go home.'

I sat straight up in bed. This was so far at odds with the rest of the evening. 'You what?'

He leaned over as he did up his shirt, tried to plant a kiss on the side of my face. I moved out of the way.

'C'mon, honey, don't be like that.'

'How am I supposed to take any of that bollocks about running away seriously when you can't stay away from her for even one night these days?' I said. He recoiled a little. Sure, I was angry, but he'd seen that before and it had never made him take a step back. I think it was because I'd repeated his plans, out loud, like they were real. It was a shock to him to have his own sweet nothings shot back in his face.

He sat down on the bed, a good old frown creasing up his face. It made him look his age for a change. 'Look, Frankie, I can't. Not tonight. Baby's getting shaky. She's convinced I'm up to something and you can't blame her. She wants me home. She deserves that, really.'

I looked at him from inside the quilt, which I pulled tighter round me.

'Soon soon, monster, I promise you. When I can plan it and have an alibi in advance.'

'Yeah, you promise.' I pulled the cover round me tighter still.

'What's that mean?' He did the loud mid-sentence thing again. I didn't find it sexy now, more threatening.

'Well you made a load of fucking promises to Baby, didn't you? And it took you, what? Not even six months to blow those ones out the water.' Even as the words came out, I knew they were too much.

Tom stood up and walked out, slamming his hand into the wall a few times along the hallway. Losing it more in each place he'd kissed me on the way in. He slammed the front door so hard as he left it shook the thin walls.

I lay back in bed, pulled the quilt right over my head and screamed. What did it matter that Baby was suspicious? So she might leave him. And? He said he loved me so surely it didn't matter. What did I care anyway? I didn't do the 'love thing'. Adultery was funny like that; it sure brought out the contradictions in people.

A few minutes later there was a timid knock on the front door. I got up and walked down the hallway. I looked through the peephole. It was Tom outside.

'I can hear you breathing,' he said.

I opened the door and let him in.

'You win,' he said. 'I'll stay.' He put his arms around me and squeezed tight. It felt like I couldn't breathe. I wasn't sure I'd won anything.

'Let's go away together,' he said.

I wriggled out from under the crush of his grip and stared at him.

'A vacation. Maybe not a week – I'm not sure I can get away with that. But a few days someplace.'

So he wasn't talking about running away. I wasn't sure whether to be relieved or disappointed.

'I'd like some proper time with you. Uninterrupted. No hassle, no worries, no Baby on the phone or trying to track us down.' He shrugged. 'Unless you don't wanna.'

'I didn't say that.'

'No one can know, though. Baby's real suspicious so we gotta be careful.'

I wanted to say 'fuck it' to Tom right there and then. I wanted to say that if people thought we'd gone on holiday together then fuck them. That if Baby found out, fuck her too. We could run away together like he'd talked about. But I didn't got the balls.

I nodded. 'Okay,' I said.

-------------------------5,794.8 ⇩35.0 (0.6%)-------------------------

I booked the holiday to Nice from the phone at work, waiting until most of the team were there to be witnesses, and giving Lorna's name as my travelling companion. Nick sneered as I spoke on the phone, a gesture that ate up all the goodness in his face. He made some comment about how everyone already knew about me winning the prize and there was no need for all this posturing. I looked at his miserable face, the plain old derision in the way his lip curled. I thought about saying, 'Where's your car, Nick?' He was keeping that story so close to his chest he could have done with a bra for it. I kept that thought to myself but it made me beam at him, catching him totally off guard and making him mutter into the air.

Meanwhile, Tom quietly arranged his business trip. Diane booked the tickets. He wrote emails to the New York and Chicago teams about what he was going to discuss in his meetings over there, and copied in all of us. There were moments when all of this felt like overkill but, if anyone had any suspicions that Tom and I were going somewhere together, they didn't say anything. They didn't show it at all.

The only person who worked it out was Jason. I saw him in a bar when I was out with Tom and we got chatting.

His opening line: 'You still seeing that tosser, then?'

A shrug from me.

'That'll be a yes, then.' A pause. 'How long you planning to be a mug for, Frankie?' Jase seemed angry.

'I'm gonna sort it,' I said. 'After I've been on holiday.'

He let out a snort. 'I see. You're going on holiday with him then.'

'I didn't say that.'

'You didn't have to.' Jase emptied the whisky from his glass. 'Listen, there's something I have to tell you, about him. You're not gonna thank me for it but it has to be said.'

'Jason, leave it.'

I was moving away but he grabbed me by the wrist, hard. He was looking all intense into my eyes. 'It's important, Frankie.'

I pulled against him but he wasn't letting go. 'Fine,' I said. 'Get it over with.'

'The UBF FTSE team doesn't need you.' Now he had my attention, but not in a positive way. He took a breath. 'I don't mean nothing nasty by that, just that it would work fine with two traders, the booth and a runner. You don't do enough business to justify the extra body. Everyone knows what the extra body is for.'

This was sounding familiar. It was the kind of talk I'd dismissed many months back. Except I couldn't help remembering that organisational chart, the crossed-out names. The exact comments made by Nick and Jack and Diane and how it all matched up to what Jason was saying now.

'He even jokes about it. All the time when you first joined he went on about what he wanted to do with you and why he'd taken you on. Sorry, Frankie, I should have told you then, but you were so happy. I couldn't burst the bubble on you.'

'I don't believe you.'

'You don't want to believe me.' Jason's eyes didn't move from mine. I would have sworn I'd be able to tell when he was lying, but I didn't feel sure. Maybe he believed his own bullshit.

'I just think you've got reasons to lie about Tom.'

Jase looked away and whistled. 'You got me on that one.' He looked back at me. 'No point denying it. But that's not what this is about and I'm telling you the truth, I swear I am.'

'I don't believe you, Jason.'

'Fine. That's up to you. There's one more thing you should know though. Him and his wife, they're trying for kids.'

Now I laughed. 'Don't be so ridiculous.' I looked over at Tom, chatting with another trader, downing drinks. It just wasn't possible. 'I don't believe I took you so seriously.' I pulled away and went back to my lover.

-------------------------5,794.8 ⇓35.0 (0.6%)-------------------------

Nice reminded me of Brighton, except that everything about it was slightly better. The shingle beaches were amazing to walk on, the stones good and strong and cold against my feet. There was cherry blossom everywhere and, although it wasn't hot there yet, it was warm enough to walk around in shirtsleeves most of the time. I bought some rollerblades and joined the parade of skaters, cyclists and joggers up and down the promenade. I'd learnt figure skating when I was younger so I could do jumps and spins. I practised them, falling and giving myself bruises but loving every minute. It made me feel eight years old.

I felt a universe and a half away from my normal life. I didn't even know what level the FTSE was trading at. Back home, the world was imploding. LIFFE was all over the place, no one knew what was happening. There were calls for senior resignations, for all sorts of changes. These issues sneaked into my food, like silver foil, and occasionally I'd bite down on them and a shock of pain would rock my jaw.

Like on my second day in France when I bought *Le Monde* and read about the MATIF and MONEP, the French futures and options exchanges. They had set up electronic trading systems to run parallel to open outcry, terrified no doubt of the Germans coming gunning for them next. The two systems ran side by side for a week before the outcry floor closed; it had been close to empty the entire time.

I read the article and it felt like seeing my own coffin on a table in front of me. I looked for distraction in the sights of Nice and made sure I took lots of photos for the record, to wave around when I came back. But underneath everything I did, the current of these changes pulled at my feet, a powerful undertow that wanted to drown me.

And I was on my own. Skating and sightseeing on my own, eating in cafés during the day, sitting on the beach with a book, all of that was very pleasant. I was chatted up and bought coffee a few times, and one guy gave me a tour of the market. But I was wary of these men, only too sure what they wanted to do to me. The danger in that? There was always the chance I would let them.

At night, the city changed; closed in on me. Going for dinner alone did not feel good. It didn't get better as time passed, but worse, and the final night was particularly bad. I walked along the seafront from bistro to bistro and nothing seemed good enough. I read mouth-watering tales of steak frites and special moules, of chèvre chaud, but I was not interested.

I heard a rumble of thunder, and felt spots of rain on my jacket. Minutes later, it was coming down in bucketloads so I ran into the nearest place, a seafront restaurant with one of those conservatories built like a tent; made of a plastic sheet and metal poles. I pushed at the door. It felt heavy and pushed back against me. The waiter pulled from inside to let me in. 'Madame?' he said, as I came inside. And then, 'Just for you?' I turned and looked behind me. Who the fuck I expected to see there, I haven't got a clue.

He ushered me over to a table in the middle of the conservatory and gave me a menu. As he walked away, I looked around. A family or two. Couples. I was the only person on my own. I studied the menu and my face was burning up, I felt so self-conscious. Yet, when I looked around, no one was taking any notice of me.

The rain made a drumming sound on the plastic sheet of the roof. It was a comforting noise, reminding me of camping trips with Dad when I was young. I studied the menu. I didn't fancy any of the food. I no longer felt in the least bit hungry. With comic timing, I got a text from Tom. 'Wish I cud b wid u there.'

I laughed out loud. He didn't know the half of it. It came to me then, with a clarity that made everything disappear except the image in my head. Me, alone at dinner, alone in foreign places, plenty. Me, alone on my birthday. At Christmas. Alone, alone, alone. It was another 'coffin on the table' moment.

I promised myself I would not be that woman. I would do something to destroy that future, smash it to the floor, no matter what it took. In my head, I was ready to get up, pack my stuff and take the first flight back. And yet I didn't. When the waiter came over, I smiled and ordered some food. Half a bottle of wine. I wasn't quite ready to sever myself from the mess that was me and Tom, not yet.

I had never felt like a mistress before. I did now.

------------------------5,794.8 ⇩35.0 (0.6%)------------------------

I flew into Newark airport, on Tom's advice. I'd never been to the States before, and he said it was the best possible introduction to his country. He knew what he was talking about.

The flight was hellish. A young baby a few rows down had cried all the way and this combined with the vibrations of the plane to make sleep elusive. But I was used to lack of sleep. It was the constant nag of the kid's wailing that got to me. It screamed when dinner was served and it screamed again later, when we got coffee and a snack. It screamed on take-off and it screamed when we were coming down to land. The thing screamed so hard that my headphones couldn't drown out the noise without destroying my eardrums. The noise of a baby crying is one of those sounds, like the tone when a TV is left on after the end of transmission; you're not supposed to be able to ignore it. When the captain announced our descent, I had a banging headache and dry eyes. I couldn't wait to get off the plane and through immigration and customs, away from the demon child.

I'd never had any special desire to visit America. Then I looked out of the window and that changed. There it was: New York harbour, the place where they catch sushi and sell it to the Japanese. A thrill lifted me in my seat. Liberty held proud her flame and greeted me with that Mona Lisa smile. Behind her was the skyline I'd seen before on so many black-and-white prints, but real, in colour and in front of me. I had no idea how many times I'd seen this view, just that it was so familiar it felt like coming home. The plane swung around, over the island of Manhattan, its grids and tall buildings like a scale model beneath us, and then across the river. I didn't hear the baby's screams again until we landed and were taxiing to the terminal building.

I'm not easily intimidated but US Immigration is something else. I think it's all the men in exotic uniforms carrying automatic weapons, or leading sniffer dogs around in apparently random circles. Intimidation wasn't the only effect these men had on me, though, and I hoped Tom had managed to come to meet me so I could drag him straight back to the hotel room. The man at the counter asked me a load of questions about my trip without smiling. I didn't try to make any silly jokes with him. I'd heard stories of the horrors they could put you through if you tried to mess with them here. There were more questions at Customs, about whether I was bringing live animals with me into the country or had been on any farms, if I had fresh food in my luggage and how much currency I'd brought along. Finally, I was allowed into America.

As I walked through to arrivals, I told myself Tom would not be there. I didn't want to start with a disappointment. There was a danger all my feelings would come out in a vomity mess when I saw him, all over the both of us, so I kept my expectations low. But then I saw he was there, waiting and holding up a sign that said 'Frankie Stein'. This made me smile so hard it hurt my face. Tom's face reflected this right back at me.

I put my arms around him and we kissed for a long time. He drew back and looked at me. 'Damn, I've missed you.'

'I've missed you too.' The words slipped out when I was not paying attention.

Tom did a comedy double take, then laughed, loud. 'Who the hell are you and what have you done with Frankie?' He pushed me back by the shoulders, then spent time looking at me, taking in every detail. 'I gotta surprise.'

We walked out into the sunshine, which hurt my eyes after hours of artificial lighting on the plane. There was a queue of yellow cabs like something out of the movies. I wanted to touch them, climb inside and feel the upholstery to check that they were real. But Tom stopped short of the taxi rank, by a white stretch limo, and opened the door.

'This is ours?'

Tom nodded.

I climbed inside and Tom made a big show of trying to look up my skirt. There were sofas lining the edges of the car, and a drinks cabinet, TV and stereo in the middle. The windows were smoked out and there was a little curtain behind where the driver sat. Tom followed me in. 'So, it's the Cosmopolitan Hotel,' he said to the driver, then he turned to me. 'Would madame like a drink?' He was putting on a silly posh voice.

'Too fucking right she would.'

Tom poured two gin and tonics, serving mine with a doily and a flourish. He put on some music, a Madonna CD. We lay back on the seats and he put his arm around me. I spilt my drink on my chest and he laughed, then mopped it up with his tongue. 'Excuse us,' he said to the driver, and he closed the curtain. I saw the driver's amused eyes in the rear-view mirror, just before the picture there disappeared from view.

'You're so bad,' I said.

'Damn right.' He unzipped his jeans. He kissed me again, winding up his hands into my hair. Then he pulled me down, below his belt, and I wrapped my mouth around his cock.

I spent my first three hours in America in the hotel room with Tom, following up on the action in the limo. We were rabid for each other.

It got dark, and we both got hungry. We showered together, then dressed and headed out of our hotel room and into the city. As we stepped out onto the 'sidewalk', Tom grabbed my hand. This gesture was against all my rules but I let it go.

As we walked and I looked around me, the strangest thing was the lack of strangeness. I had a sense of déjà vu walking through the streets; the crossings with the WALK and DON'T WALK signs, the squat yellows taxis, the subway signs, the wide gridded streets lined with tall buildings, the steel fire escapes cascading down the sides of skyscrapers and brownstones. Of course, I had seen it before, a hundred times, on TV and the movies. This celluloid familiarity gave the city the air of a theme park, a reproduction of itself.

We only had one night in New York City and Tom had booked a table for dinner at a restaurant in Union Square. He flagged a cab and we got in, treated to a recording of Eartha Kitt purring and telling us to put on our seatbelts, which we both ignored. He asked the driver to go a convoluted route so we could take in some sights. We went through Battery Park, passed by the World Trade Center, then back on ourselves to Wall Street. We stopped at the famous bull, and Tom insisted I get out and touch its

239

horns, for prosperity. I did it dirty and made him smile and smile. We headed on to the lightshow of Times Square and then, finally, to our destination. There was time for a drink before dinner and Tom ordered me a cocktail called a Cosmopolitan that I'd never heard of. It was fruity but bitter and I savoured it. I never have liked things too sweet.

Our table was booked at the Bluewater Grill for eleven. Tom said he couldn't in all conscience let me leave New York without eating a steak. It wasn't really what I wanted but I ordered one, to appease him. Tom touched my hand between courses. He'd ordered an expensive bottle of wine and halfway through the meal he proposed a toast. 'To us.' And we clinked glasses.

I went to the 'rest room' and saw my fat smile in the mirror. It made me check myself. Was I beginning to believe in happily ever after? I stared myself out. I knew I was in danger here, at risk of ending up with the life I'd had a glimpse of in Nice.

And then I thought – *fuck it*. Maybe Lorna was right and everything did always turn out for the best. If she reckoned it was some god's will, who was I to argue? Why didn't I just lie back and enjoy it?

And so I did.

-------------------------5,794.8 ⇩35.0 (0.6%)-------------------------

If you work in options and futures for any length of time, you'll end up one day visiting Chicago. It is unavoidable. Tom and I flew into O'Hare the next evening, on an internal flight. I couldn't believe how easy the experience was, like getting on a bus. Domestic arrivals at O'Hare couldn't have been more different from the international terminal I'd flown into. It seemed that, once you were inside America, no one was bothered where you went or what you were carrying, how many farm animals you had in your suitcase.

Tom had organised use of a UBF corporate apartment, a penthouse in Marina City. Tom called it 'the corncobs' and I saw why when we arrived, as that was exactly what the two towers looked like, albeit decimated, empty husks. On the lower floors, where the niblets would have been, there were car parking spaces. Further up were dangerous-looking balconies, floor after floor, holding hands and spinning circles.

Tom looked up. 'This pair, wow, I mean they used to be the world's tallest residential buildings. In fact they used to be the tallest concrete structure, period.'

'Wow. The biggest load of concrete in the world. Aren't you guys clever?'

He nudged me over with his shoulder as we walked towards the door, but he had a smile on his face. 'Fuck you.' He said this a little too loudly, making someone coming the other way give him quite a stare.

'You wish.'

Now he laughed. 'Always.' And he pushed his way through the door. He headed inside the elevator and I followed.

'Which floor?' I said.

'Sixty.'

I put on a nerdy mockney accent. 'You are having a giraffe.'

He raised one eyebrow and pressed the button. The lift shot up like a bullet.

I grabbed the handrail. 'Fucking hell.'

Tom was laughing at me. 'Thirty-five seconds all the way to the top,' he said. 'Thirty-five fucking seconds.'

It felt like less. It felt like the opposite of freefall.

Tom unlocked the apartment door and we walked in. I wandered around the flat. It was the strangest place; there were no right angles. The apartment was the shape of a Trivial Pursuit wedge, with the kitchen where it came to a point then the other rooms round the outside. There were balconies outside both bedrooms and the lounge. I went into the bigger bedroom and started unpacking my case. Tom came in and kissed me.

'Come outside,' he said.

'I'm not sure I want to.'

'Gwaan. You can't be scared of a bit of fresh air.'

'It's not so much the fresh air as the sixty-storey drop I'd be scared of.' It was a long way to fall, even if the lift could make it in thirty-five seconds.

Tom went right to the balcony rail. He turned and smiled, that killer smile of his that he thought could always get him his own way. This time it looked mocking, not so friendly. I guess the way he looked was more about my mood than his. I walked over to him. He took hold of me and stood me in front of him, by the rail, kissing my neck. He grabbed at my waist, then at my tits. I pushed his hands back down to my waist. 'No one can see,' he said. I looked ahead of me, past the river, and towards the city's skyline.

'That's the Merchandise Mart. The second biggest commercial building in the world,' he told me, pointing and nibbling on my ear. It was wide rather than stacked high and I tried to do the maths that made what Tom was saying true. He pointed to a staggered building with a big needle pointing in the air, the kind of building that invented the word *skyscraper*. 'That's the Sears Tower. It used to be the tallest building in the world, but it ain't no more.'

I couldn't imagine being at the top of that place. I've never liked heights but being so far up made me analyse it more. I was scared, definitely, and yet the way I felt wasn't totally unpleasant. In fact, if I thought about it, it gave me a bit of a thrill. It brought my breath in hard, was almost a sexy feeling. I could imagine stepping over the edge. I could see my body on the way down. Flying like in that dream I had.

I had to leave the balcony before I did something stupid. 'Take me in and fuck me,' I said to Tom. He bit my neck hard, then he did what I'd asked him to do.

Chicago was where house got invented, so we had to go clubbing. Tom took me to what he said was one of his old haunts, a huge warehouse on the east side. We arrived at about eleven and I hoped the place was going to heat up some. The dance floor was half empty and the people on it were trying too hard to look cool. It was supposed to be lofty to keep the sweaty dancers from overheating but, because it was so empty, it was chilly.

Tom went hunting for pills and it was looking unlikely. He couldn't find a dealer, which almost certainly meant there wasn't one; Tom was an expert at scoring. Then I saw him speaking with this big black guy. He sent me a thumbs-up, and signalled I should meet him in the corner, where it was quiet. I assumed he'd got hold of some Es. When we were well out of sight, he held his hand out and showed me what he had. In his palm there were several squares of blotting paper acid, with little pictures on like I'd read about. I couldn't believe what I was looking at. Acid, at a house club, in Chicago. The whole neatness of it made me laugh out loud.

I'd never tried acid before, even though there was a fair

bit around in London at the time. Jase had got hold of a dropper bottle of the stuff at one point, and the lads took it when we were out clubbing a couple of times. I was wary. Merrick had tried to persuade me, but I was too worried about ending up on a bad trip.

The squares of paper were wrapped in cling film, and Tom said this was to make sure it didn't get absorbed through his skin when he touched it and go straight into his system. Acid was different from other drugs that way, he told me. This was one that hunted you down, tried to get inside you. It could travel through the walls of human cells.

'You tried this before?' he asked me.

I shook my head. 'Not sure I want to.'

'C'm'ere,' he said, and he shoved his finger inside my mouth. 'You have now.'

I thought about spitting the blotter straight out, but I didn't want to make a scene. If what Tom was saying was true, about the cell walls, then I knew chances were I'd absorbed enough already. I went with it, chewed and swallowed the paper down. Smiled. Tom put a blotter in his own mouth and made a big show of swallowing. He offered me a second one. I said no, and he laughed, threw his head back, and gobbled up that one too.

'Might as well make the most of it while I'm away from the ball and chain.'

The club began to get busier, but the dance floor still didn't look properly hedonistic like the ones I was used to. About half an hour after I'd taken the acid, I started to notice colours were brighter, the same way they get when you take a pill. As we walked through the crowded parts of the club, it seemed like people shot towards me faster than they got there. I'd seen something similar in an advert. It was like the spirits inside the clubbers were storming off ahead of their bodies. It was like they were travelling faster than the speed of light.

After an hour or so, something changed. We were dancing and I felt a stiffness in my neck and another feeling, like my chest was fizzing. I had a stabbing pain in my stomach that bent me double for a second, but it went off quickly. I felt a bit sick. I waved my hand in front of my face to cool it down. The images didn't adjust the way they should do and I was left with a picture of everywhere my hand had been. When I noticed this I moved my hand faster and faster, until it looked like it was all floppy on the end of my arm. I was fascinated with how this looked.

I walked round to the bar, thinking about buying a drink but being all random about it because I'd forgotten how bars worked. I looked ahead of me and noticed beautiful patterns superimposed on top of everything, as if they were being put there by a pair of glasses I was wearing. And the thing that made me smile the most? I remembered the same kind of designs being on things we'd had in the house when I was growing up and was filled with a sudden understanding of what the seventies were about, but as if I'd known it somewhere deep inside all the time. It made me giggle to myself.

I didn't get a drink but went back to dance. The music sounded amazing, it shot out of the speakers and into the air like fireworks. I started pointing out things I could see to Tom. He laughed and said he could see the same things; sparks of colour in someone's glass, patterns on the wall, that kind of shit. And the other way around. Tom described the things he could see and they appeared in front of me. It didn't make sense that we were sharing the same trip, so all I could think was that the things Tom was suggesting and I was hearing, the input he was giving me, that my brain was interpreting this visually and making pictures.

I had a constant stomachache now, a grinding pain like when you get your period. I didn't think much of it; pills often upset my stomach too but when Tom said he wanted to go back to the apartment and relax, enjoy what his head was showing him, I was all for it. We went to find a taxi. A few drove by with their lights out, people in the back, and Tom started to giggle. I asked him what was funny, but he was laughing too hard to get it out. The more he tried to explain, the harder he hooted and it set me off too. We were both laughing and laughing so that we couldn't breathe. My lungs were fizzing, making a load of bubbling phlegm and I could smell plastic really strong. I coughed up a load of the fizz and spat it on the pavement. It was liked I'd breathed in a sherbet fountain.

'Niiiice,' said Tom. And that started us both off again.

Tom shot up with his arm in the air. It made me jumpy, I couldn't work out why he would do that. I turned and saw a car pulling over with a light on top of it. I breathed easy again. He was just flagging down a cab. Then I realised the taxi driver was my dad. The fear filled up my throat and, the more I thought this man was my dad, the more he looked like him. I turned away. I reminded myself I was in Chicago. I turned back to look at the driver and he was an Asian guy with a big nose. My fear melted away and dripped from my hands onto the pavement.

We climbed in and Tom recited my address in Docklands.

'This is Chicago,' I said.

'Oh yeah.' He told the driver to forget going to the Isle of Dogs and take us to the corncobs. The driver spun his finger round near his head, just where a surgeon would make the first cut for a frontal lobotomy. Tom was copying it.

The taxi driver moved like Robocop. I looked at Tom, and he looked too big. 'You look too big,' I said. My voice echoed around the inside of the cab. Tom just laughed and laughed.

We got back to the corncob apartment blocks and they looked too small. Tom paid the taxi driver with a load of green notes. I still hadn't totally got over the theme park syndrome and the green notes looked like toy money.

We went inside and got in the lift, giggling our pretty little heads off. Tom couldn't work out how to press the right button, which made us both collapse again. Then I tried to press it and had the same trouble. We were both down on the floor laughing and my cheeks were hurting from the effort of it all. Tom crawled his hand up the wall, incy-wincy spider, and managed to hit random buttons all the way to sixty. The lift went up, stopping along the way, the bell each time making us collapse with laughter. Fortunately no one else got in. Twelve stops later we were finally on the sixtieth floor, and we fell out into the corridor. Outside the apartment door I realised I didn't know how keys worked any more. I tried from all different angles, getting more and more confused, until Tom took them off me and unlocked the door.

Tom put on some music. I lay down on the floor. I felt so relaxed, almost at the stage of yogic sleep. All sorts of important things came to mind, meaning-of-life kind of shit. It all made much more sense than it usually did. I had it licked, I just had to remember it for the next day so I could tell everyone. Thinking about the next day made me a little sad, that I wouldn't be here then, this special place I'd found inside my head.

The music dripped over the room and I melted into the furniture. I drifted in and out of trippy daydreams, not focusing on much. The pain in my stomach was getting worse. I mentioned it to Tom, who suggested I go to the loo. It didn't feel like that kind of pain, but I went anyway. I sat on the toilet phasing in and out. I felt something slip between my legs and looked down.

I let out a little squeal, seeing the toilet full of blood. I didn't take in what this meant at first. I grabbed tissues and tried to clean myself up. There was a lot of blood. When had I last had a period? I could not remember. A dread filled me up from my toes to my scalp. I was making small wailing noises. I got onto my knees and looked down into the toilet bowl. I didn't see much; just a bloody red mess. Everything slotted into place. The little bit of weight I'd put on recently, the feeling that something was missing from my life, a constant nag there was something I had forgotten.

I flushed the chain. I didn't want to see what had come out of me any more. I grabbed a towel from the rack and tried to clean myself up. I didn't want Tom to know. I climbed into the bath and turned on the shower, letting it run and run and run. My legs were feeling weak so I sat down and let the water wash over me some more. The liquid going down the plughole was bright red and bubbling. I knew I should really go to the hospital. I sat down in the bath and sobbed. Why didn't Tom come? Why hadn't he noticed I'd gone?

Sitting there watching the blood wash away, I got that feeling again, the one from the dream where I'd done something terrible, the body in the garden dream. It was exactly the same fear, that my life was ruined and I would never be able to live with myself. That I had done something so bad it could never be forgiven. I tried to think about other things but my brain wouldn't let me. I wasn't in control of where my thoughts went now, like my mind was pure, unfiltered subconscious. That Chinese wall in your brain? It's there for a reason.

I stayed on the edge of a bad trip without quite going into one. Now I wanted the experience to be over, and time went so slowly I couldn't see it move. I kept checking my watch, sure it would be much later than when I looked before, but finding only seconds had passed. Sometimes the display didn't change, and I was thrown back to Dad's living room with the clock that didn't work. It had stopped working the day my mother died, I decided, and I obsessed about it. I couldn't stop thinking of her looking up at me from the bath, the way I'd seen her when I was twisted on shrooms.

I remembered Tom. Why hadn't he come looking for me? I got dressed, using the facecloth as a temporary sanitary towel. I wiped clean all the surfaces in the bathroom, then I took the bloody bath towels into the bedroom and threw them over the side of the balcony. I saw them blow away into the distance. I went to find him. He was sitting in the living room, eyes half closed and moving his head to the music. 'Boy, am I seeing some pretty pictures,' he told me. I knew it was just that he was out of it, but I still felt angry he hadn't noticed how long I'd been gone or wondered where I was. That he hadn't heard or taken any notice of my cries of distress.

I climbed onto his knee and cuddled in. I tried to blank out the badness by looking at him, but his face kept freaking me out, all his random thoughts and expressions rippling over the surface of his skin. The way my brain was processing his expressions made him look malicious. I kept kissing him so I didn't have to see.

'Are you okay?' he asked me.

'Not everso okay.'

'You can always go to sleep, if it's not going well for you, just go to sleep.'

I lay back against him. I didn't feel tired, didn't think I would be able to sleep. I closed my eyes and listened to the music. I reached for that place again, the one where I'd felt relaxed, when I'd first come into the apartment. My head screamed at me a couple of times but I breathed deep and ignored it. Then I was gone, into a sweet and dreamless dark.

--------------------------**5,794.8** ⇩35.0 (0.6%)--------------------------

I woke up in a right mess. I'd been asleep for a few hours, fully clothed. It was a strange kind of rest, full of the sort of thoughts you'd rather not consider. I knew I'd been lucky to escape a bad trip and made a vow never to do acid again. I got up and drank some water. The feeling as it went down my throat was alien. I had a moment's panic that I'd done it wrong and it had gone down to my lungs. I walked over to the window. The Chicago skyline danced in front of me. And it struck me – the sheer weight of human endeavour. I could see it all, like one of those speeded-up BBC reels of a flower opening. The people being born, eating, sweating their tits off, building houses and roads, cities and skyscrapers. I could see it, in one sequence, from the first fish climbing out of the sea, through the stages of evolution, through the meteors that destroy, it all starting again, getting better, more advanced. The millions of eyes of life looking out on the world and building it better. Bigger, faster, taller, more. Until here, in time for me being born, all this majesty, all these buildings and roads and paintings and novels and music and bright, bright lights. The vision knocked the wind right out of me and I had to sit down.

I wanted to go out, walk through the things that the world had made for me. I woke Tom up and told him. He said he'd come with me. I kissed him, and he lay underneath me with a smile on his face. His eyes darted around, like he was watching something cross the room. No, more random than that. It was like the twitch of a blind man's eyes.

It took all the concentration I had to get changed and put on my shoes. That was when I did see something that wasn't there; either I was still full of acid or it was flashback. Tom had explained to me that flashbacks weren't like people thought. It wasn't like you relived part of what had happened when you were high, but that some of the acid solidified in your spinal cord and hit you later. Like a free trip, he said. The only thing about that was you didn't have a choice about when or even whether to take it.

It started with a feeling, a familiar ache in my chest. It was a while before I pinned down where I knew this pain from. It was the feeling from that dream, the body in the garden dream. The sure and certain knowledge that I'd done something so bad my life was ruined. My heart was drumming in my chest and I was sweating.

Then I saw Mum, splashing in the bath. Not in front of me this time, but in my mind's eye. Deep inside my head I could see it. The radio on. A Beatles song was playing – 'Norwegian Wood' of course. Mum was smiling up at me, like the flash I'd had of her when I was tripping on mushrooms, but, just like then, there was something wrong with the smile. A nervousness about it that made me scared.

The radio was beside the bath and my eyes followed the wire from the back of it. It was plugged into the socket in the hallway. What was she thinking of? My dad, the electrician, he'd always drilled it into me about things like that. Water, electricity, they didn't mix. He'd gone red in the face telling me about this.

And then I knew exactly how my mother had died. The radio, playing 'Norwegian Wood', plugged into the mains. Me, standing by the edge of the bath. Her voice: 'Don't you dare, Francesca.' That nervous smile.

The smell of barbecued meat.

The thing about acid is that it fires up parts of your brain that aren't usually active. Some of these parts, they're closed for a reason. Acid can help you access repressed memories but your brain, it's a clever old thing. When it keeps its secrets, you should trust it.

The other thing about acid is you never know if what you see is a memory, dragged out and dusted down from the murky depths of your unconscious, or if it's just part of the trip and fired up by your imagination. You don't know, you can't know and you will never know.

When I'd freaked out, shouting and screaming and tearing at my hair, Tom had grabbed me and held me tight. I think he was trying to make sure I didn't damage the apartment. He stroked my forehead, and told me it was okay, like a bad dream and nothing to worry about. When I'd calmed down he put me to bed.

I hadn't slept at all that night – I'd lain awake watching the display on the clock change, its digits ticking over like they were leaves falling in autumn. I thought the trip would last forever. This morning, my clothes and the sheet underneath me were covered in blood. I changed, and rolled the bloody things up into a ball. I snuck into the hallway and threw them down the rubbish chute.

I padded through to the living room and Tom was there, drinking coffee and reading the paper. Smiling to himself as if nothing had happened.

'Hey, honey,' he said. 'It's a great day.' He got up and opened the blinds, letting in too much light. It was something I'd noticed about Chicago; the sky was higher, brighter. Rain was more dramatic and so was the light. This was welcome, mostly, but not this morning. I screwed up my eyes. How could he be so happy? So untouched? And I thought – it had all been his idea. He hadn't even given me the chance to say no, just put the fucking blotting paper in my mouth. I wanted to go back to bed and curl up into a ball, pull the quilt over my head. I wanted to scream.

Everything was different. Terrifying. Tom was an animal, nothing more, just an ape. Tongue, lips, damp nose of a beast. How could I kiss him any more than I'd kiss a dog or a horse? I was an animal too. Made of mucus and skin and fat and muscle. I was solid. I'd never felt my substance before. My throat was dry and hurt a little, but the bubbling in my lungs had stopped. There was a dull ache in my stomach, reminding me of what I'd lost. Thinking about that made me want to cry. My pain split off in two directions and the picture I'd seen of my mum in the bath stalked me too. Her words and that smell of burning. I couldn't run away from these things because they were inside me. They were a part of me.

Everything that held me together was on the floor in front of me, shattered into the tiniest pieces. I could never pick it up and glue it back together again, not if I had all the time in the world. And it was all Tom's fault.

It bubbled up in my chest then, a fury towards Tom for putting that blotter in my mouth. For not giving me a choice about taking the acid. It was a feeling so strong, I knew no good could come of it. I had to get out of there, away from him, before I did or said something I'd regret.

'I'm going to nip out to the shop,' I said. 'You want anything?'

'Nah,' he said. Then he said, 'Hey honey, actually, can you get me some cigarettes,' handing me a few of those strange green notes.

There were shops in the Marina City complex. It was one of those places you never had to leave because everything you needed was there. What designers of these places forget is that no one wants to live that life. People like going out. It was a beautiful day. I left the complex and headed down to the river. The sky above me was huge, and unreal, like a film still. I felt better, walking by the water. I watched it snake towards the lake, the way it always had since way before I was born. I saw people on bridges, in the windows of apartments and shops. The same world I'd left behind the night before.

Ten minutes later I was on my way back up to Tom, feeling so much better. I came in the door and realised I'd forgotten the cigarettes. More important, I hadn't got any sanitary towels. I shouted through to tell him I'd be two minutes, and left the door on the latch. There was a shop in the lobby and it would only take me seventy seconds to travel there and back in the superlift.

Maybe he didn't hear me shout through or he just thought it would take me longer to get some cigarettes. He definitely didn't hear me coming back in. He was talking on the phone.

'Oh honey, I am so sorry. Yeah . . . Yeah . . . I know. I know how much you want this . . . Maybe it'll be next month? Yeah . . . It'll happen soon, honey . . . I can feel it's going to happen soon for us . . . Of course you'll be a good mom. You'll be a great mom . . . I love you too, honey.'

I stood in the hallway listening. I should have gone through, made my presence known. Done the decent thing and given Tom the chance to put down the phone and pretend something technical had gone wrong when he spoke to Baby later, from the office. But I was like your classic rubbernecker, couldn't help but look no matter how much blood there was. Couldn't help but look, despite risking my own safety. And I remembered all the things Jase had said. He'd been telling the truth about them trying for a baby. That probably meant everything he'd said was true. I didn't want to think about it.

I waited until Tom put down the phone. When the living room had been silent for a couple of minutes, I shut the front door, hard.

'Hey, honey,' he said. Using the same word he'd used when he spoke to Baby. 'You got my cigarettes?'

I threw them at him and threw myself down on the sofa.

'You didn't have such a great time last night, did you?' he said.

'It was nothing. Just a bit of a bad dream.'

He opened up the packet of Lucky Strike. 'Why do I get the feeling you ain't telling the entire truth, Frankie Stein?'

I wasn't in the mood for the third degree. 'What would you know about truth?'

'Now that,' he lit up and took a drag, 'that's a bit below the belt. I gotta be careful. I don't wanna hurt the girl.'

'Right.' I couldn't be arsed with arguing that point and I definitely didn't want to talk about what I'd heard a few minutes earlier. 'You didn't give me a chance to say no last night, to that acid. You put it in my mouth.'

He snorted, took another drag. 'Like you'd have said no.'

'I should have had the choice.'

Tom shrugged. 'Why don't we talk about what's really bothering you?'

I could almost have laughed at that comment. He had no fucking clue about my mother, about the pale surface of her face and arms and legs charring as I watched, about the way she shook and shuddered and all the life got kicked right out of her. About my dad coming in and screaming, then falling to his knees and sobbing, prostrating himself like someone in a Hindu temple, and how I ran and hid behind the sofa. The way the smell of charring that I'd remembered wouldn't go away now, as if I'd been near a bonfire and it had stuck to my clothes, no, it had gone deeper and infused my skin. There was no way I was going to tell him anything about what was really bothering me.

I breathed. I thought about saying nothing, just getting on with the night and having a good time. Then my feelings towards him came pouring out in one long sentence, full of stored venom. 'I'm worried you're using me, having your cake and fucking munching it up, that you're not ever going to leave Baby, that all that is crap you spout to keep me on your little line, so you can pull at that line and reel me whenever you want to, whenever you feel the itch to fuck me.'

Tom looked me up and down and took another drag of his cigarette. 'No, Frankie. You say what you mean. Stop holding back.' The look on his face was dark as the black in the centre of his eyes.

'You gonna leave her then?'

Tom just sat smoking. The way he didn't answer right away, that said it all. He sighed. 'Thing is, I never know where I stand with you. You blow hot and cold.'

'Do you blame me? Under the circumstances?' I said, repeating something he'd once said.

He stood up. 'And what am I supposed to do? Under the circumstances? Leave my wife who loves me and break her heart, only to have you tell me in a couple of months that you don't do the love thing, and fuck off to shag the next cute guy you see in a pair of tight pants?' His voice was steady and even and he didn't shout, but there was poison there.

'I ain't like that.'

'Ainchya?' He paused. Looked down at the floor, then up at me as he blew out smoke. 'I got a question for you, Miss Quick to Judge. Answer me this, girl. Do you love me?'

That took the wind out of my sails. I sat looking at him.

'Well, do you?'

'I think so.'

Tom laughed, and shook his head, but it was the way you laugh when that last-straw-that-breaks-it thing happens on a bad, bad day. 'And that's supposed to be good enough for me is it? That's supposed to be enough for me to dismantle my life and give this thing,' he gestured at the two of us, 'whatever the fuck it is, give this thing my all.'

I still didn't speak.

'It ain't enough, Frankie, though, is it?'

I felt played. I wondered if he'd thought about this, rehearsed that little speech. I wouldn't have put it past him. I stormed into the bedroom, grabbing my suitcase from under the bed and throwing things into it. Tom followed me in.

'You gonna bail now?' he said. I carried on packing. 'This what you do, every time it gets a little bit hard?' He stood watching me for a few minutes. 'I need a cocktail,' he said, and he walked out of the room.

I let myself cry, silently, the water leaking from my eyes onto my screwed-up face. I zipped shut the suitcase, then checked around the room to make sure I'd not missed anything. I checked the other rooms too, obsessively, compulsively. What I was really doing was delaying the moment I'd have to walk out the door. Giving Tom time to get up and stop me.

He didn't. He sat in the living room sipping from a tumbler of whisky with his head in the paper.

I'd checked all the rooms about three times and I knew I had to leave then or swallow my pride and say sorry. It wasn't going to be the latter. I opened the door, put my suitcase down. I went to pick it up and could feel him behind me, his presence in the hallway. He came close and touched me on the back.

I turned. We smiled at each other.

'I don't want to go,' I said.

'I don't want you to go. We'll sort this.'

I knew we wouldn't. I knew it was all bullshit. Maybe he believed it himself, as he said it, but how could it be true? He was trying to get Baby pregnant. That picture I'd had in Nice, I could see it even clearer now. There would be kids soon, more reasons he couldn't spend time with me.

My nerves were too shot for me to sort this out right now, though. I would make the break from Tom, but I would do it when I was back home, with my friends around to help. I needed their support to sort out my head. Lorna would know the right thing to say. She'd have a mantra or seven for me, even for this.

For the moment, I thought *fuck it* – and fell back into Tom's arms. Let him kiss me and hold me and make more promises he had no hope of keeping.

Tom took me to see the Hancock Tower. 'That used to be the world's tallest building,' he said. Then he turned and pointed at a tower block that was being constructed behind us. 'That was going to be the world's tallest building, and will be for a while, but they're planning something bigger in Korea.'

I laughed. 'What is it about this place and buildings that are the ex-biggest in the world? Even the ones that aren't built yet.'

He shrugged. 'Can't explain it.' And he did his favourite smile for me.

We went for dinner at a Thai place on North Michigan Avenue. Tom ordered green curry that was too spicy to eat. He gulped at his beer, and joked about how a nuclear meltdown was happening in his mouth, then gave up and declared his meal inedible. I wasn't hungry, so I fed him most of my pad thai. My nerves were shot but that didn't stop me drinking. In fact, it made me swallow the stuff down faster. We shared a couple of bottles of wine and I was sinking it fast, so that by the end of the main course I was quite drunk.

Tom brought something out of his pocket. 'Dessert?' He opened his hand to give me a flash of what he had there. It was the rest of the blotting paper he'd bought in the club.

'No thanks.'

Tom's smile looked demonic. 'It's not for everyone,' he said, shoving a couple of the bits of paper into his mouth. The waitress came and collected our dishes.

'Was everything all right?' She looked at Tom's full plate, his red face. 'You no have Thai food before?' Thai was Tom's favourite, and he was no wimp when it came down to chillies. We looked at each other and laughed.

Tom paid the bill and we left to find a bar. We had a couple of cocktails in a posh place a few doors down, then he told me he was tripping out, and that he'd feel more comfortable at the apartment. I shrugged, said okay. There was plenty to drink there too.

We got back and I poured us both G & Ts. Tom went out onto the balcony with his and I followed. It was a beautiful evening. The slight edge in the air was refreshing. They're well designed, the balconies on the corncobs. They curl around and hold you the way a woman holds a baby, make you feel protected. The way the balcony wrapped us up, it made me feel silly for being scared out there before. We walked over to the rail and I leaned over. Tom made a loud sound and pretended to push me. It made my head spin and I had to grab the top of the railing to stay upright. He tickled me and I screamed. We both yelled and giggled and then we kissed.

I wanted to push it further and a picture came into my head. Not my mum, this time, thank fuck. I could almost close my eyes and not see that picture now, although the smell lingered. This image was of Tom, hanging from the outside of the building, holding on to me. It came to me so clearly I could have drawn it. I must have still been tripping a little. Acid, its after-effects, take a long time to properly leave you. It fades the way radioactive material decays, halving over weeks, months, years, a tiny amount sticking around for ever. A residue on your consciousness.

'I bet you haven't got it in you to climb over the side,' I said.

Tom laughed.

'I'd hold you.'

I could see he was considering it. Whether he could do it, or if he'd get close and bottle it at the last minute, end up looking foolish. Working out whether he could trust me to hold on tight enough, maybe. If it was even that logical. The amount of acid running around Tom's system, he was probably thinking elves would support him from underneath, or worried that an eagle the size of a horse might fly down and grab him with its talons.

'Don't you got the balls?' I said. A silly, loud, mocking voice.

'I got the balls.' But his voice was kind of quiet.

I looked straight down, at the road all that way below us, feeling that familiar thrill. Danger – it was sexual for me now. It hit something right at the core of me and made me want to fuck. Tom put one leg over into the darkness outside the balcony and I firmly rooted my feet at the bottom of the safety rail. I was breathing hard. I held out my hands to him and he grabbed on. My heart was a hammer in my chest. 'This is mad,' Tom said. He carried on climbing over though.

Then he was there, stood the other side of the railing, holding my hands.

'Lean back,' I said.

Tom gave me one of those intense looks and I was shot through with lust for him.

'Do it,' I said. So he did. He threw his head back and shouted. He let out yelps, a sound somewhere between panic and elation.

Then he looked at me again. 'Dare ya to let go.'

'Don't be so fucking stupid,' I said, and he laughed. His laughter echoed around the balcony, a noise that put my teeth on edge. I don't know what he was thinking. Maybe the acid inside him made him feel invincible; I'd been there before. Perhaps he had a death wish.

I was spitting. 'What the fuck, Tom. Why you pulling this shite?'

But he just laughed, this mocking horrible leer on his face. He looked like a gurning demon. 'Dare you,' he whispered, narrowing then widening his eyes.

It pissed me off that he was messing with me. Putting down the ultimate bet to try and blow me out of the water in this game we were playing.

And I thought, everyone thinks I'm in Nice. They've seen the tickets. I took the plane and I checked in at the hotel. I'm not here.

And I thought, my things are packed. My suitcase is right by the door. I could be out of this apartment in seconds flat and no one would know I'd ever been here. The lift takes thirty-five seconds to get to the bottom of the building. I could be there almost as quick as Tom.

And I thought, if I let go, and he dies, the autopsy will find him full of LSD. They'll think he was trying to fly.

And I thought about what I'd flushed down the toilet just twenty-four or so hours ago, and how he hadn't noticed or given a fuck where I'd gone. I remembered the way my life had changed thanks to the acid he'd forced on me and the pictures it had conjured up out of nowhere. I thought about my mother.

'What's ticking through your little head, I wonder,' Tom said. 'You don't got the balls, do you?' That mocking voice again.

I stared into his eyes, searching for something there. I don't know what the fuck I expected to see.

'You don't got the balls, babe. You don't got the balls to have me and you don't got the balls to let me go.' He was smiling, so sure of himself, the way he always was.

The anger that came was sudden and intense. I could feel my pulse, moving my throat. I looked into his eyes. 'You're wrong,' I said. And I let go.

He didn't believe I'd done it at first, then he realised and a look of sheer panic stretched his face. He grabbed for the railings but flipped backwards. His arms and legs shot out as he fell and then a calmness settled over him, as if he expected to drift away on a cloud, not drop like a brick, hit the ground and smash to pieces. Maybe it was the air flowing fast against his skin and pulling his face but, from where I was, he looked like he was smiling his head off. He looked euphoric, like he was having a giant starfish moment on a dance floor in his head.

Fear shot out from my throat and filled every cell in my body, it poured into my muscles and my bones and my skin as if my blood was carrying it. I couldn't move much else but I forced my eyelids shut. I pictured him, floating off in the wind like a helium balloon. I saw him in my mind's eye, fly off into the clouds like a kite. I did not hear the sound as he hit the ground.

Acknowledgements

Special thanks to Luigi Bonomi, Poppy Hampson and all at Random House.

A very specific mention has to go to Chris Lee, whose stories about the trading floor inspired me to write this in the first place, and whose help with the detail and technical aspects was invaluable. Also to Matthew Valentine, Neil McKenzie, David Norman and Philip Dove for sharing their memories.

Thanks also to Graham Joyce, David Belbin, Ross Bradshaw, Jane Streeter, John Petherbridge, Andrea Case-Rogers, Jane and Jamie D'Amico-Hutchinson, Afshan Munir, Kevin Gilholm, Joanna Lourenco, Richard Pilgrim, Maria Allen, Alastair Paylor, James Walker, Richard Berry, Darren and Clair, Bryan Brittle, Laura Browne, Theresa Caruana, as well as my family, Mum, Dad, Deb, Paul, Adam, Dan, Nat, Chad and the Murray massive, for all the different types of support a girl could ever need.

Credits

Lines from 'Insomnia', by Faithless, © Universal Music Publishing group/Warner Chappell Music Ltd/Champion Music

Line from 'Drop Dead Georgeous', by Republica, © Universal Music Publishing group

Lines from 'Born Slippy NUXX', by Underworld, © Sherlock Holmes Music Ltd

Every effort has been made to trace or contact all copyright holders, and the publishers will be pleased to correct any omissions brought to their notice at the earliest opportunity.

www.vintage-books.co.uk